gd

409 ONT Dozer

Bush Track

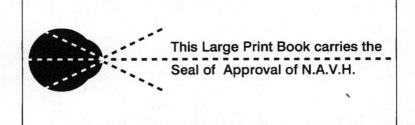

This Large Print Book carries the
Seal of Approval of N.A.V.H.

Bush Track

Fred Grove

Thorndike Press • Waterville, Maine

Published in 2004 by arrangement with Golden West Literary Agency.

Thorndike Press® Large Print Western.

The tree indicium is a trademark of Thorndike Press.

The text of this Large Print edition is unabridged.
Other aspects of the book may vary from the original edition.

Set in 16 pt. Plantin by Liana M. Walker.

Printed in the United States on permanent paper.

ISBN 0-7862-6375-X (lg. print : hc : alk. paper)

To the Pattons —
Elza, Alva Mae, and Nancy

As the Founder/CEO of NAVH, the only national health agency solely devoted to those who, although not totally blind, have an eye disease which could lead to serious visual impairment, I am pleased to recognize Thorndike Press* as one of the leading publishers in the large print field.

Founded in 1954 in San Francisco to prepare large print textbooks for partially seeing children, NAVH became the pioneer and standard setting agency in the preparation of large type.

Today, those publishers who meet our standards carry the prestigious "Seal of Approval" indicating high quality large print. We are delighted that Thorndike Press is one of the publishers whose titles meet these standards. We are also pleased to recognize the significant contribution Thorndike Press is making in this important and growing field.

Lorraine H. Marchi, L.H.D.
Founder/CEO
NAVH

* Thorndike Press encompasses the following imprints: Thorndike, Wheeler, Walker and Large Print Press.

Chapter 1

Dude McQuinn rode steadily, dogged by a sense of lateness and doubt, weary of the un- changing world about him, and glad once more to see the outscatter of another little settlement on the endless Kansas prairie. When you lost a trail already old, you had to rely on guesswork and hunches. And again he asked himself, Where could they be?

In the center of the one broad street, at the town pump and watering trough, he uncinched and refreshed Blue Grass, his long-legged Kentucky saddler, rested briefly, cinched up and rode on, drawn to the sign at the end of the street that read: Prairie Livery.

An elderly man sat on a bench by the barn's runway.

Dude drew rein and said, "Afternoon."

"Afternoon."

"Trying to catch up with some friends," Dude told him. "A one-wagon outfit. An old fellow with a white beard, an Indian jockey, and a big white man riding a smooth claybank saddler. They're carrying a blaze-faced short horse with four white socks. Likely a little string of trade horses. Have you seen them?"

"Nope."

"I was hoping maybe they'd matched a race hereabouts, maybe traded a little."

"Nope. If they did, I'd know it. Lived here since the town was borned. Camped west of here in seventy-four, last year of the buffalo." A wry smile cut his face. "Made more money haulin' bones to Fort Dodge than we did sellin' hides. Six of us in the outfit — two skinners, one cook, one handyman, two hunters. We split everything six ways."

"I see," said Dude, willing to listen.

"When all that gut-bustin' work was over, we had come out just about even. . . . Well, didn't mean to get off on old times. Nope, sorry to say I haven't seen your friends."

"Was afraid of that," Dude said, looking down, and the tone of his discouragement seemed to stir the old man, who crossed his legs and tugged on his bristly chin. His voice was obliging, "Where'd you last cut their sign?"

"In Colorado. About a month ago they won a match race at Coyote Wells. Beat a

8

horse called Rocky Mountain Joe, then headed this way, I was told."

"Rocky Mountain Joe? Hmmnn. You're talkin' about the boss hoss from Pueblo to Cheyenne."

"So they won a big race?"

"They did. Could be your friends didn't come this way a-tall. Just said they did."

"Why say that?"

"It's hard to win over there, even when you have the top horse sometimes. And when you do, it's a good idea to punch the breeze."

Things hadn't changed, Dude thought.

"Or could be your friends went around the town."

"Well, I'm much obliged to you."

Dude McQuinn put his horse into the running walk and struck eastward along the dusty road, thinking that if he failed to find them soon, he'd give up and go back to Texas.

There had been just that one terse letter. It read: "Dear Dude — Making a little swing up through Nebraska. You should see the Judge. He's running like the heel flies are gonna get him for certain. These plow-chasers sure hate to part with their corn and wheat money, but no trouble yet. Figure we'll head back for Colorado before long.

Everybody's fine. We miss you. Regards, Uncle Billy."

That had done it — that and other matters had sent him after them, knowing the odds were against finding them.

All that morning he rode eastward, meeting no one, seeing in the shimmering distance now and then, set in miniature on the level land, a neat little farmhouse, barn, corrals, and windmill. And when at last he saw movement, a string of mule-drawn freight wagons dusting up from the south and turning westward on the road he traveled, he stopped and asked the worn question of the lead teamster.

No, the man said, welcoming the palaver, he'd seen no such outfit. Just a few farmers. . . . Mighty dry. Sure need rain.

The miles fell away under the hoofs of the long-striding brown gelding. That was one of many pleasures when you owned a gaited saddler. Blue Grass could hold the running walk for hours, always ready to go on, to do what was asked of him. He relished distance. Kentucky iron — so Dude liked to think of that endurance and willingness. Blue Grass had other gaits — he could execute a pretty fox trot and a proud and rapid single-foot, which always caught the eye — but his true traveling gait was the running walk, as comfortable for the rider as sitting in a rocking chair. Many times Dude wished he knew the saddler's breeding. Acquired in a swap-and-boot deal with a cagey East Texas cotton farmer, who, unawares, received a spavined gelding in exchange for the sick saddler he was trading off; Blue Grass then had the heaves, which Uncle Billy cured with one of his medicine-chest mixtures, which he called "potions." Whatever the gelding's vague antecedents, Dude knew that he came from quality folks. After all, it was performance that counted.

He soon began seeing more and more farms, though as yet he had not come to a town. There was a little farmhouse ahead where the windmill's wheel spun like a silver disk. He would stop there, for his horse had been without water since early morning and the afternoon was a scorcher.

As he rode up to the house, a spotted dog charged out, barking furiously. Dude reined in the unperturbed gelding and spoke softly to the dog. When a man came out on the porch, Dude nodded and said, "I'd appreciate water for my horse and self. We've come a long way today."

"Just help yourself."

"Much obliged." Later Dude would inquire about his friends.

11

Blue Grass was taking his fill at the water tank when the farmer left the house and walked back, nodding as he came, a friendly man, obviously hungry for talk.

"So you've come a long way?"

"From Colorado."

"Any rain out there?"

The weather was always a prime subject of conversation, good for a beginning. "None in weeks, I was told."

"Been dry as a powder house here." The man canted his head to look at the sky. "Clear now, but I figure we're due for a change before long."

Dude grinned. "You're hopeful."

"Man has to be out here." With appreciative eyes on the saddler, "Couldn't help but notice your horse. Believe he was in the running walk when you came up."

"That's right — he was."

"Easiest gait there is. Had me a Morgan once that could get along like that. You'd almost go to sleep in the saddle. Lost him. Stepped in a prairie dog hole and broke a front leg."

"Sorry to hear that."

The friendly eyes narrowed, sizing up the horse again, and after a moment the farmer looked straight at Dude. "Would you trade this horse with something to boot?"

Dude shook his head.

"I have a young horse, younger than yours, and although he's not gaited like this horse, he can go all day. Has an even disposition and is a good keeper. I'll throw in fifty dollars to boot."

Dude's smile was understanding. "What it comes down to is, I don't want to sell him. He's too good a horse."

"That's a fair offer."

"It is. But I need him. Got a long way to go, looks like. I'm looking for some old friends." Though figuring nothing would come of it, he described the outfit and its horses.

Reflecting, the man scratched his jaw and gave a shake of his head. Dude thanked him and was riding off when, "Did you say a claybank saddler?"

Dude checked and turned his horse. "Yes — a claybank."

"Been some little time. I remember now. I saw this rider saddling along past the house, headed east. And there was a light covered wagon, I remember that. Guess they had water on the wagon, because they didn't stop here."

"When was that?"

"Some weeks ago. I wouldn't remember, except you don't see many claybanks. That

13

yellow hide sticks in your memory. A saddler, too."

At last! Dude could feel the wear of the long days of riding dropping away from him, the sudden leap of excitement. Impatience seized him. "Was there an old man and a young Indian?"

"Too far off to tell what they looked like, young or old or what color. There were two men on the wagon seat, and — come to think of it — there was another rider following the wagon."

Another rider? Four in the outfit? That didn't fit. But the claybank was enough. "What town's up ahead?" Dude asked.

"Next place is Kiowa Peak."

"How far?"

"About fifty miles, more or less."

"They been matching any horse races around there?"

"Don't know. Don't go to town but once a month, sometimes not that often; then just for a little salt, sugar or flour, and tobacco."

"How big a place is it?"

"Why, friend, it's the county seat."

"Just right," Dude said, more to himself, and heeled his horse away.

"What was that?"

Dude's reply was a flourishing wave as he

reined into the running walk and made for the road.

Even after the day had spent itself, he continued until dark before making dry camp. The prairie night had turned cool, and Dude slept under blanket and yellow slicker. At intervals Blue Grass would come in and smell of him, nosing him, as if to make certain all was well, then go back and graze. Toward morning, Dude heard the gelding lie down and sleep. Later, the night wind changed from southwest to south; rousing up, Dude felt the distant promise of rain.

By daylight he was in the saddle, hurrying under a darkening sky, the brown horse moving out eagerly. Around noon, stopping at a farmer's for water, he heard the weather-wise greeting, "Looks like rain."

"Reckon you need it."

"Need it? It's so dry the bullfrogs come in for water with the stock."

"How far is Kiowa Peak?"

"About ten miles."

"Heard tell of any match races there?"

"Just about every Saturday afternoon."

"What's today?"

"Saturday."

He hastened on.

Ahead of him the land was buckling up to

a string of rough-looking hills, like so many guardians arranged elbow to elbow, watching over the sunburned plain. One hill stood higher than its neighbors, a kind of rounded peak. Around there, he judged, should be Kiowa Peak.

About two hours onward he heard the first roll of thunder, and before long he felt raindrops. Halting, he took the slicker from behind the cantle of his saddle, shrugged into it, and hurried on. Now, dimly, he sighted the scattering of the town. As he did, the rushing wind came upon him fitfully, and a pelting rain, and the little town grew smaller and smaller, as seen through a frosted-glass window, until he lost it completely.

He was hunched against the storm, holding a stubborn course, when a rider suddenly materialized out of the gray of the rain-slashed road, pounding hard from town. For one moment Dude had him in head-on sight, before the rider cut away to the south, spurring for the broken hills, on a horse that looked yellowish through the murk. Now Dude saw him no more.

Not long afterward a knot of horsemen bulged ahead, likewise coming from town on the run. They kept coming hard, and seeing him, they raised yells.

Dude halted.

16

Rushing up, they closed in around him, outrage showing on rain-streaked faces, rifles at the ready. The leader of the posse, for Dude divined it was such, yelled above the roar of the storm, "I'm Sheriff Tug Rankin! See a rider just pass this way?"

Sheriff Rankin was a large man, a very large man, a no-foolishness man, his bulk spilling over the swell of his saddle. His size and the square, heavy face and the eyes as hard as marbles and his horse-size teeth, as even as the keys of a barroom piano, combined to give his faint lisp an unmistakable menace.

When Dude didn't reply at once, Rankin, impatient, yelled, "I said, did you see a rider pass this way! Speak up!" He kept moving his bulky shoulders as he talked. "We want him bad! He slicked the town in a horse race! He was ridin' a big claybank gelding!"

Dude caught himself on the verge of straightforward speech. But . . . but that horse? It had looked yellow — it was. So it had to be! He should have known then. To gather his thoughts, he lowered his head as if against the wind.

"Speak up! Did you see a man on a claybank? We know he came this way!"

"Was just about to tell you, Sheriff. A rider passed me going west . . . and now that

17

I think of it, he was riding a claybank. No . . . maybe it was a dun."

"Hell's fire, man, can't you tell a dun from a claybank?"

"Let me think. . . . Yes — you could call it a claybank, I guess, though it looked a lot like a light dun. As you know, the claybank is a mixture of the dun and the sorrel —"

They tore away, mouthing disgust at the delay, charging into the teeth of the whipping wind and cold rain.

Dude McQuinn heaved his relief and dallied awhile; when satisfied they weren't coming back, he dashed ahead and when he came to where the claybank rider had made haste off the road, he struck at a gallop for the scraggy hills, the wind slashing his back.

He was riding a blind trail, groping through the gray-green world of the storm, the hills just illusory shapes before him, his one certainty the feel of the good horse under him.

Reaching the foot of the hills and seeing no claybank rider, he followed along their base, in and out, peering through the mist, and on to a gap, which he entered with anticipation. But neither did he sight the rider here, which puzzled him, because he could not be far behind, and this was the logical route for a fleeing man to take. Unless, unless the rider had climbed the steeper slopes back there, or unless he had passed the gap.

He pressed on, traveling at a lope, until the gap broadened into lesser hills, barely visible through the slanting rain. He halted, while alternatives whipped through his mind. Should he keep on or ride back to the gap and look farther along the flank of the hills? Somehow the backtracking seemed wrong.

On impulse, he put his horse up the long incline of a rocky hill and onto the crest, where he took his look beyond, seeing only muddy light and the jumble of more hills. Posted there, while the wind tore at him, he became aware of a slight lessening. Was the storm passing, the light stronger? He guessed it didn't matter, because he had lost his man.

In frustration, he gazed back along the gap, and that was when he saw what looked like the eye of a campfire. Just that one tongue of flame, momentarily visible, before low-hanging clouds crossed his sight. Waiting no longer, he raced downhill, the saddler's shod hoofs clacking on rocks, and galloped over the way he had come.

After several hundred yards, he stopped short. There, he reckoned, staring, about there through that stand of oaks. And for the first time he was certain that the rain was letting up.

He ducked into the dripping timber, weaving his horse through, raising a clatter of rocks and trampling brush. A minute of this and he broke out into a clearing. Beyond, fire leaped against the lee side of a ledge, and he saw a wagon and horses, among them a claybank as yellow as the slicker Dude wore. Fire, wagon, horses — but no people.

He was slowly walking his horse across when a voice snarled at him from his right, "Hold up, buster! Grab for the sky!"

Dude halted, on the brink of laughter. That voice, that grainy, crotchety voice. He'd know it anywhere! Nevertheless, he raised his hands, calling at the same time, "Is that any way to greet an old friend?"

"Cut out the palaver. Get down off that horse!"

Dude stayed mounted, unable to see the speaker for the brush.

"I said get down!"

"Don't you recognize this saddler?" Dude called louder. "You're the one that helped me trade off that spavined gelding for him."

A pause — broken by a whoop as four men suddenly showed themselves. The white-bearded one put away his handgun and exploded a chastened voice of astonishment, "If it's not Dude on Blue Grass! Thunderation!"

Dude managed to dismount moments before they rushed him. The giant Jason Carter got there first and bear-hugged him, and Uncle Billy Lockhart clapped him on the back and howled, "You Alamo Texan, you!" and Comanche Coyote Walking whooped and, Indian fashion, grasped Dude's hand.

The fourth man held back, just grinning, a young man Dude did not know.

The trio snatched the reins of Dude's horse and hustled Dude over to the fire roaring by the rock ledge, whapping on him as they went, and there, out of the wind and rain, they stood back and sized him up and down as they might a trade horse, while he sized them up and down as well.

Uncle Billy looked leaner and perhaps a shade older, yet spry as ever, abetted by a rakish bowler and calf-hide vest, and his clear blue eyes and puckish features, set amid wreathing white whiskers and bib beard and snow-white hair worn long, conspired to present the same saintly face as of old. A trackless face, really, within it the suggestion of a past, shadowy and intriguing, that likely no man would ever penetrate, and

21

that many times had caused Dude to wonder, Was Lockhart just an alias? Texas-bred manners forbade you to ask where a man came from or what his name might have been elsewhere or what he had been, and the few times the subject of the old man's history had bobbed up in casual conversation, Dude was met with blunt rebuff or sarcastic evasion. Especially, Dude had wondered, after a heated match race and much at stake, when the other side had tried to outslick the outfit and lost, and tempers flared, and a six-gun would blink in Uncle Billy's hand quicker than the eye could follow.

Jason Carter removed his slicker, and when he faced about Dude observed that he had lost his former girth. This oversize man, radiating strength and bearing, was another person from the bartender Dude first met at the Tremont House in Flat Rock, Texas, an unhappy man then, his eyes sensitive and lonely. He had, Dude discovered, found his own true self since joining the little outfit. His oxbow mustache neatly trimmed, his soggy Stetson crimped just so, wearing a stylish frock suit of dark broadcloth, he could now pass for a man of high standing.

Coyote Walking, bandy-legged and short of stature, though deep through the chest, carried the light frame of a born jockey. Awkward afoot, he seemed an extension of the horse when mounted, riding with the stirrups up high. Of all Dude's track memories, his most vivid were those of Coyote aboard Judge Blair, Coyote whooping and the dark bay gelding running lower and faster, lengthening his stride as they tore for the finish line.

Coyote stood slouched, his blue-black braids hanging beneath a sodden black hat, the thumbs of his horseman's strong hands hooked over a silver buckle adorning a broad, beaded belt, drawn like a cinch around his lean waist. The tobacco-brown eyes, flaring wide on high cheekbones behind the proud arch of the Roman nose, kept conveying the warm pleasure of seeing an old friend again.

Dude grinned back at them all, warmed in return.

"Dude, pardner," said the old horseman, "want you to meet our new *compadre* — Danny Featherstone. He cuts a pert Irish jig and can tenor a rendition of 'Danny Boy' that would make a mean sheriff break down and cry. A play-actor by trade, temporarily at liberty, Danny has trod the boards at the Palace in Denver and elsewhere."

"Did," the young man smiled, "till the

troupe's manager skipped out with all the proceeds and left us high and dry."

Danny Featherstone was in his early twenties, Dude figured, a few years younger than Coyote and about Coyote's height, but heavier, thickset. And quick-smiling, fair-skinned, clean-shaven, blond, a round, care-free face, and gray eyes that danced. His whole aspect was that of a mannerly young man, eager to perform and please.

"That's not all," Uncle Billy praised. "Danny plays a mean harmonica."

"I'd like to hear you play and sing, Danny," Dude said.

There was a pause, a shifting of attention back to Dude, and Uncle Billy said, "Don't know how you ever found us, but we're mighty glad you did." His tone took on an appealing quality. "Maybe you've come for Judge Blair? I haven't forgotten that he's your horse."

"He's in better hands with you, Uncle, the way you can doctor a horse. You know the nature of a horse, what he wants and needs. No . . . it wasn't the Judge. I want you to campaign him. That's what he was meant to be — a runnin' horse."

"A shame he was ever gelded. Well, if it wasn't the Judge, what brought you here?"

A sheepishness seeped into Dude's face.

"To tell you the truth, I got a little homesick to see you tumbleweeds."

"Homesick! Didn't you and that pretty schoolmarm, Miss Bridget, step into double-harness?"

"Was goin' to. But about that time Bridget's mother started ailing back in Boston, and Bridget felt she'd better hurry back and take care of her. Been some months now. Bridget wanted me to go with her, but what would I do in Boston? No job, me a stranger? So I stayed in Three Springs . . . clerked for Archer & Dodd, General Merchandise. You remember them?"

"Do I? And the day the Judge beat the mighty Hondo there at Three Springs, and the local folks won enough money to build that schoolhouse?" The old gent slapped his thigh at the memory.

"After Bridget left," Dude continued, "things got mighty quiet and lonesome, though you couldn't ask for better folks than those at Three Springs. Then one day came your letter from Nebraska. I made tracks north the very same morning." He kicked at a pebble. "I was just a month behind you at Coyote Wells."

"Had us a little skirmish there." The eyes in the saintly face acquired a kind of glitter.

"They tried to steal the Judge after he threw dust in Rocky Mountain Joe's face all the way to the finish line. Breezed the quarter mile in twenty-two flat, he did. This fella came up with a false bill of sale — claimed he'd owned the Judge in Wyoming and we'd stolen him. Imagine that! Me takin' another man's horse."

Dude made a little face. "Of course not, Uncle."

"The sheriff was in on it."

"How'd you tumbleweeds get clear?"

"Simple. Jason knocked heads together, took their guns, and we tore out for Kansas, avoiding all towns till we came to Kiowa Peak. . . . Go on with your story, Dude. Afraid I took the bit in my mouth and ran with it."

"That's about it. I was hoping . . . till Bridget comes back . . . that maybe I might help out a little."

"A little!" Uncle Billy roared and swung his arms. "You're just in time. Jason aims to go into business for himself. Got his eye on a steady little saloon in Alma, Nebraska." A roguish jiggling of his head and a deviling wink. "Combination place, you might say. Hotel overhead. Girls."

Jason colored. "Now, Uncle, the hotel will be run nice and proper. Sheets changed every two weeks, whether they need it or not, and no more than three to a bed. I got my limits."

"I don't want Jason to leave on my account," Dude insisted.

"He's stayed on now longer than he should have."

"Not that I minded," Jason said, "unless it was today, when Rankin's posse took after me." He fixed Dude a puzzled look. "Something happened. Never saw 'em again after I cleared town. You must've come that way."

"I did," and he told them of meeting Sheriff Rankin and the posse, and sending them on west.

"Whew!" Jason whistled. "That explains it. Much obliged, Dude. That was close."

"That sheriff was mighty mad, I tell you."

"No wonder," Jason said, pursing his lips. "It was his horse we beat."

"Boys!" Uncle Billy exclaimed, waving his arms like a country preacher. "This calls for a little toddy," and he broke on top for the wagon.

"None of your horse potions," Dude called after him. A drink was never just a drink with his old mentor. It was always "a little toddy," so called, never a big one, as if that curative caption absolved the imbiber of any sinful intent.

"Just what all happened in Kiowa Peak?" Dude asked, while they gathered around the fire and took pulls at the clay jug now and then. Jason, Coyote, and Danny looked to Uncle Billy, who cleared his throat and began, "You see, we'd matched Texas Jack twice in Kiowa Peak on Saturdays, and he'd lost both times as expected."

"Texas Jack?"

"That's our new slow horse — that dark bay gelding over there with four white-sock feet. The spittin' image of the Judge, except he's without the Judge's blazed face, and except he can't outrun a hoptoad. Same horse I showed you I bought off that trader fella the day we left Three Springs. If anything, he's a shade slower than Rebel." The old eyes lit up. "And how is ol' Rebel hoss?"

"I retired him. Got him boarded out with a ranch family. Now the kids ride him to school. He's fat and sassy. Just an ol' pet."

"As smooth a looking racehorse as I ever saw, and one of the slowest, but ideal for this kind of campaigning," the old man reminisced. "I thought a lot of that horse. Once we schooled him in the swingin' start, he could hold his own pretty good up to a hundred yards. Trouble is, they don't match races that short. I'll say this for Rebel, though — he could look better behind by daylight than some horses do three lengths in front. . . . Well, like I said, we'd matched Texas Jack twice and he got beat both times. So word soon got around that he was no bolt of forked lightning. That evening after the second race, there was a little bunch of us in the saloon, Sheriff Rankin included, jawing about racehorses, and Jason says to me, 'Uncle Billy, did you notice how much faster Texas Jack looked today?'

" 'Faster,' says I, 'when he lost by two lengths?'

" 'It was four lengths the first time,' Jason comes back. 'I do believe he's finally looking like his old speedy self, finally coming around. He broke pretty fast.'

" 'Not fast enough,' says I. 'However, he seems about recovered from those bucked shins,' letting that excuse drop.

"Jason then says, 'I'd like to match him just one more time around here to prove what he can do. I've got my pride.'

" 'Well, it's your money,' says I. 'Leave me out of it.'

" 'Of course, I'd have to have odds,' he says.

" 'Odds won't make Texas Jack run any faster,' I tell him, an' everybody laughs. You should have heard 'em.

" 'I'll put up a hundred dollars right here

and now,' Jason brags, 'that Texas Jack is on the improve enough to beat any horse around Kiowa Peak at three hundred yards. I mean *any horse*.' He takes out the money and lays it down on the bar and smooths it out. It looks big — a twenty on top, a bunch of fives and ones under that.

"Now this Sheriff Rankin is a proud man. He owns a four-year-old stud called Nugget that's never lost a race around Kiowa Peak. The moccasin telegraph on Nugget is that he's a fair-to-middling horse at one furlong — no farther. We figure we can dust him. . . . Well! Rankin swells up till his face gets red as a side of beef. He blusters, 'I'll just call you on that, but it has to be one furlong and even money.'

"Jason just laughs at him. 'Whoa, now,' he says, 'I said odds. I mean three to one at three hundred yards.'

" 'No odds,' this Rankin holds, 'and we'll run one furlong.'

" 'Can't go,' Jason says. He picks up his money and rattles his hocks for the swingin' doors, and the sheriff calls, 'Wait a goldurned minute. I'll give you two-to-one odds, but it's still one furlong.' You see, this Rankin is cagey as a treeful of owls. He's trying to match his horse at his best distance, and when Jason strolls back and

30

hangs his head . . . just like I've schooled him and you . . . and says, 'Did you say two to one?' why, Rankin nods, figuring he's got the advantage, and they shake on it and have a drink." Uncle Billy had another tip of the jug and passed it around.

"What went wrong?" Dude asked, going along with the telling, while pretty certain that he knew.

"Plenty. You see, it starts raining hard . . . and I mean a real toad-strangler . . . just as the horses break. But I figure we'll get through. Coyote, like always, knows what to do. He keeps right on riding past the finish line, heading east, pretending the Judge has taken the bit and is running away. Once I see that the Judge has it won by daylight, I and Danny pull out fast in the wagon, headed south, all of us having agreed to rendezvous here.

"Jason has already collected the bets from the stakeholder and is in the saddle, when some smart-aleck . . . believe me, there's one in every town . . . hollers out that dye was running down Texas Jack's face when he crossed the finish line, and that it wasn't Texas Jack's bay face at all, but a blazed face, and that we'd brought in a ringer. You know the rest."

"Didn't Rankin see the dye was running?"

"That was the one piece of luck we had. He was back at the starting line, fussin' over his stud to see that he got off right. That gave us a little start, you see. . . . Rankin even tried to outslick us at the last minute. Fella came up, said he'd just heard about the race and wanted to enter his horse, winner take all . . . a big, rough, part-Percheron stud so rank it was all the jock could do to hold him on the track. Well, we saw right through that little dido. That stud was a put-in horse to knock the Judge down at the break."

"I've heard that song before."

"When we said no go, the new fella tried to make it sound we's afraid of his horse, but he eased off pretty quick and the sheriff stayed mum, figuring he already had it won against our sorry horse. How he wanted our money!"

"Hope you're putting something back for your place by the f'ar, Uncle. And your own hotel, and you on the front porch, watchin' folks go by. Like you always wanted."

"Easy now, Dude. That really means end of the track, and I'm not ready for it." He seemed to shake off the thought. "I tell you the Judge ran himself a good race. He broke first and ran on down there as straight as you could draw a line. Daylighted that

Nugget horse all the way. Coyote didn't have to whoop at him once."

"How many lengths?"

"Four."

"I've got to see him," Dude said eagerly. Rising, he crossed to the horses.

Judge Blair had never looked more in his prime, Dude thought, as handsome as a quarter horse could be. The four white socks and that distinctive blaze on his face, which could be a problem sometimes when you had to race him under another name because you couldn't match him under his own because veteran horsemen never forgot a sprinter with his speed and markings.

Dark bay, the Judge, strong of jaw and the eyes large and clear and set wide apart, the fox ears ever alert. The good withers. That long, sloping shoulder and powerful front and hindquarters. Long-hipped. Short cannons. Short back and deep girth. Legs straight and well-muscled. A balanced horse. About him, somehow, the look of eagles. Put simply, Judge Blair was a runnin' horse, as well-known as any Texas outlaw.

Another mystery horse, won in an all-night poker game at San Antonio; nothing known of his breeding beyond the whiskey-fume brags of the cowman-owner, who had won the horse the previous night off an Arizona cowman. Why, the man carried on, Judge Blair was sired by none other than the famous Buck Shiloh, a hard-knocking son of the legendary Shiloh, and his dam was the equally legendary Mexican sprint queen, Lolita. . . . What! You've never heard tell of Buck Shiloh or Lolita? Man, you just haven't been around the big tracks. . . . Unconvinced, but figuring he had little to lose, Dude had played on, and when morning came he owned a sure-enough racehorse, he soon learned, faster than he had ever dreamed of possessing. So fast that he couldn't match the gelding anymore around San Antonio. The one alternative besides selling his horse, which Dude couldn't bring himself to do, was to travel around, picking up a match race here and there, and pickings were lean as the Judge's reputation as a speed horse preceded him.

Enter William Tecumseh Lockhart — trainer, veterinarian, raconteur, and possibly a good deal more — who had put the outfit together. At his suggestion Dude had bought the smooth-looking Rebel, a dark bay look-alike of Judge Blair, except for the white markings.

Afterward, on the lookout for fresh money, traveling northeast across Texas, using pick-up jockeys, if need be running the Judge under an alias, or matching the "slow horse" Rebel, and losing, and then matching Rebel at high odds and switching to the Judge, his markings painted or dyed to resemble Rebel, and winning, meanwhile careful not to get slicked in turn, the outfit had found by chance the jockey it needed in Indian Territory — Comanche Coyote Walking.

These thoughts coursed through Dude's mind as he gazed at the horses: Texas Jack another look-alike, another Rebel; Jason's claybank saddler, which took Dude back to Flat Rock and the touch-and-go business there; the fast-stepping sorrel team, and Judge Blair.

He stepped in and began rubbing the broad blaze that came to a point between the velvety nostrils, and talking to his horse, he stroked the black mane and the good neck and the heavily muscled shoulder. He thought, It's really just a game grown-ups play. Never dull. A gamble, true, but a whale of a lot of fun. Racing's give and take kept Uncle Billy young, provided him with challenge and purpose. You took the advantage when you could and the other side tried to do the same to you, fortifying the old horseman's often-repeated assertion, "All's fair in love and war and horse racin'."

Hearing steps, he turned to find Coyote Walking there. Of all the diverse persons in the outfit, the Comanche was the most unlikely: a graduate of Carlisle School, in Pennsylvania, better educated than many of the whites settling the small towns just now emerging from their frontier infancy. When not working with the horses or helping with camp chores, Coyote could usually be found engrossed in a book. Though educated like a white man, he remained a Plains Indian, very much so, irrevocably tied to the old ways through loyalty and sentiment, and to some primitive superstitions such as the powerful "Owl Person," so that sometimes his talk became an entertaining mixture of English and signs and Indian thinking, perhaps on purpose, perhaps not; in another moment a memorized quotation from the classics, spoken flawlessly, with expression — until you wondered whether it was he and not you that was amused.

"How you been, Coyote?"

"Like always, white father — good."

"Mighty glad to see you," Dude said, smiling at the paternal salutation. There was nothing patronizing or servile about it, rather an amiable thing, a half-teasing sobriquet between friends.

As they started back to the fire, the Indian stopped and turned, head uplifted, listening toward the woods and beyond. Dude heard it also, and waved a silencing hand at the others, and saw Uncle Billy quickly grab a piece of wood and tear the fire apart, while Jason and Danny ran to the horses.

With Coyote, Dude darted into the dark timber, not stopping until they could see the open gap. There, Dude heard the racket distinctly, for the wind had lessened: the thudding of trotting horses, the squeal of saddle leather, and the musical *clink* of spurs and bridle bits. Controlling his excitement, he crouched down beside Coyote.

Slickered horsemen appeared, hunched against the weather. A big man rode out front — Sheriff Rankin. Dude stiffened when Rankin threw up a halting hand. The horsemen flowed around him, stirring indecisively. Thunder rolled and the quiescent rain let down again, cold on the skin. One rider pointed south. Rankin's jaws moved. He shook his head in negation and gestured impatiently to the east.

They jawed some more, then spurred away to the east, their bobbing shapes gradually fading; now the gray gloom of late afternoon swallowed them.

"Just like white men," Coyote sniffed.

"Comanches our wood-smoke would have smelled."

They ran to the camp.

Uncle Billy listened and said, "We'd better pull out as soon as it's dark. Track south for a few days. Some nice little towns on east with bush tracks. One in particular called Lost Creek. You with us, Dude?"

"I am."

"I'll be drifting," Jason said.

Chapter 2

Lost Creek.

Dude squinted across the brassy distance at the little town, hardly more than a gentle ripple on the heaving sea of rolling prairie. One lonely church steeple. A scattering of trees, probably planted by some hopeful pioneer yearning for the green hills of his eastern youth. Yet, in all, an inviting place after the days of riding. Yesterday's rain had left a sparkle on the land.

"More there than meets the eye," Uncle Billy said. "At the far end of town there's a big wagonyard. Past that, there's a nice campground and good well water."

"Many saloons?"

"Enough for a sportin' man to wear calluses on his elbows."

"Don't see a courthouse," Dude said, unimpressed.

"I've been in county-seat towns not half as lively."

"Wonder why they call it Lost Creek?"

"Because the creek disappears underground south of town near where the track is."

"It sure looks small. Don't believe it's any bigger than Three Springs."

"Three Springs was big enough, wasn't it? A lot happened there. Lost Creek's a regular hub on Saturday. They swap and sell horses and mules and match race, and once a month they stage a Sale Day. All kinds of stock. That really draws 'em. Best time of all to match an unknown horse. . . . Now let's pull off here and change clothes. Want to stash this fool bowler and vest before folks take me for some Denver slicker on the make. By the way, did you happen to bring a plow-chaser's getup?"

Was that slyness creeping into the guileless face? Dude said, "No room for such. Had to travel light to catch up with you tumbling tumbleweeds."

"I remember how you, brought up as a cowboy, hated to put on farmer's duds. Like it was a comedown." The slyness was still there; if anything, it was deepening. "But you can't get out of it."

"Chew that a little finer, will you, Uncle?"

First, a meaningful pause. Next, "Your

getup's still in the wagon, just like you left it in Three Springs."

"Like I left it?" It came back to Dude now. With all that had happened, he had forgotten. "And you've kept everything? Wasn't because you schemed a little so we might be pardners again?"

"Let's say I was hoping we might match another race or so."

"And your letter?" Dude said, half accusing.

"First time I'd taken pen in hand in years. A long shot, I knew at the time, but it came through."

"You hoot owl, you," Dude said, a surge of affection rushing over him. "You knew all the time I couldn't stay away!"

Gone was all funning from the seraphic face. Uncle Billy seemed like a child, almost, open and repentant. "I didn't know. I sure wanted you and Miss Bridget to step into double harness. I'm sorry you didn't."

"We will someday."

"You see, Dude, once a horseman, always a horseman. Once he's raised 'em and schooled 'em, doctored 'em and raced 'em, a man never gets horses out of his system."

"Guess that's why so many old horsemen die in the poor house," Dude replied ruefully. "It's as bad as too much whiskey."

41

Uncle Billy had no retort for that observation. He turned his head, a going back in his blue eyes. He was, Dude saw, about to reminisce. "Used to know an old fella back in the early days who always had good horses. Wouldn't keep a sorry horse around. Always had a boss stud that could pass on the credentials. After he quit the racing circuit, he continued to raise and sell horses. That is, he might sell you one if you could qualify. He wouldn't sell to just anybody, say some well-heeled greenhorn that didn't know sic 'em. Finally, when he got way up in years, he sold out the last of his horses . . . a little bunch of mares and his last old stud . . . sold 'em to a long-time friend." He paused.

"What happened?" Dude asked, taking the familiar cue.

"Well, the old gent started pining away." Again the measured pause.

"Pining away?"

"For his horses. Got down and couldn't get up, just like a mighty sick horse. Was off his feed." Another long silence.

"I can understand that. What then?"

"Well, one day his friend that bought the horses happened by and read the situation. He didn't do a thing but pack the old fella up, take him home with him where he could be near his horses. He lived at his friend's rest of his days . . . had his place by the f'ar."

"Where was this, Uncle?" Dude asked, not meaning to pry.

A watchful laugh. "Did I say? . . . Dude, pardner, let's get into these plow-chaser duds. Your stuff's still in the old leather-covered trunk behind my medicine chest."

When Dude opened the trunk, he found his worn denim overalls, blue flannel shirt, straw hat, and work shoes of the clodhopper type — heavy, square-toed, high-topped. Behind the wagon, he struggled out of his tight-fitting cowboy boots, and, not without a modicum of lost status, his trousers, checkered vest, string tie, and cherished flat-topped planter's hat, his one true indulgence next to the handmade boots. He guessed it was the straw hat, purchased at Uncle Billy's insistence, that bothered him most. Not because it was straw, because straw was cool, but because of its chimney-pot crown, which small-town folks associated with rubes. On second thought, though, wasn't that what this was all about? For some reason, people seemed to think all sod-busters were too honest to take the advantage in a match race. Uncle Billy was right!

Ready, and amused at himself, he saw the others likewise dressed, except the legs of

Uncle Billy's overalls, too long for his short, wiry frame, were rolled up above his shoe tops, and Coyote Walking's straw hat rode low on his ears. Danny, having a better fit all around, had the appearance of an apple-cheeked farm lad. Ever the performer, he let a straw droop from his lips as he hummed the "Little Brown Jug" and shuffled his ever-restless nimble feet.

"There's one more thing," Uncle Billy told Dude. "We've added a new little wrinkle since Three Springs. Got the idea from an old mountain man who used to match races with the Utes and won plenty ponies. In fact, that was what the Utes called him — Plenty Ponies. It worked right well for us in Nebraska. Get the Judge ready, Coyote."

While Dude watched, Coyote, using a curry comb, tangled the bay gelding's black mane, added some cockleburs, then strapped on a rough, canvas pack, whereupon the Judge hung his head and stood hipshot, tail-switching flies.

"Ever see the likes of that?" Uncle Billy chortled, gesturing. "He knows what to do. Put a pack on 'im, he acts like an old pack-horse. Put a light racing saddle on 'im, he's a runnin' horse . . . carries his head high, primed to fly."

"He looks pretty sorry," Dude admitted. "Sorrier than when you used to put that ol' blanket on him and that beat-up stock saddle. He didn't look like he could outrun a fat man. It worked good."

"Still does, but I like to vary things. Now, Coyote, you and Danny dab on the peroxide. Bottle's right there on the tailgate."

Dude, remembering, watched the two smear and rub. Streaks of peroxide on the shoulders made the poor horse also appear to spend long days in the toil of heavy harness.

"Now tie him to the wagon," the old man instructed after Coyote had carefully set the peroxide bottle on the tailgate — not, Dude noticed, in what Uncle Billy called his "medicine chest," which was off bounds to the others. He would put the bottle away.

"Why don't I lead the Judge into town?" Dude suggested, when they were ready to leave. "Like he's my packhorse?"

"Dude, pardner, you're beginning to think again!"

Plodding into Lost Creek, the ground soft after the rain, trailing the wagon as he led the sorry-looking Judge Blair, Dude could not have been less impressed. Except for one lone customer entering the general store, the street was as lifeless as the road the outfit had followed here. And save for a freighter banging away on a wheel rim, the wagonyard was empty.

"Just wait till Saturday," the old man promised. "This place will look like a bee-hive. And I'll give you three-to-one odds that before the sun goes down somebody will come over to look at our horses and stand around and chew the fat. You have to remember that life is dull in these bush-track towns, that the arrival of a traveling short-horse outfit and trader means enter-tainment."

They had no more than entered the campground when Uncle Billy pulled up. He snapped out, annoyed, "Looks like we've got us some competition. Just hope they haven't skimmed off all the cream and left us the blue john."

Dude saw at the same time: a two-wagon outfit, some trade horses, and a three-man crew. He said, "Let's camp over there. That will put the well between us, and we'll be in the shade of those elms."

They had just finished watering the horses and set up camp when Dude saw the trio approaching.

"I don't like this," Uncle Billy said, scowling. "They either want to borrow something or they're nosying around." He

46

planted himself on the wash bench and pretended to be busy braiding a quirt.

The first man, Dude could see, was obviously in charge. Tall and rawboned, he was about forty years old or more, his walk loose and sauntering, and he wore one of those mechanical smiles you saw on itinerant peddlers selling small wares. His beard-fringed face was craggy, built around a bold hook of a nose. Coming into closer focus, the face had a roguish look. And the eyes, which at a distance had seemed a mild brown, now became those of a traveling horse trader: roving, intent, foxy, nervy, seldom fooled. He kept nodding and smiling that pasted-on smile, gauging the camp and its contents as he came.

The second man, whom Dude took for the outfit's handyman, showed a round and heavy face suggestive of an owl. A head shorter than the first man, he was thick through the middle and shoulders. Though younger, he seemed less alert, almost sleepy-eyed. He also was smiling, a loose-lipped smile that was no more than a vacuous grin.

The third man, in his late thirties, had the quick movements of a monkey. His fine-boned face looked drawn down, his under-sized body as well. Sun and wind had weathered his skin to the hue of mahogany. He also was smiling, a kind of roving smile. The whole outfit had the smiles. Their jock, Dude knew. If he weighs ninety-five pounds, it's soaking wet with a brick in each hand.

Something besides the smiles had been bothering Dude as they approached. Now it hit him. The trio was dressed like farmers, too, straw hats and denim overalls and clod-hopper shoes, only they didn't look like farmers. Instead, exactly what they were: traveling horse traders, here today, gone tomorrow with the wind, and you stuck with that spavined gelding you'd bought or traded for, or outslicked in a race. And, boy, were they inventorying the horses! In fact, everything in camp — the well-kept harness, saddles, blankets, bridles, down to the last cooking pan.

They came right in without so much as hesitating and the lead man boomed, "Howdy, there. Saw you boys pull in. Mighty glad to have neighbors."

"Howdy," Dude said without invitation. Uncle Billy didn't glance up from his work.

"Guess you boys will be here a spell?"

Dude shrugged a reply.

Unabashed, the tall one spread on the smile and said, "I always say a man should be neighborly," and coming forward, hand outstretched as if he meant to grab Dude, "I'm K. C. 'Sugar' Kyle — the K.C. stands for Kansas City. I was born there, and the old man named me for the place. Folks call me Sugar Kyle."

"I see," said Dude, giving Kyle's hand a brief shake.

Kyle's getup looked as how it hadn't seen soap and water for a long, long time, so sweat-streaked and greasy, it was, and the whiff Dude got of the man as they shook hands made him wish to be upwind.

"And this here," Kyle went on, pointing to the owl-faced man, "is Rufus Swink." Next to the lightweight, "And that there is Spider Gentry. Best jockey that ever crossed the finish line."

There's no getting around this, Dude thought, seeing the last two crowding up to shake hands, and smiling, and so he gave his name and said, "This is Dr. Lockhart . . . Mr. Coyote Walking . . . and Mr. Featherstone."

Uncle Billy rose stiffly and shook hands stiffly, a cold dislike framing his face. As the trio moved on, the man called Swink, seeing a pan of leftover cold biscuits on a camp table, preparatory to supper, started to help himself.

Before he could, Coyote Walking drew the

pan back, murmuring, "White man take —
Comanche spank," and smiled from the
teeth.

Swink just returned that empty grin, and
with the others went to eyeing the outfit's
possessions, fingering the team's harness,
neatly hanging on the side of the wagon, and
each saddle and bridle, touching everything
with acquisitive hands. Swink peeked into a
box of groceries, sniffing.

Dude's anger popped. This bunch would
take over if you'd let 'em. You couldn't in-
sult 'em. He called sharply, "You fellows
ever see horse and camp gear before?"

They eased off, and Kyle, unruffled,
boomed, "You got a mighty nice outfit. Sure
have." He took several objects from a shirt
pocket and bounced them in his hand,
playing with them as a boy might marbles —
they were sugar cubes. "Mind if I take a
gander at your horses?"

"Go ahead," Dude said.

Up close, the threesome ran appraising
eyes over the sorrel team, then the Judge,
then Blue Grass, then Texas Jack. Casually,
Kyle held out the sugar cubes for Texas
Jack.

"Get away from that horse!" Uncle Billy
exploded.

Kyle drew back and turned, unoffended,

still smiling. "No harm meant. An old way of mine. Never saw a horse that didn't like his sugar."

"Never saw one that sugar made faster."

Kyle shrugged and eyed Texas Jack again. "Guess this 'un is your runnin' horse. He looks smooth." When no reply was offered, Kyle spoke expansively. "We're matched up for next Saturday. Our Rattler horse against the pride of Lost Creek, a stud they call Pardner. Been hard to match 'im till we came along. Seems he's run the legs off ever'thing else around here."

"What distance you matched?" Uncle Billy asked.

"Three hundred yards for three hundred dollars," Kyle said and lowered his voice to a confidential tone. "Here's a little tip for you boys . . . bet on my Rattler. He'll win by daylight." Winking, "Always like to be neighborly, y'know. Maybe you'd like to run at us later?"

"We're in no hurry," Uncle Billy let him know, following the outfit's established rule of never appearing too eager to match a race. "Our horse is just getting over the colic."

"Laws alive, I'm sorry to hear about that, neighbor. Now I've got a sure cure you're welcome to —"

"Don't believe you heard me right. *He's getting over it.* Just needs a few more days of rest."

"If I do say so," Kyle kept on, tilting his head back, "I've done considerable in the way of doctorin' horses in my time. Was schooled in it by my old man, and what a marvel he was with herbs an' such . . . him havin' lived as a boy among the Kickapoo Indians an' learned their secret healing ways. Everything had to come straight from Mother Nature. Sometimes he'd go off in the woods an' stay for days. . . . Been known, I have, to sling a lecture now and then on various ailments that stump the ordinary vet that goes by the book." (He had the habit of chuckling to himself over what he had just said. It was plain, Dude saw, that Sugar Kyle loved to hear himself talk.) "Been a jack of all trades, you might say. Even stood for county office once."

"Mind telling us where that was?" Dude urged him on, and met with a killing glance from Uncle Billy for encouraging the windbag. No, Dude thought, let him blow. Let's hear his spiel.

"Don't mind a-tall," Kyle obliged, off and running with the bit. "It was back in Caldwell County, Missouri. Ran for county surveyor and put on a right smart campaign,

I did. Almost got myself elected. Me just a stranger, too. . . . Four-square preachin' of the gospel was my line when I was young and rasslin' with the devil. Ran a batch of temperance revivals — made it hot for the rumheads, believe you me. An' did the sufferin' womenfolk cotton to that! A clean young sprout like me, standin' up there, punchin' away at demon rum — ever' blow a knockout. Did well enough with collections. Always saw to it that a youngun whose old man was a rummy passed the hat. That was the key! Some nights we'd take in enough to fill a gunny sack, mostly widders' change . . . though from time to time some sneaky cuss would pitch in a wad o' Confederate money." He was chuckling again. "Trouble was, the womenfolk took such a powerful likin' to me an' my four-square ways that things got out o' hand. In one little burg, word got about that the banker's wife . . . a pretty little thing with big brown eyes . . . was havin' me over for late snacks an' hugs an' kisses an' such." He winked suggestively. "All this, mind you, while 'er spouse was tied up at the saloon. Good times never last long. What happens, but one night he staggers home early. He comes in the front, I slips out the back. It was close — but I won the break by daylight. . . . Got like that just about ever'where, it seemed, the womenfolk makin' a pet o' me an' fools o' themselves. So I cut out. Gave up my callin' entirely."

"That's a shame," said Uncle Billy, heavy on the sarcasm.

"After that, I took up school teachin' — the three R's, you know."

"Believe I've heard tell of 'em," Uncle Billy said dryly.

"If I do say so," Kyle said, not batting an eye, "I had a way of coinin' catchy sayings, such as . . . 'A pound of pluck is worth a ton of luck.' . . . 'Not only strike when the iron is hot, but make it hot by striking.' . . . 'Little things are great to little men.' "

"Those are bell ringers, all right."

With scarcely a pause, Kyle recited, "Another 'un was, 'A good name is better than bags of gold.' "

"You said it there," Uncle Billy badgered him.

"And uh, 'A crank is all right if you turn him the right way.' " He chuckled long on that one. "And . . . 'Honor and profit do not lie always in the same sack.' "

"You have a remarkable gift."

"Thank you, neighbor. I do pride myself on that. And there's yet another good 'un that comes to mind. 'Conceit may puff a man up, but it will never prop him up.' "

"Truer words were never spoken."

"But the schoolhouse is no place for a born horseman," Kyle continued, effecting a go at humility. "Not for a vet who cures by natural means."

Dude saw Uncle Billy perk up on that cue. If there was anything the old gent relished, it was verbal jousting connected with horses.

"Natural means, you say?"

"Laws alive, yes. Herbs an' such, like the old man taught me. Take my cure for the colic I was about to pass on to you free of charge. A cure derived from nature's bounties."

"Let's hear it."

"First off, the digestive organs should be kept in as healthy condition as possible. I recommend wild prairie hay, well shaken up."

"Believe they teach that in the primer."

"One teaspoonful of lobelia," Kyle said, unruffled, "once a day, given with the hay for a week, will often relieve the animal."

"Get down to the particulars, man."

Kyle slipped on his peddler's smile. "Didn't think that was all, did you? Here it is, neighbor. Two common tablespoonfuls of saleratus — never heaping — mixed with one and a half pints of frest sweet milk — administered in one dose."

"Milk!" snorted Uncle Billy. "The only time milk is ever needed is for a foal nursing its mammy. As for saleraturs, its common name is baking soda."

The battle was joined, Dude saw, and leaned back to enjoy the tilting.

"That's a home remedy. Here's one I call my Four-Square Remedy, which should always be kept on hand — one ounce each of chloroform, sulphuric ether, and laudanum."

The old man sneered. "They spooned that to babies where I grew up. Won't cure a colicky horse, just put 'im to sleep. Tally this remedy in your memorandum book . . . take one pint of sour-mash whiskey, add three heaping tablespoonfuls of common gunpowder. Give in one dose. If not better within an hour, repeat the dose and throw in a pint of linseed oil."

Kyle drew back, adopting a lofty posture. "I never give whiskey to a horse. It's not four square."

"Well, let me tell you something. Sour-mash whiskey, properly administered with other potions, is a dang sight closer to Mother Nature than chloroform and laudanum." Kyle shrugged and the old man, becoming thoughtful, cocked a challenging eye at him. "How would you go about treating bone spavin? Chew on that?"

"Easy, neighbor. Equal parts of wormwood, sassafras, and capsicum. Rub in briskly. If the animal shows signs of distress, add a few drops of laudanum in his water for relief."

Dude crossed his arms and hand-covered a grin, thinking that the way Sugar Kyle rattled off remedies without so much as a moment's hesitation, his mentor had finally met his match this once.

Uncle Billy said, "I see you're still strong for that laudanum, which is a fancy name for a tincture of opium. If I'se going the Mother Nature route, I'd apply hot water and vinegar, and give the poor critter plenty of bran and flaxseed. Every schoolboy knows that the seed of flax is the source of linseed oil and of emollient medicinal preparations."

As Kyle blinked on that one, Dude heard a slap and a crash and, turning, spied Swink stepping back from the biscuit pan and Coyote Walking, hand upraised, ready to administer another slap.

"Rufus!" Kyle called. "Where's the manners I been tryin' to learn yuh? Now stand back there — behave like a proper gentleman. And you — Spider, take your hands off that new bridle." Swink and Gentry

57

backed away with sickly grins, and Kyle, in apology, said to Uncle Billy, "Sorry, neighbor. They're just backward country boys. I've tried to learn 'em."

"Believe you need to try some more. I've seen mules with better manners."

Dude supposed the duel was finished, Uncle Billy holding the edge, when the old man spoke again to Kyle. "I can see that you have done considerable in the way of doctorin' horses in your time, as you say. What would you recommend to stop the heaves quickly?"

Dude sensed a trap.

Yet, Kyle answered easily, without pause. "Two ounces each of gentian, Spanish brown, and lobelia — no more, mind you — three ounces of resin, eight of Jamaica ginger. It's only a temporary relief and will not cure, but —" He checked himself.

" — is good to trade on," Uncle Billy polished it off, winking at him.

"You said it, neighbor, I didn't," Kyle came back, again presenting that straight face.

"You got it down pat," Uncle Billy agreed, and added his possum grin, "except you left out your laudanum."

Dude laughed, everybody laughed, including Kyle, who, motioning for Swink and

Gentry to go, said, "You boys come over and play with us, now. Mighty good to have neighbors. And don't forget to bet on Rattler."

After the trio had gone, Uncle Billy muttered, "A mangy, sticky-fingered outfit, if I ever saw one. We'll have to keep somebody here in camp all the time, or they'll carry it off."

"How do you figure Kyle?" Dude asked.

"A blowhard — but a cagey one — and he's done some doctoring, like he claims. But I can't take that four-square gospel stuff." He was looking toward town as he talked. Suddenly his face wrinkled expectation. "Look! What did I tell you? We've got company on the way. You talk to 'em, Dude. That Sugar Kyle winded me."

A little bevy of loafers, Dude saw, whittlers and chewers and likely domino players, come to see what the new horse trader had brought to town. Aimlessly, one by one, they seemed to float up to the camp's edge, lodging there like pieces of driftwood, while they sized up the horses, nodding all the while. One man stirred himself after a bit, a brown-eyed little man whose ears stuck out like flaps on a winter cap. He was chewing on a matchstick and he spoke around it now, as friendly as Kyle was foxy. "Guess you carry a racehorse?"

"That dark bay yonder," Dude replied, pointing to Texas Jack.

"Looks like he can run," the little man said.

"A little. That is — sometimes he can — sometimes he can't."

The other grinned and paced slowly around Texas Jack and stopped to consider. "Yes, I'd say he can. What's his best distance?"

"Oh, anywhere up to three hundred yards. Depends how strong a tailwind he's got. He's no long-distance horse."

"I see you're not one to brag."

"Braggin' never won a horse race."

"But it sure helps get one started." When one onlooker uttered a chuckling laugh, the rest joined in concert.

Dude decided to open the ball. "You got a horse you want to match?"

"Reed Neale's got the only real runnin' horse around here, and he's matched Sugar Kyle next Saturday."

"So we heard. We're not plumb eager to run, anyway. Been on the go. All wore out, and Texas Jack there is just gettin' over the colic. He'd have to go short."

"About how much would you want to bet . . . say you did run?"

"Twenty-five dollars . . . maybe." By starting low, you didn't scare the other man off; besides, if you ran your slow horse first and lost, which you almost always did unless the other horse fell down or broke a leg or jumped the track, to set the stage for a second race and your look-alike fast horse and hoped-for odds, you didn't want to lose enough to hurt.

The man took the match from his mouth, spate and dug the toe of his heavy shoe into the soft earth. "I see you're not one to wager much," he said, slow-grinning.

"Not," said Dude, matching the grin, "on a horse that's just gettin' over the colic."

"By the same token, you don't stand to win much, either." With that, like a choir following every move of its director, the loafers clucked and nudged in unison.

Dude was likewise enjoying the easy-going exchange. Catching Uncle Billy's eye, he suddenly remembered something. At this crucial point in the dickering, it was proven strategy to pretend that you really had no hankering to match your horse at any distance for any amount. And so he circled some more. "By the way, who's favored Saturday?"

"Reed's stud is."

"That the horse they call Pardner?"

"He's the one."

Dude ribbed him gently. "Favored just because he's the local horse?"

"Pardner's taken the slack out of so many horses around Lost Creek that Reed can't match him anymore, and we've never seen this Rattler horse run."

"Not even work out?"

"Not even once. See, Kyle works him early of a morning . . . takes him way out."

"Where?"

"Never the same place twice."

"Maybe he's slickering you. Maybe you boys better be careful."

"You always bet the favorite, don't you?"

"I do most times. Depends."

"Depends on what?"

"If I think the favorite's gonna win."

"Why not?"

"Things can happen."

There was a pause between them, and Dude realized that the preliminaries were over, and although nothing had been decided, he sensed a concealed hanging on by the other. He figures he has the advantage, Dude thought, and he's getting impatient. If he only knew the advantage he does have!

Waiting him out, Dude saw the man circle Texas Jack again, noting every feature, more observant than the first time. Coming back, he dug out his pocketknife and a plug of tobacco, opened the knife and cut off a big wedge and plopped it into his mouth off the blade. He closed the knife and returned it and the plug to an overall pocket, wallowing the bulging cud until he settled it in his jaw as he might a piece of hard-rock candy. He bent and scooped up a wad of the soft loam and pinched it thoughtfully between thumb and fore and middle fingers, examining it. For all his eagerness, Dude saw, he was a cautious man. He said all at once,

"I might run my old mare at you."

"Oh," said Dude, feigning surprise. "Bet she's a real breeze-burner for you to challenge a stranger."

"Guess Sister Nellie is like your horse — she's off and she's on."

"How much you want to bet?"

"Fifty dollars — if you're interested?"

"Well . . . reckon you've run at Pardner?"

"Tell you the truth, I never have. You can ask these boys." He turned to the loafers and Dude saw them nod as one, just as he knew they would. "Seems like we never could get together," the man explained. "Something always happened. One time we's all ready, had everything set, and dog my old cats if Pardner didn't come up with bucked shins! Next time, Sister Nellie got the thumps. Too, she's generally been in foal till this year, when she didn't settle. Another time, Pardner had the heaves."

Dude thought, Boy, can this plow chaser lay it on! More excuses than a last-place jockey.

"Another time," Sister Nellie's owner continued, "my old mare got wire cut morning of the race. Another time —"

Dude raised both hands high in mock surrender. "You've convinced me, friend. I just wondered if you'd run at Pardner. Maybe we can match this race." He turned, calling, "What do you think, Uncle? Is Texas Jack on the improve enough to run a little?"

"Well," Uncle Billy began, coughing and assuming a serious manner, "he took his last dose of medicine this morning. He's lost that sleepy look, he's quit pawin' with one foot, his legs and ears are normal temperature, and he's not gassy. In my opinion, he's in condition to run a tol'able short race."

"That's what I want to hear," Dude exclaimed, and to the other, "Dr. Lockhart is helping out as our vet and trainer. He's an old friend of my daddy's, down in Texas. We call him Uncle Billy. He's come out West for his catarrh, which is clearing up nicely. On leave from the Kentucky School of Veterinary Medicine, where he graduated magnet come loud and now teaches. . . . So we might run at you Saturday, Mr. . . ."

"The name's Jake Bowman. I run the hardware store."

"Glad to make your acquaintance, Mr. Bowman. I'm Dude McQuinn."

They shook hands formally.

"Only I can't run you Saturday," Bowman said apologetically. "Be a great big old crowd there — lots of hollerin' and goin' on, and my old mare is high strung. She'd throw a wall-eyed fit. We'd never get off."

"Let's see," said Dude, considerately. "Today is Thursday. Can't run you today, when Texas Jack is just finishing up on his medicine. What about Friday?"

"Friday will be just dandy, Mr. McQuinn."

Boy, Dude thought, he took that and ran with it. Almost too fast, on second thought. There was something here that didn't quite meet the eye, yet the outfit had to establish Texas Jack as a horse that could be beaten, and it mattered not whether he went against Sister Nellie or Rattler or Pardner. Dude said, "The track may still be a little soggy by Friday."

"That's all right. It's that great big old crowd that bothers Sister Nellie. Why, Saturday this place will look like the Fourth of July. Now, guess you want to take a look at my old mare?"

"I sure do, before we cinch this up and decide on the distance."

"Well, sir, she's tied up behind that big old empty building next to the old Jayhawk Saddle Shop. Always like to keep 'er away from crowds."

"Believe you could tie her just about anywhere today in Lost Creek, Mr. Bowman, and it wouldn't upset her. . . . Uncle Billy, I wish you'd go along with us, if you feel like it?"

"Pleased to." Joining them, Uncle Billy shook hands with Bowman. "As a matter of academic interest, Mr. Bowman, may I inquire as to the pedigree of Sister Nellie?"

"Well, Doc, about all I can tell you is that she's by Avalanche, the stud on the old Pid Jenkins farm west of here, and out of a sprint mare on the old Jiggs Brady place east of here."

"Most interesting, Mr. Bowman. Can you tell me what line Avalanche traces back to?"

"You've got me there. All I know is that Pid bought him off an old trader comin' up from Texas."

"Ah! Texas short-horse blood. Excellent! And Sister Nellie's dam?"

"That's Sister Sue. Jiggs bought her in Missouri. She ran pretty good till she bowed a tendon. . . . Reminds me. My old mare has moon blindness sometimes. Anything a man can do about that?"

"Ophthalmia," Uncle Billy said, summoning his lecturing tone, "commonly known as moon blindness, is a periodic thing. An inflammation of the eye, especially of the conjunctiva. Seems to come and go with the changes of the moon. I suggest that you institute special care when you notice this condition so she won't injure herself, and give a condition powder with warm bran mashes."

"Thanks, Doc. I'll remember that. Sure appreciate it."

Brown Sister Nellie, Dude soon saw, walking around her, looked anything but an "old mare." She couldn't be more than five or six, although he didn't examine her teeth, and she mounted up well in the withers, had long, strong muscles, a nice head, clean, flat bones, a short back, and well-muscled hindquarters. She stood straight except for her left front foot, which was somewhat twisted and enlarged around the hoof and pastern. Dude pretended not to notice. He said, "Like to go three hundred yards?"

Bowman knifed off another wedge of tobacco before he answered. "A little too far down the track for my old mare. What say, one furlong?"

"A little too short."

"You see that left front foot?" Bowman dickered.

"I see it. But I reckon you wouldn't run her if it hindered her any, would you, friend?"

Bowman let that pass. He took a pinch of the soft loam and let it dribble away.

Then Dude shrugged and said, "Tell you what I'll do. I'll run you two hundred and fifty yards." Not that distance made much difference when you were going to lose; still, you didn't want your horse to look ridiculous. Texas Jack might look a little better losing at two-fifty.

"It's a race," Bowman came on fast. "Would — would you like to raise the ante a notch . . . say up to seventy-five dollars?"

"Don't believe I can, Mr. Bowman." Why hand this plow-chaser merchant another twenty-five dollars?

"We'll go at fifty then. What time Friday?"

"Anytime."

"Two o'clock?"

"Fine."

"The track is south of town."

"What about our starter?" Dude asked,

noting that Bowman, in his anticipation, had overlooked that also.

"We can get Van Clark. He runs that old livery down the street."

Dude appeared to study on that.

"Van's started every old race around here for the last twenty years. That right, boys?"

They nodded, like always.

"Van Clark is agreeable with me," Dude said.

"Is it all right with you if Reed Neale and Alf Tinker are the judges?"

"Who's Alf Tinker?"

"He runs the old general store. We call on him to catch the finish when he can get away from the store, and on Reed when Pardner's not running."

"All right," said Dude.

They shook hands.

Turning for camp, Uncle Billy said, "I got a hunch that mare can run."

"So have I. She's a walkin' picture except for that foot. I didn't argue about the judges. Might have looked better."

"No matter, when we know pretty well how the race will go."

Chapter 3

It was like old times to Dude as they sat around the campfire that evening, listening to the horses cropping the good grass, the "hoomhoom" of the hoot owls, and the high wailing of the coyotes beyond town. Tonight, he thought, especially tonight, the wild notes seem to go straight up to the sky. Maybe that's a good sign.

Coyote Walking, his expression teasing, leaned back and commenced singing, and as he reached the highest drawn-out pitch, the coyote voices chimed in, man and prairie wolf harmonizing, until the human singing could hardly be distinguished from the coyote chorus.

When he ceased, the wild voices ceased. After some moments, one by one, as if waiting for their newly found caroler, the coyotes resumed singing.

"They want you to sing some more," Dude said.

The Comanche shook his head. "They will sing all night, those coyotes."

"Maybe Danny will play us a little tune," Uncle Billy suggested.

Danny hastily finished a cold, sourdough biscuit; it seemed that he was always eating. The old man and Coyote teased him about his appetite, which, Danny explained, had grown during his hungry days in Denver and was not yet appeased.

He snapped to his feet and flashed a broad smile, ready to please, harmonica in hand. "What would you like, Uncle?"

"Let's hear 'The Girl I Left Behind Me.' "

Danny blew tentatively on the harmonica and swung into the tune, keeping up a lively foot-tapping, while Uncle Billy beat time against his leg, his whiskery face alight. Likewise, Coyote nodded to the beat, clapping his hands, his dark eyes shining.

Dude found himself feeling the music, swinging his arm back and forth. Son of a gun, how this Danny could play!

And then, with a flourish, Danny brought the song to a close and struck into a pert jig, never missing a step, snapping his fingers and jiggling his head, perfectly balanced, a horseman might say, as light on his feet as a spring colt. Tap, tap. That boyish smile. Now, toe and heel. Now, the toe-and-heel click. Finished, he smiled and bowed to the outfit's applause.

"Mighty fine, Danny," Dude sang out. "Never saw or heard better."

"Danny can play just about anything," Uncle Billy said.

"I can't read music," Danny amended. "But once I hear a piece I can remember it most times."

"It's a gift," cried the old man. "That's what it is. Now play 'Lorena' for us. And I want Dude to hear you sing it."

"You're sentimental tonight, Uncle. 'Lorena' it is."

Slowly, softly, Danny breathed into the harmonica and Dude began to hear the strains of the Civil War song, and, shortly, Danny's young tenor, warm and appealing, the words clear and tender:

The years creep slowly by, Lorena,
The snow is on the grass again:
The sun's low down the sky, Lorena
The frost gleams where the flowers have been.

Danny's sweeping smile dispelled the somberness of the song, as if he could not long abide sugary melancholy; and Dude, to guy his old mentor, frowned and said critically, "Isn't that a Johnny Reb song?"

Instant denial rushed to the old man's face. But Danny spoke first, mannerly and placating. "Believe it was sung by both sides. So my paternal grandfather used to say."

"Your grandfather?" Uncle Billy echoed.

"He was in New York City's Irish Brigade — the 88th Regiment. Their flags were emerald green embroidered in gold, and, you might know, with an Irish harp, a shamrock, and a sunburst. He said they sang 'Lorena' . . . 'My Old Kentucky Home' . . . 'Old Black Joe' . . . 'Nellie Gray' and lots more."

"See!" A cackling, chortling laugh. "You Alamo Texans can't claim everything. Now, Danny, give us 'Danny Boy.'" And for Dude's benefit, "First time I ever heard him sing it was in Denver. Seemed everybody in the saloon broke down and started buyin' drinks for everybody else, fellas who'd been in a brawl only five minutes before."

Danny played a stretch of the slow-paced, pining notes, drawing them out to the fullest yearning, and then he sang, and then he played some more, switching back and forth like that.

Dude's eyes were moist before Danny took his bow.

No one moved for moments. It was Uncle

Billy who broke the hush. "Danny, you need to be where many people can hear you."

"Right now," Danny laughed, "eating is more important. Denver can get mighty cold and hungry. Besides, I like where I am."

When no one spoke after some moments, Coyote Walking shifted his feet and looked around at them, on his high-boned face a recalling expression that Dude knew was prelude to a story told in lingo. Coyote then said,

"Eating every day is good times on the prosperity for Comanches. Not so, soon after buffalo-gone days." His voice changed to a singsong tempo, "Little bird was told me when one old woman her first garden did she plant on reservation — reservation white mans say they give Comanches, though funny thing, 'cause Comanches own land already." He shook his head, deploring. "Little bird was told me on the springtime it was when old woman her garden did she plant. Many melon seeds in Grandmother Earth she put." At this point dramatic gestures: digging, planting, hoeing, bending to watch the plantings grow, a beatific expression filling the Roman-nosed face. "Hard she work, doin' just like white mans tell Comanches: work hard, be good Injun, stay outa Texas. . . . Time pass. Moon come. Moon stay. Moon go, by and by. Melons grow. Old woman hungry is she.

"One morning this old woman her garden when she go to it got was all pulled up. Hmmmnn. Who this bad thing all melons pulled up? But old woman White Wolf knows, and this White Wolf he's a big championship eater on the village and when he can he eat a white mans' coffee in bed, too. Old woman to his lodge go she did. Sure enough, White Wolf devil in belly got. Stomach all tipped over." He paused and looked around, awaiting laughter, but the others had fallen silent.

"What did the old woman do?" Dude asked, finally.

"No garden in Grandmother Earth she put again," Coyote answered, beginning to shake with mirth, holding his sides.

"Didn't she get hungry?"

Coyote nodded. "But fool that championship eater on the village she did. No more melons for him on the springtime!"

"You know," said Uncle Billy, scratching his chin, "guess I never will savvy Injun humor."

"Just like white man," Coyote retorted, twirling a forefinger alongside his head.

"You mean just like Injun — not funny."

"Want me to tell it again?" Coyote obliged, falling back on his Carlisle School English for clarity. "Well, little bird was told me when one old woman her first —"

"Heaven forbid! Spare me any more of that Comanche gibberish."

"But don't you see, Grandfather Billy," Coyote struggled, "there were no more melons for White Wolf to pull up on the springtime? Imagine his surprise! Imagine the old woman's feeling of triumph! Don't you see, Grandfather?" He was beginning to quake again.

"I don't see," came the testy reply, "and don't call me Grandfather." He turned in disgust to Dude. "He's still at it. Still calling me Grandfather. I'd rather try to break a horse of a bad habit."

"He's merely showing respect for an elder — that's all, Grandfather Billy," Dude badgered him.

"Now you're both at it. When I'm ready for my place by the f'ar, I'll tell you."

And thus the evening progressed, the give-and-take bantering, and, uppermost, the everlasting talk of runnin' horses. Short horses that Uncle Billy said could "run a hole in the wind," scorpions like Dan Tucker of Illinois, sire of the famed Peter McCue; Barney Owens, Butt Cut, Jack

Traveler, Hi Henry, and Sykes Rondo, to name a few. Dude could have listened all night as the old man drew on his never-ending store of reminiscences.

"Judge Blair," Uncle Billy stated, "could run with any of 'em."

As Dude listened, it occurred to him that at last one William Tecumseh Lockhart, off guard, had let drop the whereabouts of his original stomping grounds, and Dude could not resist venturing into that forbidden area. "Remember Dan Tucker's breeding, Uncle? I know he was a boss horse for sure."

"He was a Shiloh-Steel Dust cross. By Barney Owens, out of Butt Cut."

"That's mighty interesting." Dude seemed to ponder. "Believe Dan Tucker was from around Petersburg, Illinois, wasn't he?"

Somewhat warily, "He was. His home was the Little Grove Stock Farm, run by a man named Samuel Watkins. Why?"

"Just wondered, maybe, if —"

"If I ever lived there? Wouldn't be prying, would you, Dude, pardner?"

"Just interested, is all, since you said you saw Dan Tucker run."

Gruffly, "I saw Dan Tucker beat his half brother, Sheriff, in a famous match race over the quarter mile. Dan Tucker ran on down there in twenty-two seconds."

"Whew! Where was that, Uncle?"

"St. Louis, Missouri." The saintly countenance was a study in dry amusement. "Don't recall saying I ever lived there, either."

And that's that, Dude thought, grinning back. It was like a game between them, a game that was never resolved.

As suddenly, the old man's tone was relenting. "That was the fastest official quarter mile ever run in Missouri up to that time. I believe the record still stands. You see, Sheriff had dusted a heap of top horses in Texas and Kansas, and his owner had come in there on the look-see for fresh money. I remember because I won five hundred dollars that day. Went home singing."

"Home?" Dude hung on, probing.

"Did I say where?"

And they both laughed, struck by the absurdity of their fencing, and Uncle Billy said, "Believe that calls for a little toddy before bedtime."

Chapter 4

After breakfast, continued clinking sounds drew Dude to the rear of the camp wagon. Uncle Billy was bent over his medicine chest, that odorous and mysterious wooden box redolent of pine pitch, turpentine, camphor, oil of hemlock, wintergreen, and sassafras. These familiar smells Dude could identify; there were others more subtle he could not.

Like its owner's past, the box was hands off. Once, early in the partnership, Dude was caught rummaging for liniment. Uncle Billy let go a pantherish yell; thereafter, Dude had not invaded the old man's domain again.

Coyote Walking regarded the off-bounds box as something mystical, through the reverential eyes of a superstitious Plains Indian. "Grandfather Billy," he had told Dude afterward, "is a medicine man. Medicine is power and not to be handled by everyone. That box is like a Comanche's medicine bag, secreting objects known only to the Grandfather." The dark eyes widened. "Should you or I touch the sacred objects, Uncle Billy might lose his power. Sometimes I wonder, though I would not dare look, whether Grandfather's box does not contain a handful of sweet grass or cedar twigs or some beaver oil or the gristle of a bear's snout or a deer's tail, or something from the all-powerful Owl Person, a claw or feather."

"I know one medicine that's in that box," Dude said. "It's called sour-mash whiskey."

The old horseman was intent as he measured and mixed and poured into a whiskey bottle, and held the concoction up to the light and cocked an eye. "Just about right," he said to himself, ignoring Dude.

"We got a sick horse?" Dude asked, concerned.

"Just mixing a little pick-me-up for Texas Jack. Don't want him to look too slow. Some of Professor Gleason's Original Sure-Shot Conditioner. A horse, you see, is like a human in the respect that he needs an occasional tonic."

Dude, leaning in to study the brownish mixture, got an unmistakable whiff. "That smells like whiskey and" — he gagged — "asafetida. What else is in it?"

Impatiently, "Mean you don't remember? Besides one ounce of asafetida, one ounce each of Spanish fly, oil of anise, oil of cloves, oil of cinnamon and fenugreek, and two ounces of antimony. Ordinarily, I'd use brandy to add, but Kentucky sour mash does as well. Ten drops daily of this conditioner in a gallon of water will make an old horse get up and howl and a young horse want to fly."

The old man, who kept everything in his head, had recited the mixture without pause. Dude had yet to see him refer to a list of ingredients.

He was, Dude could see, in fine fettle for so early in the morning. His crotchetiness would recede after a pull at the clay jug and his arthritic joints loosened up as the day advanced.

Coyote and Danny drifted over to listen, whereupon Uncle Billy, never loath to ignore an audience, no matter how small or how familiar, cleared his throat and gestured toward Judge Blair — the signals for a lecture.

"I doubt," he began, "that you will ever see more perfect conformation than this horse has. I like to say, and you will find other horsemen of the same opinion, that Conformation Foretells Performance." (Once Uncle

Billy coined a dictum he used it over and over, Dude remembered.) "However, heart is equally important and although you can't measure it, it is the one indispensable force needed to make a horse come from behind and win. I like to say this about a good horse: He never lost falling back, he was always coming up. . . . So conformation alone won't make a runnin' horse, no matter how smooth he looks — if a horse doesn't hanker to get on down there and outrun the pack, if there's not speed on both sides of his breeding. An example was Rebel. As smooth-looking as they come. Yet his heart just wasn't in it, bless him. But, in most cases, conformation tells you whether a horse can do what you ask of him."

He moved closer to Judge Blair. "Conformation can affect a horse's behavior. For example, consider the Judge's eyes, which are large and clear and set wide apart. Eyes placed close together limit a horse's side and rear vision, and what he can't see may bother him . . . cause him to throw a fit. Furthermore, good conformation means balance and equilibrium, which calls to mind what Professor Gleason termed the center of gravity in a horse."

Danny held up a questioning hand, as curious as a schoolboy. "Who was Professor Gleason, Uncle?"

Ah, thought Dude, we're getting on queasy footing.

"Professor Gleason," Uncle Billy replied, never pausing, "was an old and trusted friend, since gone to his just and final reward. Inventor of Professor Gleason's Eureka Bridle for subduing horses made vicious by the inhumanity of man, and discoverer of various remedies to ease the suffering of man's most noble fellow creature."

"Where'd you know him?" Danny exclaimed, impressed.

Dude listened with a smile, wondering how the old man would parry that innocent query.

"Oh, back in the early days," came the evasive reply.

"What's your formula for speed?" Dude asked, enjoying this.

"There's only one — breed speed to speed. That way you won't take anything away from the break, and the break is everything in a short-horse race. Conformation will take care of itself if you stick to proven bloodlines. . . . Another thing. All most greenhorns can see is the stud. They overlook the dam's importance, when the dam is the main wellspring of any union — I'll say sixty per cent or more. You can put that down as gospel."

An exceptional thoughtfulness softened his voice, turned it wistful. "I've owned some top horses, and not just runnin' horses, that had as much sense as I did, and in certain situations better judgment than I had. If a good horse can't make it to heaven, blamed if I want to go there, either."

He walked back to his medicine chest. The lecture was over.

Later this race-day morning, Uncle Billy suggested that Dude accompany him to pay a call on Sugar Kyle's outfit.

"Always like to be neighborly," the old man said, mimicking Kyle's booming voice.

"What you mean is, you want to take a look-see at Rattler."

As they approached the camp, Dude saw the little bunch of trade horses tied under the trees. They looked poor and drawn down. And closer to the wagons, in the shade, he saw a light bay gelding haltered alone. That would be Rattler.

The outfit had been here for some time, judging by the litter of tin cans, bottles, rags, and pieces of leather. An unwashed pot hung over the dead campfire; tin cups, plates, and cutlery, also unwashed, were stacked on a wooden crate. Hordes of flies circled stickily. A set of harness, flung over a wagon wheel, showed numerous patches, as did the wagon cover. Rufus Swink and Spider Gentry lounged on bedrolls under the farthest wagon, talking and smoking. Kyle dozed in a chair by the nearest wagon, straw hat pulled over his eyes.

At the sound of footsteps, Kyle snapped awake and Dude saw the peddler's smile draw across his face like a window shade. He heaved to his feet, shaking hands and greeting, "Howdy, neighbors. I hear you've matched yourselves a race today."

"That's right," Dude said. "Two o'clock."

"Maybe I'd better put down some money on your horse?"

"I never tell a man how to bet. Might lose a friend."

"Well, my tip still stands on Rattler. Take it or leave it. Funny thing, when I heard that Bowman had that sprint mare, I tried to match him. But he wouldn't take me on at any distance . . . gave him his choice, too. That was three weeks ago. Guess he was afraid of Rattler."

"Rattler is what we've come to see," Dude said.

"Always glad to show my horse. Like to be neighborly. Wait just a minute." He took long, charging steps to the other wagon.

Swink and Gentry sat up suddenly, but before they could crawl out, Kyle was upon them, kicking their feet, yelling, "Get up! We've got company! Where's the manners I learned yuh!"

They scrambled out and stood chastened by the wagon.

Striding back, no dent in his neighborliness, Kyle escorted the visitors toward the light bay, talking every step, Swink and Gentry trailing like obedient hound dogs. "This horse will fool you. He looks small and measures big. Know what I mean? Perfect proportions, if I do say so. Just a little over fifteen hands high. Strong through the shoulders. Good hind legs and forelegs — long-muscled. Good middle. Good back. Good head. Good bone. Stands right up there, believe you me. What more would a man want in a runnin' horse?"

We're off again, Dude thought, amused. However, you had to admit that this Sugar Kyle could stretch the blanket and then some.

Upon reaching Rattler, Kyle fed him a handful of sugar cubes. The gelding munched them eagerly. "He sure takes to his sugar," Kyle said.

Uncle Billy's response was a look of disapproval. He rounded the horse and stopped, still appraising. "What's his breeding, Kyle?"

Dude got set for a windy blowup of the gelding's ancestry, all kings and queens; instead, Kyle said, "Just wished I knew, neighbor. Bought him two years ago in northern Kansas off a cowboy, who'd bought him off a farmer, who'd bought him off another farmer, who'd bought him off a Nebraska trader, who'd bought him as a yearling off a party of folks from Iowa travelin' through to take up homestead land out Wyoming way. . . . I bought him the same day I saw him take it all at one-quarter mile. Believe you me, he never let up. If the other jock had throwed a rock, he'd never touched Rattler's dust."

"If he's that fast, we'd better not talk match race."

Kyle's face changed with the tone of Dude's voice, and his mouth opened like a cave. "Laws alive, neighbor. I didn't say he'd outrun everything. Just *most* everything — now and then." He looked down, his face confessional. "I have had one trouble with this horse. Sometimes he gets off his feed. When he does, a fence post could beat him."

"And," Uncle Billy said, quick to take up the challenge, "I suppose you restore his appetite by natural means?"

So they were at it again, Dude saw.

But Kyle was ready. "Just mix four ounces of each of pulverized caraway seeds and bruised raisins, two ounces each of ginger and palm oil."

"All right as far as you went," the old man sniffed. "I never bruise the raisins. Furthermore, I give twice as much of the first part as I do of the last. One ball a day is sufficient. Use warm mashes at the same time."

"Neighbor," said Kyle, showing no offense, "you do cut it fine." He seemed of a mind to discontinue the sparring.

Uncle Billy persisted, "Since you say you have done considerable in the way of doctorin' horses in your time, which I do not doubt, what is your cure for halter pulling? Answer me that, Kyle."

"Why'n't you give me a tough one, neighbor? Just take an ordinary rope strong enough to answer the purpose of a halter and long enough to pass between the forelegs and under the surcingle — using the surcingle to keep the rope in place — tie with a slipknot to one of the hind feet. A few trials will satisfy any horse that pullin' is a total failure. He'll soon throw himself. A few experiences will be enough to break him for all time."

"Or a leg," Uncle Billy countered. "Because it's safer, I much prefer to bore a hole through a plank and spike it upright in front of the manger, with the hole about six feet from the floor. Take a strong rope, tie one end to the halter and run it through the plank hole; then tie a two hundred-pound stone to the other end of the rope. He'll get mighty tired lifting on that stone, and your horse won't break anything except his bad habit. How's that for natural means?"

Kyle was raising a disputatious finger when the shuffle of hoofs intruded. Dude saw a farmer leading in two trade horses.

"Got a customer," Kyle said, obviously glad to get away. "Don't run off. Stay and play with us some more. Always good to have neighbors come over."

"We have to go," Dude said.

"There operates a true horse trader, Dude," Uncle Billy mused, watching Kyle greet the farmer. "Now he's passing out the sugar cubes. He'll skin that farmer so many ways, the poor fella will be lucky to get out with his galluses." Shaking his head, he gazed hard at the camp as they walked away. "Notice how that harness was patched — with rawhide? Wagon covers, too? This is a rawhide outfit, Dude. That tells me something about Kyle and those two clowns."

"Tells you what?"

89

"Back in the early days people who kept on the move from one section to another were called rawhiders because they used rawhide for just about every purpose."

"Don't we move a good deal?" Dude came back at him.

"There's a difference. Rawhider was not exactly a complimentary term. Some rawhiders had sticky fingers. They'd latch on to chickens, loose hogs, milk cows, buckets, washtubs, plows, ropes, saddles, blankets, bridles — anything that wasn't tied down — and that included horses, which they'd trade off fast in the next town."

Dude could hear Kyle's extolling voice as he worked up to a swap-and-boot trade. Dude said, "You didn't seem taken with Rattler. Why?"

"His neck and back are too long and he stands with his feet out behind him, not squarely under him."

"So you don't figure he can run?"

"Don't mean that a-tall. Just don't like his conformation."

"Another thing, Uncle. Why was Jake Bowman so all-fired eager to match us when he wouldn't Kyle?"

"We'll know why about sixteen seconds after two o'clock. Which reminds me, we'd better slick up Texas Jack for the race."

Chapter 5

Lost Creek's race track was what Texas horsemen called a "bull ring" — a small, circular course. But in lieu of the usual half-mile strip, this one was only a quarter mile, with sharp turns that many horses couldn't navigate. Some straight-ahead sprinters would "run blind," smash through the outside guard rail unless pulled up. Judge Blair could take the turns, though seldom had the outfit matched him on an oval. Compensating here, however, and to Dude's preference, was the long straightaway on the prairie, smoother than most, he judged, still soft from the recent rain, yet not slippery. It flanked the vanishing tree-lined creek that gave the town its name.

Bowman was waiting with his mare and jockey when the outfit arrived minus Danny, left behind to keep an eye on the camp. They shook hands with Bowman and Van Clark, the starter, a smallish, friendly man past his middle years, pleased to have today's official duties.

"I'll drop my hat and holler go only when the horses are closely lapped," he said. "I want them head to head as much as possible when they walk up to the line."

Everybody nodded agreement.

"Are you gentlemen ready?"

Everybody was.

"All right. Take your horses down the track and back and we'll run this race. Good luck."

Coyote, stripped to breechcloth and moccasins, trotted Texas Jack away, and Bowman's jockey, a kid looking about wet-gunnysack weight, jogged Sister Nellie downtrack. The noisy crowd, strung along the course, considerably exceeded Bowman's prediction, and the brown mare merely displayed friskiness as she danced along, eager to run, behaving like a lady, the twisted foot no hindrance. If the crowd bothered her, she didn't show it.

Dude positioned himself. Bowman's friends were nearby, chatting and gesturing. They kept looking at him. Did he see smirks? A sudden suspicion warned him.

Shortly, the horses trotted back and Clark waved the jockeys to the head of the track to commence the walk-up to the broad line drawn across the race paths. Ready, they turned and moved forward, fairly well lapped, the mare as steady as a work horse in harness.

Suddenly, Texas Jack broke early, half a length in front, and the patient Clark called the jockeys back. Coyote had to pull hard to bring the gelding about, while the gentle mare reined as easily as a cutting horse. Once more the walk-up, the horses lapped as they approached the line.

All at once Clark dropped his hat and shouted.

Dude tensed, seeing the horses break together. A few jumps and daylight opened. The mare was gone, streaking on the soft path. Coyote whooped at his horse, a sign of early trouble. On that impetus Texas Jack moved up, trying hard, but the catch-up speed wasn't there and the mare was tearing away, lengthening stride.

After one hundred yards, she was building a two-length lead. Coyote whooped again and this time he whapped his quirt across the gelding's rump. Nothing changed. Texas Jack could run no faster. Coyote didn't hit him again. The mare was really taking hold by now. Her lead looked three lengths.

In a wink it was over.

Head down, Dude started walking to the

finish line. He hadn't expected Texas Jack to win. Still, he had honestly felt that the dark bay could give the mare a decent run, which he had not. Passing Bowman's friends, he heard one yell, "She did it again!" The man grinned like a tomcat at Dude.

Going on, Dude waited for Coyote and when the Comanche rode up, he shook his head, muttering, "She just ran off and left us, that mare. She likes this soft track."

Sugar Kyle drifted by, loud as usual. "I can see now why Jake Bowman wouldn't run me on a dry track."

Uncle Billy was at Dude's shoulder when he turned to go. The old man wore a dryly humorous look. "Man's never too old to learn. Like never match a sore-footed mare on soft ground. Fella just spilled the milk to me back there. Said she suffered a deep wire cut on her foot when she was a yearling. It never healed right. Grew crooked. On hard ground she has to tiptoe around — it hurts her. Bowman never matches her unless the track is spongy. So he took the advantage today. I'd do the same." The clear blue eyes narrowed. "Now what Jake Bowman ought to do is take that mare to Louisiana or Mississippi . . . race her in those river-bottom towns where it rains a good deal. Why, he'd clean up!"

"And once you'd raced her you couldn't match her anymore in that place."

"I'm thinking of a man's place by the f'ar. What he could do on one big sashay down through there with an unknown speed mare. Here, Bowman can't match anybody but strangers, and sometimes it goes months without raining. First time he's been able to match her this year."

"Come on. Let's find Bowman."

They found Bowman surrounded by back-slapping friends. Dude paid him. "Doubt if there's a horse around here that could catch her today," he said and fixed Bowman his grinning rebuke. "Funny, the crowd didn't seem to bother her one little bit. Suppose they would tomorrow, when the track's dry?"

"You're a good loser, McQuinn," Bowman said, not one to rub it in. "Maybe you ran your horse too soon after the colic?"

"Don't figure that made any difference."

"Want you fellows to meet an old friend — Reed Neale, Pardner's owner."

Dude saw a square-faced man of about thirty, his hazel eyes affable, his manner straightforward. The creases at the corners of the eyes, the weather-scoured cheeks and mouth, the slight stoop of the sturdy shoulders, bore the stamp of a hard-working man.

"Meet Dude McQuinn," Bowman said, "and Dr. Lockhart, the vet from back East I was telling you about, Reed."

They all shook hands.

"We'd sure like to see your Pardner horse," Dude said. "Understand he's the boss sprinter around here."

Neale hung his head a little. "Maybe we've been lucky, too. He's a sound horse. An easy keeper. You're welcome to see him. Come out in the morning. We'll just be waiting around for the race. I'm camped at the south edge of town."

By ten o'clock Lost Creek overflowed with milling farm families, a variety of vehicles, and riders. Loose-reined country kids darted here and there like steers out of chutes. Some, caught by the ear, were led protesting back to the wagons.

"See," praised Uncle Billy as he and Dude strolled toward Neale's camp, "these are horse folks come to town."

"It's also Saturday."

Dude whistled when he saw Pardner, a dark sorrel stallion, big and powerful in all departments: heavily boned and muscled, well balanced, standing on well-set legs, and as gentle as a dog, unmindful of the constant going and coming of his admirers.

Again and again someone would come up and pet him.

Neale was constantly shaking hands or being waved at and called to.

"Tell you one thing," Uncle Billy observed, after they had greeted Neale, "I wouldn't want all those people fooling around my horse. Some are strangers come in here for the race. Somebody could fix that horse some way. Reed Neale's too trusting. Visiting with folks, he's not where he can see his horse at all times."

"You're mighty suspicious."

"You bet I am!"

"Maybe his jockey's watching?"

"Thunderation if he is! There he is over there. Got his back turned. Look!"

Turning, Dude saw a pint-sized youngster in riding boots talking to a girl. "Pardner's all right — he's just a big ol' pet," Dude said. "He's got it all over Rattler in conformation. That tells me where to lay the money down."

It took some moments for Uncle Billy to reply. He continued to scrutinize the crowd. Finally, he spoke. "Rattler draws my money."

"Why?"

"Conformation has nothing to do with it."

"What does, then?"

"Just a hunch, Dude, pardner. Kyle is mighty certain he will win. Never saw a horse trader more certain. Just a hunch."

"Well, I'm staying with Pardner. I like his looks."

"You'll have to look hard to find any local Rattler money."

Dude was staring beyond him. "Wish you'd look what's coming."

It was Kyle's handyman, Rufus Swink, meandering along with the flow of the lookers from town, smiling that careless, loose-lipped smile, his owlish face sleepy-eyed as usual.

"I'd better go make that bet on Rattler," the old man said, moving off.

"I'll look around here for mine."

Everything his mentor had predicted about Lost Creek's fervor for horse racing was true, Dude could see that afternoon, standing with Uncle Billy not far from the finish line. The festive crowd lined the sides of the track from starting line to finish. And the town's little band, strutting the red-gold uniforms, marched and tooted proudly, if not harmoniously, on jerky renditions of "The Old Gray Mare" and "Home on the Range." Townsmen kept busy herding the frolicsome youngsters off the track, drying fast after Sister Nellie's triumph of yesterday. Dude had to smile at Bowman's cagey timing. Just right. Today's track, hardening to clods, would hurt the mare's tender front foot.

"Still think Rattler will take it?" Dude chided the old man.

"Still my hunch. Did you bet?"

"Couldn't find any Rattler money."

"Then you didn't look hard. There's a saddle-blanket gambler taking Pardner money at the Union Saloon."

"Didn't go there and I steered clear of that windy Kyle."

Down the track paraded the runners. Pardner first, led by Neale on a pony horse, followed by Rattler, Kyle on the lead rope, riding a gaunt trade horse. Pardner's appearance set off a storm of handclapping. Neale waved at the friendly crowd, his crowd. Kyle played his peddler's smile around. A cool one, Dude thought. The horses were behaving, Rattler more nervous than Pardner, shaking his head at the annoyance of the lead rope, and dancing from side to side. Spider Gentry swayed in the irons, his body crablike. Pardner seemed unconcerned. His kid jockey was white-faced and tense.

They turned and headed for the starting line.

"How do they look to you, Uncle?"

"It's not how they look, it's who wins."

Van Clark, standing in the track's center, waved the get-ready signal, and the townsmen cleared the track and the finish-line judges took position.

The crowd stilled to low-voiced murmurs and shufflings and craned necks for better views of the getaway.

Watching, Dude saw Clark instructing the jockeys and then the jockeys reining their horses back for the turnaround and the walk-up start. On they came.

Clark dropped his hat. His simultaneous shout arrived late and muted on the wind.

To Dude's surprise, Rattler took the break, took it by half a length. Gentry so low in the saddle it appeared that Rattler ran without a jockey.

They were coming hard now, Rattler still out front. He opened daylight — one length, two lengths. Dude kept waiting for Pardner to surge, to close, to hit his stride, but he was just hanging there.

At two hundred yards Pardner, under the boy's whipping, made his bid. He tried gamely, but could not close the gap. They ran like that, Pardner getting no stronger, no closer.

Was there time?

As Dude silently asked that, the horses pounded across the line and the race was over. Pardner simply didn't have it today. Dude heard Uncle Billy's voice, strangely cheerless for a winner, "First time I ever won money I kinda wished I'd lost."

"Pardner couldn't get untracked," Dude said.

"That," said Uncle Billy, "is just why many an old horseman can wind up without a place by the f'ar. There are a thousand ways to lose a horse race. I had a horse on the lead get hit by lightning fifty yards from the finish. That's the worst luck I can think of. The next is when the other fella's horse flat outruns yours, such as we just witnessed. Notice how that Rattler moved down the track . . . his long neck stuck out like a New Mexico road runner? He can bend the breeze, all right."

"That's an interesting comparison. When did you ever see a road runner, Uncle?"

"Did I say?" An abiding vexation trickled across the irascible yet likable face. "If I mentioned Bohemia, would that mean I'd been there? Let's go have a little toddy in town."

The "little toddy" at the Union Saloon became two, and by the time they reached camp an hour or more had passed. Coyote was waiting for them. "Jake Bowman's looking for you," he said.

"Something wrong?" Dude asked.

"Didn't say. Asked for you and Grandfather Billy to come to Reed Neale's camp pronto."

They walked fast to the south edge of town. Neale's camp was deserted except for a few friends still lamenting the outcome. Bowman drew the two aside. "Dr. Lockhart, Reed wants you to take a good look at his horse."

"Is he hurt?"

"Don't think it's that." He looked around. "Wait till everybody leaves. Won't be long."

They stood around and talked awhile, killing time. "That race just about cleaned out Lost Creek," Bowman informed them. "Reed not only lost his three hundred, but he bet Sugar Kyle another two hundred that Pardner would daylight Rattler at the hundred-yard mark. Kyle cleaned up. He was all over town this morning, takin' bets. Lot of country folks bet, too. Altogether, I'd say five thousand dollars was lost here today."

Neale was fussing over his horse. When the last hanger-on left, Neale waved them over, a usually mild-mannered man now bewildered and angry over the condition of his horse. "Pardner didn't run right. Wasn't himself, I know. One thing, he was left standing at the break, which he's never done before. He's a fast breaker. I'll appreciate it if you will look him over, Dr. Lockhart."

"Glad to help if I can. Sometimes these things are difficult to pin down." He eyeballed the stud. "You mean you think your horse was fixed? Is that it?"

Neale looked pained. "Don't want to accuse anybody in public unless I'm dead certain. Right now all I want to know is what was wrong with Pardner."

"Here," said Uncle Billy, stepping forward, "let me have this fine young gentleman."

He took the halter rope and led away. The sorrel followed obediently, yet sluggishly, it seemed to Dude. "Now," said Uncle Billy, circling back, "you lead him around, Dude, while I give him a long look-see." After Dude did so, the old man said, "He moves about right, though he's not quite as alert as I like a horse to be." And he went to examining the forelegs and shoulders, stroking back the hair, peering closely. "Thought maybe he'd been jabbed or something, but he shows no marks or tenderness. Of course, he will be soring up from running."

He stood back and folded his arms,

frowning, assessing. Stepping in, gently running his hand along the strong neck, he turned his head to listen to the sorrel's breathing. Puzzled, he felt under the jaws and took out his watch. After an interval: "His breathing is somewhat uneven and his pulse is a little slow. Normally, it should beat thirty-six to forty per minute. In a feverish horse, it will run as high as forty-five to seventy."

He put back his watch and, gently murmuring assurance as one might to a sick child, he peered into the wide nostrils. Some moments of that and, "In fever or inflammation of any of the internal organs, the color inside the nose is red. His is pink, which is just right." Gradually, firmly, yet without struggling, he opened the sorrel's mouth and examined his teeth. "The black cavities of the center nippers are disappearing. This horse is coming six years old." He stepped back.

"Well, what do you think, Doctor?" Neale asked anxiously.

"I'm not finished yet," was the curt reply.

He folded his arms, eyes narrowed, concentrating. Suddenly pointing a reminding finger, he went to Pardner's head and peered steadily at the dark eyes. For long moments he peered. Then, stepping clear,

"A horse's eyes are mirrors of his inner self. His are dull and glassy."

"What does that mean?" Neale demanded.

"I cannot say. But they are not clear and full. Did you give this horse any medication before he ran?"

"Nothing. He's in good condition — or was," Neale added bitterly. "What shall I do?"

"Keep him on warm mashes until the dullness leaves. Add linseed meal as a digester. No exercise. Come by the camp this evening and I'll fix you up a tonic. On your way, stop at the Union Saloon for a quart of Kentucky sour mash."

"Whiskey — in the tonic?" Neale's surprise said he was a straight-laced man.

"For medicinal purposes, my friend, which is the way whiskey should be used. Never to the extreme. There will be other ingredients in the tonic as well. If the eyes do not clear up within forty-eight hours, you'd better get in touch with me at once." His stern, professional manner easing, he slapped Neale on the shoulder. "Your horse will be all right. A few days of good feed, tonic, and rest will bring him around."

"What do I owe you, Doc?" Neale asked gratefully.

"Not a thing. Just take care of your horse, and be sure to come by for the tonic."

They were some rods beyond the camp when Dude spoke. "You didn't tell him the truth, did you, Uncle?"

There was silence.

"Why didn't you?"

"Why tell him that his horse was fixed, when I can't prove it? Only make him feel worse. What he wants to know now is will his horse be all right. He will be in a few days, if not sooner."

They passed the livery stable and the general store, where families were loading the last of their purchases. The street, jammed before the race, was emptying rapidly. Noise from the Union Saloon swelled louder than usual.

"Sounds like a celebration," Dude said. "Let's take a look."

They entered. Across the smoke-fogged room, Kyle was holding forth, around him a crowd of hangers-on and the ever-present Swink and Gentry.

Nearby, a short, smooth-faced man observed the celebration like a tolerant fringe presence. His neat dress made him stick out: impeccable gambler's black, white shirt, string tie, flat-topped gray hat. A close-barbered brown beard framed his straight mouth. His cool gray eyes seemed to regard nothing in particular, yet everything.

Dude turned to an onlooker. "Who's that in the gambler's getup?"

"Mile-High Hanley. He bets 'em big. New in town."

"How new?"

"Showed up a little while after Sugar Kyle did. Real friendly fellow."

Dude looked at Uncle Billy, whose affirming nod as much as said, "That's the saddle-blanket gambler I told you about."

Kyle was braying, "When did I know we had it won?" He roared with laughter. "Why, when we took the break — that's when. Rattler's never been headed once he got off first. An' farther he goes, faster he runs."

The approving crowd hung on each word. A slurred voice spoke. "Let ol' Spider tell us how he won it."

Kyle slapped the jockey's shoulder. "Tell the man, Spider. Tell 'em all how you rode that race. Then we'll have another round."

Gentry hung back and lowered his gaze, a model of modesty.

The wizened man stepped forward, his eyes race-experienced and shrewd. "I'd like to say I was as sure as Mr. Kyle was, but I wasn't. Bet'cher boots, I wasn't." That got some laughs. "All I did was hang on. Rattler did the rest. He knew what to do. He runs his heart out every time he goes to the track." He left off, eyes downcast, then looked up. "That Pardner made a stout run at us there at the last. You bet he did. That just seemed to make my horse run all the faster. Don't believe there's a horse in the whole country that could've caught Rattler today." He waved and stepped back. The throng hooted and clapped.

He's every bit as slick as Kyle, Dude decided. Telling the local boys how Pardner came on and made his late bid, so they won't feel so bad, while Kyle sets everybody up to free drinks.

Just then Kyle bellowed, "Another round of drinks for all the boys!"

On that, the pack charged the bar, elbowing for places, laughing and talking.

That round soon downed, the crowd shifted toward the victorious horsemen again. Kyle had not yet ceased talking, his coarse voice dominant over the hum of the crowd, while Gentry, responding to questions, hunched shoulders and brought his strong hands up, clenched, pantomiming how he had ridden the mighty Rattler. Swink was owl-faced over a mug of beer.

Dude and Uncle Billy shared a knowing

look. "I think," said Dude, speaking low, "it's about time somebody took the slack out of one Mr. K. C. 'Sugar' Kyle. What do you say, Uncle?"

"What are we waiting on! I'd like to see a clean young fella like Reed Neale get his money back somehow. It's one thing to take advantage of conditions that favor your horse. We've all been outslicked that way. But to fix another man's horse!" He snorted contempt. "Dude, I've never told you this till now. Didn't think it necessary. But I've never fixed a horse in my life."

"Hell's fire, I know that. Where would be the fun if a man did that?"

"Just wanted you to know."

"I'm goin' over there, see if we can't match us a little four-square gospel race." Dude crimped his hat and squared his shoulders."

"Now, wait! Even with Pardner not right, Rattler was beginning to fade at three hundred yards. So match Kyle for as long as you can. Nothing under three hundred."

They weaved through the crowd and listened for a short while before Kyle, who was constantly gesturing and turning, laying on the talk, peddling that smile, noticed them. He erupted into geniality. He shook hands like a man grabbing the rung of a ladder.

"Glad you came over to play with us, neighbors. Have a drink on me."

"Much obliged, Brother Kyle," Dude boomed back at him. "Right now just want to coyote 'round the rim with you."

Kyle's craggy face went blank. *Coyote 'round the rim?*"

"That's Texan for wantin' to mix the medicine."

Kyle's face was still blank. *"To mix the medicine?"*

"That's Texan for wantin' to talk."

"I see," Kyle said, emitting a honking hee-haw.

"Guess you know I'm a Texan?"

"That, neighbor, is not hard to cipher out. What you want to chin about?"

"Oh," said Dude, smiling, "just a little four-square horse race."

"Horse race? What you got to run at me?"

"Texas Jack."

Kyle couldn't believe it. "After that clubfooted mare daylighted him three lengths?"

"Texas Jack," Dude replied, "is just recovering from the colic. I made the mistake of matching him too soon. Can't blame my horse. Another week or so and he'll be back in condition."

"You're stringin' me, neighbor."

"Why, Brother Kyle!"

"I can't see a man matching a horse as slow as Texas Jack." The trader's eyes were keenly wary.

"He's a far better horse than he showed. And I doubt that Rattler could beat Sister Nellie on soft ground." Dude folded his arms and rocked on his boot heels. "However, since your horse would be a heavy favorite, I'd have to have odds."

"Odds?" Kyle burst out laughing. "Something like three to one?"

"Sounds four square to me. Didn't Rattler beat Pardner two lengths?"

"I wouldn't give three-to-one odds if I ran Rattler at an old milk cow. Anything can happen. You know that." He put on his face of humility. "Money comes hard for this ol' country boy."

How many times Dude had heard that! Used it himself to advantage. He said, "Not afraid of my ol' horse, are you, brother?"

Kyle's face showed heat. The voices around them stilled. Then Kyle, chuckling, evading, said, "You are strong on that Texas Jack."

"You wanted to match us."

"Let's have that drink," Kyle said, draping an arm around Dude's shoulder. With Uncle Billy, they marched to the bar. Kyle ordered the drinks. A man barged up to Kyle, slapping him on the back, wanting to know more about the race. As Dude finished his drink, he became aware that Kyle was drifting away with the backslapper, pumping up his horse.

"So he didn't go for it," Dude said, outside.

"We rushed him a little, and he figures we've got the advantage on him somewhere."

"Think he'll run at us?"

"Will . . . soon as he works out a way to get the advantage on us."

Chapter 6

Sunday morning.

The sun was a copper ornament stuck against the blue dome of the great sky. The capricious breeze out of the southwest came laden with grass smells. Church bells called Lost Creek's faithful to worship. Afterward, the town settled down for an afternoon of comfortable drowse.

There was little movement over in Kyle's camp. Once, Dude noticed Kyle leading Rattler back and forth. That, and the camp sank back into deep lethargy.

By late afternoon, Dude was restless and doubtful. "Uncle," he said, "if Kyle doesn't accept our challenge pretty quick, we might as well move on to another town."

"Thunderation!" The old gent was pawing through the bowels of the cavernous, smelly medicine chest. "Seems I'm always short of linseed meal . . . good digester, you know. Have to make a little memorandum on that. . . . What was that, now?"

"I said we might as well move on if Kyle fails to take up our challenge."

"You worry too much, Dude. Kyle is feeling high and mighty right now. Playing us cagey. I'll give odds he runs at us."

"You're more patient than I am."

"I've lived longer and I've seen more of the world." And then, as if anticipating Dude, "But I'm not sayin' how long or where."

Impatient, Dude walked to Neale's camp and found him hitching up to leave. "That must be some tonic Dr. Lockhart mixed up. My Pardner horse is his old self again. Wants to run. I'm taking him out to the farm. Thank Doc for me."

"Will do."

"In case I don't see you fellows again," Neale said, holding out his hand, "good luck. I won't be back till Sale Day."

"When's that?"

"Week from Saturday." His voice picked up hopeful interest. "Hope you'll still be around."

"Maybe. We're trying to match Texas Jack against Rattler."

Honest surprise sprang into Neale's eyes. "Texas Jack? Well . . . I know he's a pretty good horse." He was, Dude sensed, too courteous to say otherwise.

"He'll be a heap faster than he was against Sister Nellie, now that he's fully recovered from the colic. We matched him too soon."

"Luck to you. Don't forget to thank Dr. Lockhart. Pardner is like one of the family."

Monday started off like Sunday, the two camps following unvarying routines of watering and feeding, and the crews lounging around the wagons. While Coyote and Danny busied themselves with the harness and racing tack, Uncle Billy delved into the medicine chest, checking supplies, muttering and humming to himself, bent over the bottles and cans and jars like some ancient sorcerer.

It was ten o'clock when Dude saw Kyle walking toward town. The trader flung up a neighborly wave. Dude waved back. Kyle returned at noon. Around midafternoon he walked to town again.

"Wonder what he's up to?" Uncle Billy puzzled.

"Probably goes for a snort at the Union," Dude said.

"A long time ago — when I first learned never to approach a mule from the rear, I also learned that a horse trader shows you only what he wants you to see."

"Meaning what?"

"That I trust Brother Kyle no farther than I could throw a bull elephant by the tail uphill against a stiff wind."

For the remainder of the afternoon and evening the old man was reflective and preoccupied, less talkative than usual. He scowled a good deal.

Well after midnight, Dude heard him get up, grunt on boots, britches and shirt, go to the rear of the wagon and scratch a match. Dull lantern light glowed, carefully shielded, it seemed, while he rummaged in the medicine chest. Glass jars *tinkled*. A pause, as if he might be measuring. Another pause. Muted stirrings became audible. He was mixing something. When the stirrings ceased, Dude heard him go among the horses and lead two to the tailgate and tie up.

A period passed in which Dude caught only the now-and-then stamping of the horses, after which Uncle Billy led the horses away. Returning, he blew out the lantern and came to bed.

Dude started to ask what was up. On second thought, he lay back, thinking, humoring. It will come out in the morning, he thought. But not till he's ready to tell us. It was, he knew, just the old man's nature, a peculiarity, some would say; partly secretive as well, as established as the guarding of his vague past; partly keeping you in the dark for his own amusement or cussedness, like a storyteller who withholds the outcome till the very last. Another game that helped keep an old man young.

During the outfit's customary early breakfast, neither Dude nor the old man referred to last night. The latter then placed his favorite canvas-backed chair where he could watch Kyle's camp, took out his memorandum book, and began writing.

Dude waited, his curiosity mounting. The sun was climbing when he heard getting-up sounds across the way, the slap of a coffee pot, curses, the bang of a skillet, Kyle's coarse voice chousing Swink and Gentry for their lie-abed habits.

Still watching, Uncle Billy put away his little book and pencil stub. When woodsmoke mingled with coffee and bacon smells over there, he turned and said, "Coyote, let's saddle up Texas Jack."

"The stock saddle, Grandfather?"

"Do you exercise a runnin' horse with a stock saddle? We're going to the track."

Coyote Walking went to the horses, led the gelding to the rear of the wagon, bridled him, laid on blanket and the light racing saddle and cinched up. While Dude saddled Blue Grass, the old man readied Judge Blair.

He told Danny, "If Kyle heads for town while we're gone, you follow him and see where he goes and what he does. But don't let him see you."

"What about the camp?"

"If anything's missing, we'll sure know where to find it."

They mounted.

Kyle and his crew were wolfing down breakfast as the outfit passed and waved. Kyle flapped a long arm. At this untidy hour he reminded Dude of a scarecrow. Swink and Gentry did not glance up from their plates.

Coyote Walking spoke disdainfully, "It's good times on the prosperity for those white men, eating before they water and feed their horses," and glared in their direction. "Just like mean white men. We Comanches always feed our horses first. We live with our horses."

"Just like cowboys," Dude grinned.

At the track the old man kept glancing behind. "Let's wait awhile. We might have company. Somebody in the creek brush back there clocking our horse to see how much he's on the improve."

"Wouldn't it be wiser to act mysterious?" Dude suggested. "Like we're hiding something? Breeze the Judge out early in the morning . . . earlier than usual . . . say just at daybreak?"

"The Judge?" Uncle Billy inquired innocently.

"Figure you could fool me, Uncle? You covered over the Judge's blaze to look like Texas Jack, and you painted a blaze on Texas Jack so he looks like the Judge."

"Surprised you didn't catch that back at camp. Proves the old man's still got his touch."

"You have. Only a mother could tell the difference. That eagle look in the Judge's eyes, the way he moves, with go on his mind, the way he picks up his feet — and that long shoulder."

"Proves, too, you haven't forgotten everything I've schooled you in." He looked off toward town again. "Nobody's coming. Take him down the track, Coyote. Let him out pretty hard over three hundred yards. He needs the work." And to Dude, "My idy is to make the point that Texas Jack is coming back. Not scaring anybody, but on the improve. As foxy as that Kyle is, he'd sure figure something was wrong if we agreed to match Texas Jack as slow as he looked against that soft-ground mare."

Coyote trotted the Judge to the far end of the straightaway, turned, and took him on, simulating a walk-up start. Suddenly, they were off and breezing, the Comanche riding with a light hold. On they came, one hundred, two hundred, three hundred yards and more, a blistering pace, now down to a gallop, a lope, now trotting, now walking.

"I'm in a happiness to relate," Coyote reported, lapsing into an excitement of lingo, "the Judge wants to run today, he does, this horse. Gives me good feel to riding him I am. Pull him up, this Comanche could, but hurt his mouth, this Comanche would not."

Dude said, "The Judge breezed faster than Texas Jack ran against the mare."

"But not all out," Uncle Billy said. "Fast — but not too fast. That's what I wanted."

They were in no hurry, jogging north for town, the road taking them along the green line of the creek, when Dude spied a distant flutter of movement. A man's figure, shrinking as he climbed down from a tree and retreated into the brush, now lost in the dusty passage of wagons where the creek bent, giving way to the road entering Lost Creek from the west.

"There's our company, Uncle," Dude said. "Let's slow down. Give him time to make camp."

They found Danny gone. In Kyle's camp, Swink and Gentry were loafing under a wagon as usual. A breathless Danny hurried in half an hour later. "I followed Kyle to the Union Saloon."

"Did he see you?" Uncle Billy asked.

"Don't think so. I watched from the back door. He was talking to a gambler-looking man."

"That would be Mile-High Hanley we told you about."

"Kyle was still there when I left."

Dude turned to the old man. "So it was Swink or Gentry at the creek. Likely, Gentry."

Kyle did not show until nearly noon. He waved as he walked by to camp. At sight of him Swink and Gentry quit their grousing over the meal they were cooking.

"He won't be over till tomorrow," Uncle Billy predicted. "He needs time to figure how Texas Jack has improved so much, colic or not. I kinda wished Coyote had held the Judge in a bit, 'cause he looked mighty fast."

At three o'clock Kyle was observed going to town once more. He waved, like always, fluttering that long, preacherlike arm.

"By now," said Uncle Billy, "he knows about the workout. He and that slicked-up cardsharp will be jaw to jaw all afternoon on ways to get the advantage."

Darkness was near when Kyle made his way back. The outfit was fixing supper. Kyle waved, as neighborly, Dude thought, as somebody bent on borrowing a cup of sugar.

"Think he'll come over this evening, Uncle?"

"No."

"What if it rains tonight and the paint runs?"

"Dude, you're always worrying. It's already rained once this summer. Regardless, we still have one blaze-faced horse and one brown-faced horse."

During the night Dude heard Uncle Billy get up and he saw lantern light, saw it briefly, and heard the faint shuffle of horses. Well, it wasn't unusual for the old man to see about the horses. Dude rolled over and went back to sleep.

At breakfast the old gentleman looked sleepy-eyed, his avuncular face as noncommittal as the tin cup of coffee he was blowing on between sips to give spring to his arthritic joints. Dude let the nocturnal doings pass unsaid, his mind on Kyle & Company.

Breakfast was scarcely over and the camp cleaned when Dude saw them coming, all three.

"Morning, neighbors," Kyle sang out. "You boys still serious about that four-square horse race?" This time he stopped politely at the edge of camp, on his manners instead of barging in as was his wont, Swink and Gentry trailing along like the tail of a kite.

Dude waved them in. "Oh, we might listen to a four-square set-to. What's your notion, Brother Kyle?"

"First off," the trader said, hawking that smile about and coming forward, "I want another gander at Texas Jack."

"There he is. Rid of the colic and feelin' his oats."

Kyle stepped to where the gelding was tied, standing quietly. That was another good feature about the Judge, Dude assured himself, he never showed that let's-run look unless you slapped the light saddle on him.

Circling, Kyle studied the dark bay fore and aft, his professional eyes intent. He stopped abruptly.

Dude stiffened. Had he detected a difference in the two horses?

Kyle opened the gelding's mouth and eyeballed the teeth, and ran his hand along the neck and shoulder. Circling again, he scanned the short back and the hindquarters. He studied the withers. Apparently satisfied, he strolled back, chuckling, "Remarkable how a horse can improve sometimes."

"It is," Dude said. "Just takes the right cure. Dr. Lockhart gave him another round of . . ." He turned inquiringly.

The old man shot out the words. "One pint of sour-mash, three tablespoonfuls of gunpowder. Heaping."

"Oh, yes," said Dude, snapping his fingers. "Three tablespoonfuls. Heaping. I forgot."

"I've been thinking we might run that race," Kyle opened.

"Sounds interesting."

"Figured it would be."

"Depends. We're about ready to pull out for fresh country."

"Just when prospects get better?"

"That depends, too. How far and how much you got in mind, Brother Kyle?"

"One little bitty furlong for all of five hundred big bucks."

"That's a heap of money for a small outfit like ours."

"Five hundred will buy a lot of grub and horse feed."

"I won't match Texas Jack that short."

"You ran him two fifty last time."

"That was last time. His best lick is the quarter mile when he's right, and he's on the improve. I found that out today. He's stronger, and he knows who he is."

Kyle brightened. "Lost Creek's bull ring is exactly a quarter mile."

"I'm talking about a straightaway race." Too many things, he realized, could happen on turns.

"True, neighbor. But a straight quarter is not to my liking." He gazed up at the early-morning sky and inhaled deeply. A beatific smile filled the crevices of his long face. He held that expression for so long that, for a moment, Dude could imagine him making it hot for the rumheads. Then Kyle, beaming at Dude, purled, "Would three hundred and fifty yards strike your fancy?"

"I like four hundred better."

"For five hundred dollars?"

Dude swung his right arm, a gesture of decision. "Tell you what I'll do, Brother Kyle. I'll put up the five if you'll give me three-to-one odds."

Kyle flung up a disdainful hand and executed a circling dance. "Laws alive, neighbor. You're takin' hide an' hair. I can't do that."

"Your horse is favored."

"I might give you two to one."

"If I put up the five hundred?"

"Let's settle the distance first. Four hundred yards is still a mite too far away."

He's angling for three hundred yards or less, Dude figured. He said, "Three-fifty?" deciding he would go no shorter.

"Now you are bein' neighborly. And we could run that around one turn."

"You don't run three-fifty on a turn."

"I have."

"I don't."

"I like to be four square. All right. It's three-fifty down the straightaway."

Dude nodded. "That distance at two-to-one odds. I'll put up five hundred."

Kyle thought hard, his craggy face compressing. "It's a go," he said and that immutable smile washed over his uneven features like balm. "Though I'd still like to run you around one turn."

"No turn," Dude said firmly, thinking that he was fifty yards shorter than he was jockeying for and that Kyle was fifty over his horse's best distance.

"We'll forget the turn," Kyle conceded, smiling, and in an obvious display of candor, "I see I can't get the advantage on you there. Makes no difference. Rattler can change leads for the turns or he can stay in the same lead runnin' straight." He pulled on an ear and scratched his jaw. "What about forfeit money?"

"What about it?" Dude smiled back.

"Say, two hundred dollars?"

"One hundred."

"It's a go. Posted at the Union Saloon? The stakes, too?"

"I like to leave my money where I know it's gonna be after the race," Dude dickered. "I prefer Alf Tinker at the general store."

"If you say so."

"If it rains, the race is off. Texas Jack is no mudder. You saw that." Happened the Judge was a mudder, but you had to keep your horse in character and, of course, the paint would run.

"Rattler's no mudder, either."

"We'd agree later on a dry-track day?"

"Suits me."

"Brother Kyle, you are fair." Was the man too agreeable? Dude had to wonder a little.

"I always aim to be four square. Goes back to when the gospel was my line and I was rasslin' with the devil. Any druthers for the starter, good neighbor?"

"I like Van Clark."

"I had another man in mind."

"Your horse won when Clark started."

"Oh, all right. I won't wrangle."

The thought kept growing on Dude that Kyle wasn't truly concerned about these minor details, that his mild dickering was actually a smoke screen to conceal the advantage he now figured he had or he was maneuvering to get.

"For one finish-line judge," Kyle said, his voice smooth, "I want Mile-High Hanley."

"Wup! Hanley, the gambler?" Slick, Dude thought, giving on race conditions that hardly could be disputed, now trying to slip in Hanley. In a close finish, that could mean trouble. "I won't agree on Hanley," Dude countered. "I will on Alf Tinker, Jake Bowman, and Reed Neale. We can't get fairer judges."

"Tinker and Bowman — fine. But Neale is out."

"Neale's honest."

"I don't deny that, but I beat his horse. Remember? A man might . . ." Kyle shrugged, leaving it unsaid.

Catching Uncle Billy's almost imperceptible nod, Dude said, "I'll flip you for it."

"All right. You toss the coin."

"You call it in the air."

Dude flipped a silver dollar. As it fell spinning, Kyle called, "Heads." Dude caught and slapped the coin on the back of his left hand. He looked. "Heads, it is," he said.

Sugar Kyle had won some ground in the event of a nose finish.

Weights? Dude asked himself. What about the weights? In many bush-track races, you mounted your jockey and the other man his, no arguments raised. But the way this race was shaping up, each condition a fine point, why give Kyle the bulge when Gentry looked several pounds lighter than Coyote. Therefore, to counter that advantage, Dude said, "I figure each horse should carry the same weight."

"Was afraid you might come around to that," Kyle said, his smile like a pucker.

"We can weigh each jockey and his tack at Clark's livery right before we go to the track," Dude pursued, primed for Kyle to hem and haw and complain that he was already giving odds.

"I guess," Kyle grumbled, "it's only four square to even up on the weights, even though I am giving up the advantage, good neighbor."

"I wouldn't match you, otherwise," Dude said, surprised that Kyle had agreed so readily. "Another thing is what each jockey will be allowed to carry on his horse."

"All Spider carries is a bat."

"Coyote uses a quirt."

"So what's the fuss?"

"None, Brother Kyle. But just so you'll be satisfied and I'll be satisfied, what say we inspect the other man's jockey on the track, before we start the race? You know . . . no chain links to put wings in a horse's feet. No barbed rings." Dude smiled graciously, shaking his head. "Not that either of us would use such a thing."

"Why, no — never. But as you say, we'll both be satisfied. Guess that's all except the day. When do you want to run?"

"How about Sale Day — that afternoon — a week from Saturday?" Dude was thinking they had better train the Judge carefully for this outing.

"You know," Kyle boomed, "you took the words right out of my mouth. You did. That day is four square with me, good neighbor." He clutched Dude's hand and pumped. "May the top horse win."

"Whew!" Dude exhaled when they had gone. "For a minute there I was afraid Kyle might notice the Judge's long shoulder."

Uncle Billy swung about. "What do you think I was doing up last night? That was Texas Jack he looked at!"

Chapter 7

Next morning the outfit decided to shift camp away from prying eyes, south of town where Neale had kept his horse, and began exercising the Judge on alternate days just before dawn in a remote pasture to the east. Later the same workout morning they would take Texas Jack to the track, working the gelding lightly for the benefit of local railbirds and saloon loafers. Meanwhile, Jake Bowman informed the outfit Kyle was working Rattler undercover on a road north of Lost Creek.

To break the monotony of waiting, Dude would saddle Blue Grass each afternoon and go for a long ride into the country. Tuesday before the race on Sale Day, which was next Saturday, he took the long-legged saddler on his accustomed outing east of town. By this time Dude had shucked his farmer's getup for his horseman's attire: trousers, checkered vest, string tie, planter's hat, and cowboy boots.

As he glanced back, Lost Creek appeared to shrink with each stride of his horse, a Lilliputian collection of white houses and smaller outbuildings, except for the red barns, which were larger than the houses, a picturesque tableau on the endless sweep of this Kansas heartland. A place of nods and drowsings, rousing only when the daily stage hurried in, paused briefly, hurried on, and on Saturday, when folks came to town.

On they went in the running walk, now the fox trot, now the single-foot, the gelding's ears flicking. My, Dude thought, pulsing with pleasure, how this horse likes to show what he can do!

About four miles out, where the mirror of a spring glinted amid mossy rocks at the foot of a rounded hill, and some oaks grew, he watered and rested the gelding and idled about. It was another cloudless day, the sky a great archway of blue, the southwestern breeze rippling waves through the short grass, singing as it roamed.

It was time to go. They swung away, the eager saddler rocking along in the comfortable running walk.

A mile or more onward, he saw a rider stopped on the road, apparently fussing with the saddle cinch. A woman rider. Dude felt a spark of interest, for he had seen no woman riders around Lost Creek. Only farm women in wagons.

She continued to pull at the cinch as he rode up.

"Having trouble, ma'am?" he asked, touching fingers to his hat-brim.

"I'm afraid so," she said, turning with some exasperation and embarrassment, enough to flush her pretty cheeks. Her stylish riding habit of dark blue looked of the best material, her perky little hat jaunty with feathers, her brown gloves open at the wrist and flaring — everything genteel, foreign to Lost Creek. He wondered at her presence here.

Her oval face was carefully made up, her eyes a deep violet, her mouth bow-shaped. About thirty or more, he guessed. Sure no young filly, but pretty. Dismounting, he dropped the reins and stepped to the side-saddle and inspected the cinch.

"The cinch is loose," he said and tightened it snugly, forcing the horse to grunt.

"It seemed all right when I left town," she told him, perplexed. "When the saddle started to slide, I got down."

He glanced at her. Up close, she looked more than thirty or so, a full-bodied woman. Lines were beginning to edge down her throat and crinkle at the corner of the wide eyes, but nothing that marred her good looks, which made him realize how long since he had been around a pretty woman. At the same time he got the scent of something: jasmine, he guessed. Pretty strong, but not unpleasant.

"You did the right thing," he assured her.

"But how in the world . . . ?" She placed a hand at her throat, a gesture of feminine helplessness.

"May I ask where you got this horse?"

"At Mr. Clark's livery."

Dude smiled. "This is one of his regular rent horses. These ol' boys will fool you sometimes. They'll swell up when you saddle 'em, make the cinch tight. After you get down the road a piece, they'll draw in and the saddle is loose. It's their way of gettin' back at you for ridin' em."

He stepped back for her to mount.

"Thank you so much," she said. She had a way of looking at a man, a sidelong way, and of holding her full mouth just so, barely parted, which he found somewhat disturbing. As he gave her a hand up, their bodies brushed and he got the smooth feel of her beneath the dark blue habit and caught the scent of her perfume again.

"I do believe I've gone far enough today," she decided, and turned her horse for town.

Dude mounted and held up, waiting for her to go ahead. But her horse was slow and lazy, while the spirited Blue Grass seethed to be gone. So Dude was soon riding alongside her. Again he held up to let her proceed, and again the irrepressible Kentucky saddler took him beside her.

She smiled. "Please don't hold up on my account. But I'd be pleased for you to accompany me."

"Thank you. I'd be glad to."

So they rode together.

"I'm not used to so much open country," she chatted. "It frightens me a little."

"This is one of the safest places you could be. About the wildest thing around here is a jackrabbit."

"It's silly of me, I know. Coming from the East, I yearn for green hills and valleys. Perhaps you can tell me all about Lost Creek?"

"I'm new here myself."

"I should have known," she said in a tone of self-reproach. "You don't look like a farmer." Her voice conveyed approval and mannerly inquiry.

"I'm a horseman and trader. Here with a small outfit." He could have shrugged and no more, instead of volunteering that much, and supposed it was hunger for feminine company.

"Oh, I do love horses, though that's about as far as it goes. I'm what you would call a green hand at riding."

"You don't ride like a greenhorn."

The violet eyes moved over him. "Thank you. But I am. And you are a gentleman to say that. Would you also happen to own a racehorse?"

"My horse is matched for a race next Saturday."

"Oh, I do love horse races . . . the few I've seen," she added, almost hastily, he thought. Anticipation filled her voice. "I hope to see that race, unless my Uncle Jim arrives early. He's on business down in Indian Territory, selling goods to traders at the various Indian agencies. I'm to meet him here. It's been a long and tiring trip, and I shall be so happy to see him again . . . the first time since my dear husband, Jedediah, passed away last year." She gazed down at her gloved hands on the saddlehorn. "I ought not be saying these things to a total stranger, I know." She looked across at him, the violet eyes wide and earnest.

"Sorry about your husband, ma'am," Dude said, touched.

"Uncle Jim," she said, a plaintive quality softening her voice, "is all the family I have left. Uncle Edgar — that was Uncle Jim's only brother — used to ranch in Wyoming. Oh, what a spread he had! And, oh, the tales he used to tell when he came East to visit us." Her voice descended to a monotone. "The big die-up in the blizzard of eighty-six and seven ruined him. He just couldn't take it. They say he died of a broken heart."

"That die-up busted many a cowman," Dude said.

"However, one ought to shoulder one's own burdens," she said, admonishing herself, eyes downcast again. She turned her head away, as if to hide the onrush of tears.

His sympathy soared. He could never stand a woman's tears. "As much as we can. But it helps to talk to someone, and people should listen to one another."

"You are very kind, Mr. . . . ." She tilted her face as she spoke, smiling as she had not smiled. Yet, behind that smile, did he see tenseness? An underlying hardness? Grief could cause that; of course, it could, and he dismissed the thought.

"My name is McQuinn — Dude McQuinn." He touched his hat-brim to her.

"Mine is Victoria Todd. My friends call me Vicky."

"Mighty pleased to make your acquaintance, Mrs. Todd."

"*Vicky.*"

He was beginning to feel at ease. "About when do you expect your uncle?"

"Any day now. When he comes we'll go to St. Louis, where he and Aunt Mattie live. After visiting them for a few days, I'll be going home alone." She was somber again, eyes downward. Of a sudden she looked up. "I shouldn't talk like that, I know." She seemed to force a wan smile.

A questioning crossed his mind. "Seems like quite a trip, to meet your uncle here, then go back so soon?"

"I took the train to Hays City, the stage from there. It's a vacation of sorts . . . to get away . . . to see new country. I thought Uncle Jim would be here by now. I get so bored waiting at the Blue Front Hotel. That's why I decided all of a sudden to go riding yesterday, inexperienced as I am at handling horses."

He spoke on impulse, "I ride out here every afternoon about this time," and saw her hopeful look. "I'd welcome your company."

"That is very kind of you, Mr. McQuinn."

"*Dude.*"

"Perhaps tomorrow, then . . . *Dude.* You are most *ga-llant.*"

Well, he hadn't heard that one in many a moon. Her voice transmitted a kind of intimacy, and she was holding her mouth that way again.

He escorted her to the livery; tipping his hat, he turned south for camp, his being filled with the raw, physical pull of her. Somehow he could not place her in this town. And that story about her Uncle Jim? The more he thought about it, the more it struck him as a long shot in credibility. Still, here she was. Certain fantasies began to disturb him.

Before dawn Wednesday.

Dude's mind kept rambling back to her as he lay flat beside Uncle Billy on a grassy knoll overlooking the north road, waiting, they were, for Kyle & Company. At this same time Coyote and Danny were working the Judge east of town.

The old man clutched his stopwatch, his attention unwavering on the road.

The sky was changing from dark gray to fawn. The heavy pungency of the prairie was sweet incense.

Long ago, Dude had learned, thanks to the schooling of his salty mentor, there was more than one way to get a line on the other fellow's horse, and the most reliable was to clock the horse while being worked in secret — if you could.

Directly, shapes materialized on the dim road: three riders. They halted, the low murmur of their voices indistinct. Slowly, one left the others.

Dude stared. That was Gentry on Rattler.

Another rider backtracked some hundred yards, posting himself in the middle of the road.

Dude watched. That was Swink, stationed there to halt any nosy railbirds come to sneak-view the morning workout.

Gentry was walking and trotting Rattler. Way down there, as the light strengthened, he wheeled and brought the gelding back galloping past the third man, Kyle. Gentry turned and slowed, approaching for the walk-up start.

Kyle dismounted to play the role of starter. He dropped his hand and shouted.

Rattler shot away, a fast break. Reaching his stride within a few jumps, the gelding ran straight and powerfully.

"This is no breeze," Dude warned. "He's blowing him out." He watched, peering through the muddy murk.

Far down there, Gentry suddenly shut off his horse and stood up in the stirrups. The little guy could ride.

"That was three hundred and fifty yards if it was a foot," Uncle Billy said. It was too dark yet to read the stopwatch.

"Come on," Dude said, tugging on his arm. "It's fixin' to light up pretty quick."

The old man didn't move, his attention riveted on horse and rider.

"Come on! They'll spot us."

Uncle Billy turned and they crawled back. Below the knoll, they hastened to the horses and drummed off. Minutes later they rode into camp. Neither had spoken.

"Well, Uncle," Dude said, tying up, "what did Rattler run it in?"

Scowling at the stopwatch, "I said three hundred and fifty yards. Blamed if that horse didn't run on down there in . . . in . . ."

He eyeballed the watch again, holding it farther and farther away from his eyes, squinting, grimacing, until he held it at arm's length.

"You hoot owl," Dude said, disgusted, "why don't you get some glasses?"

"Don't need 'em — that's why."

"Give me that."

"If you insist."

Dude took the watch and looked at it. He continued to look, struck speechless.

"Well, Chief Eagle Eye, what does it say?" rasped the huffy voice.

"You sure it was three-fifty?"

"You telling me what I saw? Guess I've

measured a few common distances in my day. They ran that horse three-fifty."

"All right, now," Dude soothed him. "Just wanted to be sure. Here it is. . . . Rattler ran it in eighteen and change." He swallowed. "I knew it was fast, but not this fast. To be exact — eighteen and one-fifth seconds." He whistled tunelessly. "What do you make of that?"

"That Kyle matched his horse at his best distance."

Dude cocked an eyebrow. "Thought you said Rattler faded at three hundred against Pardner?"

"Looking back, I'd say Gentry eased him off. He already had it won, didn't he? Had it won from the start with Pardner fixed." The old man was grinning, a tight, mirthless grin. "All the time Kyle was pretending he wanted to go real short and around one turn — that was dust in our eyes — when he was angling for three-fifty. Dude, pardner, we've got a horse race on our hands. This Rattler's a real scorpion at three-fifty. That's Kyle's advantage."

"There could be one more."

"What's better than a fast horse at his fastest distance?"

"Kyle fixin' our horse. Way he fixed Pardner."

★ ★ ★

It was two o'clock, close to the usual time for his jaunt into the country, when Dude took the east road aboard Blue Grass.

Not far beyond town he saw her walking her horse. Coming up, he noticed that she was dressed as before except for a bright red scarf. She was riding the same livery saddler.

"No trouble today, I hope," he greeted.

"This time I made certain the saddle was cinched tight," she answered, giving him a tinkling laugh.

"Any news of your uncle?"

"Not one word. If he doesn't come in a few days, I'll have to go back alone."

Alone.

Once more that intimation of loneliness. He wondered about her and where she had come from. Back East, she had said. Kinda vague. Wouldn't most people say what state, what place, especially if it was a big city? Well, it was none of his business and he hadn't been brought up to pry into another person's past, one William Tecumseh Lockhart excepted.

"There's a little spring a few miles out," he said, for conversation purposes. "Like to ride that far?"

"I have nothing but time on my hands."

Dude considered the livery horse. "I guess this ol' boy here can make it."

They struck out smartly, the livery saddler answering as best he could the challenge of Blue Grass's ground-eating gait. Although the day was hot, the wind was not unkind for this time of year, a condition Dude hoped did not portend rain on race day.

A jack rabbit jumped up beside the road. Without warning, the livery horse shied violently, narrowly missing Blue Grass.

Dude stuck out a restraining hand, expecting her to grab leather.

Quite coolly, she yanked the horse's head up and brought him about on a straight course, settling him at once. Her face was set and determined.

Dude regarded her with admiration and some question. If she was a green hand as she claimed, she hadn't reacted like one. Instead of letting her mount have his way while she clung to the saddlehorn, she had moved on instinct, on the experience of a skilled rider.

"You straightened him out mighty quick," he complimented her.

She sagged and placed one hand to her throat, that gesture of helplessness he recognized. "I thought you said this was safe country?" she laughed. "That jack rabbit turned out to be dangerous."

Thereafter, no more jack rabbits jumped up to startle the placid horse, and save for random exchanges on the weather and the road, they rode in silence the rest of the way to the oak-shaded spring.

Her expertness back there continued to cling to his mind.

He assisted her down. They watered and tied the horses, and as they turned away from the pool she seemed to stumble on a rock.

He caught her before she could fall. For one long moment she swayed off balance, fully against him. Her body felt heavier and older than he had imagined. Her jasmine loaded his senses. He saw that look come into her face, her bow-shaped mouth parted and waiting. He bent and kissed her experimentally, almost before he thought. She met his kiss, her lips cool and firm, not really giving. She drew back, murmuring, "This country is more dangerous than I thought possible," and showed him an odd smile that could mean much or little.

"Not dangerous — just friendly," he said, smiling in turn.

"What a lovely place," she enthused.

"The water is so clear. Is it all right to drink?"

He started to say that if it was fit for a good horse, it was for a human. But, being on his manners, he said, "Just get above where the horses drank."

She kneeled to drink. He did the same. Rising, she dabbed daintily with a tiny handkerchief. As she rose to sit on a mossy rock, she revealed an ankle. Belatedly, it seemed, she pulled down her skirt.

A mighty trim fetlock, Dude judged, thinking in the appropriate horsey term. He took the rock next to hers.

"This calls to mind a little story," he began. "It's a cowboy story. You might not want to hear it."

"You mean it's naughty?" She flung him that sidelong expression, eyelids half shuttered.

"Anything but naughty. You could tell it in church."

"Tell it anyway," she said, affecting disappointment.

"Well, these two cowboys, Shorty and Slim, had been out long before sunup, riding hard. It was hot and dry. Along toward sundown they come to this little hole of water. They get down. Shorty on this side, Slim on the other. Shorty's horse goes

146

right in to drink, muddying up the water. Shorty is down on hands and knees, slurping it up, regardless.

"Pretty soon Slim sees what's happened. He calls across, 'Shorty, why don't you come over here where it's not so muddy? My horse didn't wade in like yours.'

"Shorty goes on filling up. After a bit, he raises up and says, 'It don't make a dang bit o' difference, I'm gonna drink it all anyhow.'"

Her laughter pealed forth. "Horses," she said, "all you talk about is horses."

"Guess you're right. Next to people, they're the most interesting things around."

"Since that is so, and since it looks as though I'll be here the day of the race, would you suggest I bet on your horse?"

He shook his head. "I never tell a person how to bet. They might lose. If so, they'd be mad at me."

"You mean you think your horse will lose?"

"Don't mean that. I just won't tell folks how to bet."

"You're an honest man, Dude. I'd bet however you suggested, and I wouldn't get mad if I lost. Isn't that what it's all about, winning or losing?"

"A big part of it, Vicky. That and the enjoyment you get out of working with horses." So she was a good sport. Many women, including Bridget, didn't like horse racing . . . thought it cruel, when it wasn't if you didn't race a horse too young and took good care of him.

Her voice changed. "I'd better tell you what I heard at the Blue Front." She let him think about that for a moment before she went on. "People wonder why you would match this man . . . what's his name?"

"Kyle — Sugar Kyle."

"Why you would match him, when his horse . . . what's his horse's name?"

"Rattler."

"And yours?"

"Texas Jack."

"Why you would match Texas Jack against Rattler, when Rattler daylighted that other man's horse, and Texas Jack lost to that mare? Why, Dude?"

"Because my horse is on the improve. He was just getting over the colic when I matched the mare."

"So that's it?"

"I made a mistake matching the mare." He smiled without rancor. "I got slickered, too. I didn't know Jake Bowman ran her only on soft ground. She's got a crippled foot."

"Anyway, Dude, people aren't betting your horse." She kept saying his name, giving it a special intimacy.

He said, "That's their choice. I put up *my* money."

"Texas Jack must have improved a great deal in a very short time."

"He can run a little," Dude said, going down the middle.

"You must think he can run a whole lot to take Rattler."

"Depends how he feels Sale Day."

"For a man betting his horse, you don't act very confident."

He fashioned his face into mock humility. "I'm cautious for a Texan."

She rose and settled herself beside him, bringing a wave of jasmine, and leaned toward him. "I'm beginning to like you, Dude." The violet eyes played over his face. "You're so different . . . so honest . . . and understanding."

"Just an ol' country boy a long way from home," he averred, with a slow grin. Boy, that jasmine was strong enough to gag a mule! Still, she was the first good-looking woman he had been close to in months, in fact, since Bridget left. That awareness smote him.

She leaned closer, until he could see the heaviness of her mask of powder and rouge and mascara. Her lips parted, heavy and red. There also was that underlayer of harshness in her face that bothered him.

As she stirred again, her skirt crawled up. It exposed a ruffled purple-and-white garter above her black-stockinged knee, a disarrangement of which she seemed unaware or not to care. Now she leaned against him.

He found his hand on her knee, feeling the warmth of her. She made no protest, and he could feel his pulse hammering. Sweat started to his forehead. *Here — now?* He was astounded at himself.

She was murmuring, "Dude, I want to bet your horse . . . but I'm like anybody else, I guess — or more so. I have to win. My circumstances are modest. If I lose, I may be stranded here."

"Don't bet," he said, meaning it, aware of a headlong sensation.

"But —"

She slid her arms around his neck. She lifted her face to him. She kissed him, this time with fervor.

"Dude," she sulked, staring up at him, "you hardly kissed me back. Is something wrong? Don't you like me?"

"Sure, I like you. Just don't bet. It's safer."

"Just as a matter of interest, because I like

you, won't you tell me how you figure you'll win?"

"Any horse race is a gamble. All a man can do is hope he wins."

She drew back sharply, a pouting upon her. She disengaged his hand from her knee, deliberate about it. "I thought we were friends . . . good friends." She swished her shoulders, a suggestion there that he could not miss, that they could be even better friends.

"Aren't we friends?" he said back. She was playing games now, he suspected. That was all this was, a teasing game.

"I didn't mean that. Only —"

"Only what?"

"Before I put my money down, I need to be fairly certain your horse has a chance. I'd like to know how you plan to win that race . . . tell me."

"I'll tell you — my horse will win because he'll run faster — that's all," he said and saw the expectancy dull and leave her face.

Piqued, she sat farther back on the rock, turned her eyes downward on her clasped hands. "Guess I've made a fool of myself, acting this way. Kissing you . . . wanting to bet on your horse . . . asking those silly questions . . . when I shouldn't." She looked up, eyes glistening. "Old memories come over me. It's only been a year now —" She did not finish.

Dude stood up, conscious of an enormous reprieve. Guilt flayed him. What had got into him? Had he forgotten Bridget? He hadn't. But —

He viewed her with a new awareness, his sympathy diluted. Why the questions about the race? And he wondered how she could turn on the teardrops like that, quick as the snap of your finger, whereas a moment before she had seemed — well. He shrugged mentally. He could think of nothing to say.

The creaking and rattling of a wagon and the jingling of heavy harness invaded the stillness about them. He turned. A farmer coming to town. And whatever might have happened here between them, Dude realized, could not happen now. In a way he regretted that it hadn't, in another he was glad.

After the farmer passed, they mounted and rode down the road. Their silence held until they reached the edge of town. She stopped her horse. A making up smoothed her face as she said, "You still haven't told me, Dude."

Thank God, he thought, she's not reaching for more of that stuff about dear

Jedediah and Uncle Jim. "Yes, I have," he said.

She looked confused. "I don't understand."

"I have told you — don't bet."

Her eyes bit into him. Lashing the horse, she tore away.

He sensed a further escape. *My friends call me Vicky.* Boy!

Chapter 8

He did not ride into the country on Thursday, deciding that one Dude McQuinn had come near enough to making a damn fool of himself, if he hadn't already — this Dude McQuinn who talked too much, who let sympathy lead him into uncomfortable situations, who might know runnin' horses and how to palaver when setting up a match race and getting favorable odds, but who didn't know beans about women. Such a nice-looking gal, too! He could only wonder about her.

And there was no time for a horseback ride Friday as Van Clark, the official starter, drove a buckboard up to camp to chin about the race. He got out limping. Clark was a soft-spoken little man, now tending to tallow around the midsection, whose mane of graying hair flowed straight back from a broad forehead to the collar of his shirt. He had been a jockey back in Missouri, he said, hence the gimpy leg suffered in a tangle along the rail at Springfield. He reminisced at length on Black Ball, a stud whose progeny spelled speed. A true scorpion, he said, right up there with Peter McCue and others.

Amenities over, Clark suggested they go over the track with Kyle that afternoon so both parties would be satisfied as to its condition.

This they did, and found that the straightaway needed dragging, which Clark said he would have done. In addition, while the horsemen looked on and assisted, Clark staked the track at every common distance up to the finish line at 350 yards, where he put up flags on slim poles on both sides. The starting line, also staked, was just that — a line drawn across with a stick.

Kyle was agreeable on all points, shaking hands with everyone, spreading his good-neighbor talk, and as usual bragging about his horse.

Racetime was two-thirty o'clock, Clark reminded them, give or take a little, if that was to both sides' liking.

It was.

He said there would be a few saddle-horse races before that. He would haul a scale to the track to weigh the jockeys and tack, easier there than at the barn, because of the crowd and noise on Main Street. Sale Day's livestock auction, he expanded, held at the pens behind the livery, would start nine o'clock and be over by noon.

Any questions?

Kyle shrugged.

"We don't have any," Dude said. "However, we did agree to check the jockeys for what they'll carry. That can be done before the horses parade downtrack."

"*After* they parade," Kyle dissented. "Not that I don't trust you, good neighbor. Just never been up against an Indian jockey before."

"You won't find any chain links in his moccasins — that's for sure. But we agree to that condition, and we want you to oversee the inspection, Mr. Clark."

"Glad to. There'll be men stationed at intervals along the track to keep the crowd back. Be quite a crowd here, gentlemen. It will surprise you. Folks from all over the county. And they'll all want to see your horses before the race."

They went their respective ways.

In camp, the outfit fashioned a rope corral from tree to tree next to the wagon, scattered plenty of straw for litter and turned Judge Blair inside at Uncle Billy's bidding.

"I don't want him tied with the other horses hours before he runs. He might get kicked. A runnin' horse needs to relax. Have his own bailiwick, where he can roll and lie down when he wants to. Where he can get up and look off when he wants to. In case you don't know it, the horse is a very curious creature. It's part of his enjoyment of life. . . . Look at him now. Ears up! He sees those horses tied in front of the Union Saloon. He wonders who those fellas are. Where they're from. Besides, I want him up close where we can keep an eye on him."

"Why don't you take the first watch tonight, Uncle?" Dude said, thinking of the old man's rest. "I'll stand the last one."

He got an irascible glare for his concern.

"You sound like I'm ready for my place by the f'ar. Not by a jugful I am! No — I will take the last watch like always. That's when they try to sneak in if they aim to fix your horse, when an outfit's sleeping the soundest."

He marched to the wagon, every step emphatic, and reached inside the medicine chest, wheeled, and a revolver blinked in his hand.

It was, Dude knew, Uncle Billy's old Colt

157

single-action Army .45, its walnut stock as natural in his hand as another man would hold a pipe or flip a playing card. Dude had grown up hearing that many old-time gunfighters, the real ones, packed a single-action instead of the faster firing double-action. For it was the first shot, Grandpa McQuinn used to say, that counted when your life was at stake. That flicked through his mind now.

"If there's one varmint in this world that's worse than a horse thief," William Tecumseh Lockhart sermonized, "it's a horse fixer. If one shows up around here, they won't have to call the doctor — just call the undertaker." He twirled the Colt, settled it in his hand again, at that moment seemingly gone back in time, a reminiscence building up through the clear-blue eyes. It vanished almost as Dude glimpsed it, which he had before, though rarely. Danny was wide-eyed, Coyote like stone.

Then the old man walked to the medicine chest and back, his hand empty, the saintly features in place, once again their Uncle Billy.

"I don't look for any trouble," Dude appeased him. "Not with one man on guard and the rest of us bedded down under the wagon."

Uncle Billy all but sneered. "I've schooled you better'n that! Reminds me of a little story. . . . This outfit — just about the size of ours — was all set for the big race. Sackfuls of money bet. They figured they had it won because they had the top horse. . . . Well, they tied the horse to the wagon that night and set out guards and the rest went to sleep." He paused. He always paused for the "kicker."

"What happened?" Dude asked dutifully.

"Next morning their horse was sick. Somebody had slipped in and fixed him . . . fed him something, when one of the guards fell asleep."

"Where was that?" Dude wasn't prying this time.

"Did I say? Point is, it happened — and it can happen to us."

Danny stood the first watch, the Comanche the second. When Coyote touched him, Dude pulled on pants and shirt over his underwear, grunted on the always-tight cowboy boots, and posted himself by the rope corral.

Judge Blair, who was lying on the hay, got up and shook himself, making a rumble. What was that old story? That when you heard a horse shake himself and it sounded like thunder, you knew you had a runnin' horse. True or not, Dude liked it just the same.

Leaning over the rope corral, he stroked the soft nose and neck, then the forelock. The Judge was as gentle as a sheep dog, therefore as vulnerable. Anybody could pet him, anybody might fix him.

Bands of wind-whipped clouds obscured the moon off and on. A good night to fix a horse, Dude brooded. Walking to the road, he viewed the sleeping town. Not a light shone. By this hour even the rowdy Union Saloon was closed. He paced back and sat on the wagon tongue, feeling the unruly wind, smelling the dust off the road.

His horse stirred restlessly. Was that something beyond the corral?

Dude rose and crossed over there. Nothing there, just the blinky darkness of an empty cow pasture. And yet, he thought that he had heard something. Going back, he stood by the corral for a long, long time, unmoving. After that he eased over to the tied horses, eased back, never straying far from his horse, his eyes scouring the darkness. Uncle Billy was right. You'd better watch.

Nothing happened.

Long later, he struck a match to look at his watch. Time to wake up Uncle Billy.

The old man came out of his blankets like a panther on the prod. In moments, he was up and dressed and heading for the corral. Dude, drifting off to sleep, heard him prowling around for a while. When those sounds ceased, he heard only the wind and sometimes the horse stirring on the straw litter. He slept.

A shot exploded him awake. He jerked up, blinking, staring. He could hear horses dancing nervously. It seemed like such a short time had passed since he had fallen asleep, but dawn was no more than minutes away.

Scrambling from under the wagon, he rushed to the corral only feet away. His horse met his eyes, standing watchfully, turned toward the tied horses.

Dude's whole being surged with relief. But Uncle Billy?

A figure jutted up beside the corral.

"What was it?" Dude called as Danny and Coyote closed in.

"I saw something," the gruff voice growled.

"A coyote — a cat — maybe? A dog?"

"It *was* a man. Think I don't know what a man looks like! He was sneaking straight for the corral." Pointing; "He was right over there."

"And you missed him?"

"He vamoosed, I tell you!"

Right over there, Dude saw, happened to be about fifteen yards away. He said, "You missed him at eyeball range. Wouldn't have anything to do with the fact that you need glasses, would it?"

"Me? Listen here! I was just about ready to bore that fixer some new buttonholes when the Judge gave a great big snort — that threw me off."

"Which way did he run?"

"For town."

With pink light breaking, Dude scouted over the place where the intruder was shot at, pacing back and forth, and on to the road and up it some distance toward town. Returning, he said, "Didn't see any blood on the road."

The old man slapped his leg, his face a summary of disgust. "Don't see how I missed him. Now back in the early days . . ."

"Let's eat breakfast," Dude sighed. "This is gonna be a long day. " He studied the rope corral. The three strands were stout enough to keep a horse in, but not tight enough to keep a man out. "Danny, I'd like for you to stand guard today."

"You bet."

"Don't let him out of your sight for a single instant," the old man cautioned.

"Uncle Billy's right. Furthermore, don't let anybody pet him or touch him or get close. Not even kids. Keep 'em back. There'll be visitors."

Before eight o'clock Dude heard the first rumble of farm wagons and the bawling of cattle being led and driven to the auction. Looking uptown, he saw strings of horses and mules destined for the sale, and vehicles headed for the wagonyard and the campground.

Reed Neale and Jake Bowman were the outfit's earliest visitors.

"How's that burn-the-breeze stud of yours?" Uncle Billy greeted Neale.

"Worked him out yesterday, and he ran so fast it took his shadow ten minutes to catch up with him."

"Tol'able fast, I'd say. Tol'able."

"Just came from Kyle's camp. Offered to match him again at any distance, anytime, and you know what?"

"He wouldn't run at you."

Neale's jaw fell. "How did you know?"

"Figures."

"How?"

"Kyle's not fool enough to count on your

horse coming down sick twice in succession, is he?"

Neale's face darkened, angry and baffled. "It's still a mystery to me what happened. But . . . looks like Kyle is having some of the same kind of luck. He told us Rattler's left foreleg swelled up. That's what we came to tell you."

Dude moved in a step. "You mean he's gonna forfeit?"

"He didn't say."

"How serious you think it is?"

"Seems Rattler kicked himself. Kyle's doctorin' him. You can smell the liniment a mile away."

Bowman said, "Word's already reached town. They're starting to bet your horse. Some are giving odds. Mile-High Hanley is busier than a coyote in a chickenyard covering Texas Jack money."

Uncle Billy folded his arms and rubbed his cherry-red lower lip. "Did you see Kyle walk Rattler around? Sorta test him out?"

"No, he kept him tied."

Deeply musing, "The left foreleg, Kyle told you. Did you see the swelling, friend Bowman?"

"Kyle's got Rattler wrapped from fetlock to knee."

"I see."

Just then more visitors arrived. Neale and Bowman seemed to know everybody. Bowman proudly informed one farmer, "Dr. Lockhart tells me Texas Jack's got Himyar blood — comes straight down the ladder."

"Himyar?" The man looked blank.

"You know, sired the Kentucky Derby winner —" He couldn't remember.

"Plaudit," Uncle Billy helped, and Dude felt like hiding.

"Yes, Plaudit. Sure makes my Sister Nellie look good, her takin' the measure of Derby blood."

As the morning wore on, the lookers multiplied, stringing down from town, looking at the horse, visiting with neighbors, and idling back to their wagons.

Danny, exhibiting good-natured tact, shooed back a boy trying to sneak under the ropes to feed the horse a tuft a grass. When a rather haughty woman inquired as to the gelding's "antecedents," Danny referred her to Dude, who referred her to "Dr. Lockhart," who, at Bowman's insistence, was reciting before a bevy of farmers the extraordinary restorative powers of Professor Gleason's Sure-Shot Conditioner for both racehorse and man.

She shrank back, flushing, and strode to

the road, head high.

After a bit, Neale and Bowman left for the Union Saloon. At eleven o'clock they came back. As yet, Bowman reported, Kyle hadn't forfeited, because Hanley was still covering Texas Jack bets.

"Then he's gonna run the race," Dude said. "He'd know by now if Rattler wasn't fit."

By noon the crowd had thinned for lunch. But by one o'clock a new wave of visitors engulfed the camp as more late-arriving farm families rolled into town.

A face in the chattering, gawking throng took Dude's eye, an owl-faced man, spilling that empty grin: Rufus Swink. He meandered among some obvious saloon idlers; judging from their loud talk, they had found some Texas Jack money. As they moved on around the corral, eyeballing the horse, Dude dismissed Swink from his mind.

Neale moseyed over to Dude. They talked horses. Uncle Billy was visiting with a young farmer and his wife, citing the benefits of warm mashes for a mare in foal. Thanks to the admiring Bowman introducing him around, the old man was in his element today as "Dr. Lockhart from back East." He was constantly bowing, shaking hands, gallant, sermonizing, dressed for the occasion:

166

frock coat, white shirt, the inevitable string tie, brushed bowler, polished boots. It was hard to tell which was the major attraction, Uncle Billy or the racehorse.

Coyote Walking was polishing his tack. Danny stuck to his post by the corral. Neale joined Bowman and Uncle Billy.

Dude glanced at his watch: five minutes until two o'clock. He was starting to fidget, which he always did shortly before a race. A scattering of visitors still tarried in camp. A sound from the road pulled him about. A murmur of excitement. He saw heads swiveling. Kyle was leading Rattler by, Gentry aboard.

True enough, Rattler's left foreleg was wrapped. Even so, he wasn't limping.

He's early, Dude thought. Some horsemen said that helped accustom a horse to the crowd. Others said it made a nervous horse more nervous.

Kyle had no more than passed when it happened. Tipsy voices rose. Two drunks bound for the track started pushing each other. The pushes became swings, the voices wrathy. A strapping, bush-bearded man wearing a red shirt reeled into the path of a rider whom Dude had not noticed. A woman rider.

Her horse seemed to spook. The woman

fought the reins, but the horse reared and kept rearing. Women shrieked. Men on the road rushed to help — stopped short, unable to get in close to the fractious horse. The woman rider began calling for help.

The camp emptied of the remaining visitors, also Uncle Billy and Coyote, Neale and Dude.

By now the horse had quit rearing and the woman was pulling it in a circle. If the fool woman would only quit jerking on the reins that way! Dude thought. At that, she was doing a mighty good job of riding.

Dude shouted for her to ease up, as other men were shouting. To quit fighting the horse. As he did so, Dude recognized her.

It was Vicky Todd, in the same dark-blue riding habit, astride the same livery horse, normally so sluggish he had to be prodded into a trot. After his initial scare, the gelding should have settled at once, which he had on the road that day.

The red-shirted man had vanished.

Before Dude could wonder further, a yell sounded behind him. That was Danny's voice shouting alarm. Dude ran that way, Neale with him. They rounded the wagon to the rope corral.

Dude saw the Judge apparently unharmed, but no Danny. Movement through the trees past the corral. Danny was chasing a man, gaining on him with every stride. Danny, sprinting faster, closed on the man and tackled him, threw him to the ground. As Dude and Neale rushed there, Danny flung the man over, face up.

Rufus Swink glared up at them. He struggled to free himself. Danny punched him down. Swink lay there.

"He" — Danny gasped — "he tried to feed the — uh — Texas Jack some sugar cubes." (Danny was excited, Dude saw, but not enough to give the game away.) "I was — watching that woman on the horse."

"Did Texas Jack eat any?" Dude was almost afraid to ask.

"I'm sure he didn't. Swink was just leaning over the ropes when I saw him. Had his hand out. When I yelled, he took off."

"Sugar cubes? Where are they?"

"He threw 'em away just before I caught him. Back there."

"Sit on 'im. Don't let 'im up."

Dude ran back. On the ground he found a scatter of white cubes. He was gathering them when Uncle Billy and Coyote hastened up. Dude told them.

"Sugar cubes?" The old man's huffing voice hurled suspicion. "Give me one."

Dude held out his hand and Uncle Billy

munched one, cautiously, experimentally. Suddenly he spat. He made an awful face. He roared, "Sugar cubes, hell! They're loaded with laudanum!"

"Laudanum?" Neale puzzled.

"Tincture of opium. Now," Uncle Billy said gravely, "we know what was wrong with your Pardner horse."

"Swink hung around our camp. I remember." Neale's face was twisting. His eyes blazed. "By God, I'll —"

Dude, seeing his impulse, said, "Hold on. Don't say a word — yet. Don't let on. Listen —"

Neale wouldn't let Dude finish. "I want Kyle, and I want him now!" Fury shook him. "He fixed my horse!" He made a sudden turn to go.

Dude blocked the way. "Listen to me. Here's your one chance to win back what you lost. Find Hanley. Bet all you can. They're in this together — they have to be! You can settle with Kyle after the race. Go on! There's not much time."

Neale's face hardened with purpose. He began to nod, faster and faster. He took off running.

Dude glanced at Danny, sitting on Swink, and turned to Uncle Billy. The glittery blue eyes seemed to read his mind. The old man said, "We can't let Swink go. He'll spill the beans to Kyle — Kyle will forfeit. All bets will be off. Neale won't get his money back."

"Only one thing to do. Gag Swink — tie 'im to a tree till after the race."

"Better leave Danny on guard to make certain Swink stays put."

Dude broke for the wagon to get rope.

Chapter 9

Jogging trackward with Uncle Billy and Coyote, Dude had ample time to review what had just happened. They still had a race to win. They still had to beat Rattler, who had gone 350 yards in:18-1/5. That was travelin'! His mind swung to Vicky Todd. Visualizing the antics of the spooked horse, which hadn't acted so spooky after all, he saw with the clarity of hindsight how skillfully she had ridden. An expert . . . (he groped for the correct word) . . . equestrienne. That was it. Far from the helpless female she pretended.

Everything, he fretted, was just too well-timed to be accidental: the drunks, their fight that looked staged, somehow; her needless jerking of the poor horse; her cries for help. Was the whole thing a diversion to empty the camp, while Swink fed dope to the Judge? Swink had refused to talk. Yet how could she fit into this?

Seeing Van Clark cut short his second thoughts. Clark was waiting by a spring wagon, and by the wagon stood a platform scale.

Kyle rode up leading Rattler, with Gentry mounted. The gelding showed not the slightest sign of pain in that wrapped foreleg.

Dude's suspicions grew.

The trader laid about his peddler's smile. At the same time he sent the Judge a sizing-up appraisal. It was all Dude could do to hold his temper. The big fake! he rankled silently.

"Who's first?" Clark asked amiably.

"We don't mind," Dude said.

Coyote Walking dismounted, unsaddled, and stepped upon the scale with his tack. He was copper-bright naked above the waist, down to breechcloth and fringed Comanche moccasins. His blue-black hair was cropped neck-length. His aquiline nose and slim body gave the impression of poised swiftness. He was without visible tension, as calm as the horse he rode. He seemed to gaze far off, above the mundane dickerings of mere white men.

The way a chief ought to look, Dude thought.

Clark moved a weight on the crossbar,

nudged it a trifle, some more, peered, and announced, "Hundred and twelve pounds."

Gentry, his face as inscrutable as a piece of rawhide, got on the scale. After adjusting the weight, Clark announced, "Hundred and nine. We're pretty close." From a small box in the wagon he took three lead weights and inserted them into pockets on Gentry's saddle, motioned Gentry back on the scale for confirmation.

"There you are, gentlemen," Clark said, checking the scale. "Even weights. Any questions?"

Dude, set for Kyle to complain about something, saw him shake his head instead. Actually, Dude knew, adding three pounds of dead weight to Rattler's back meant little in a short race like this. Up around 125 pounds, however, especially in a long race, it could be a factor.

After the jockeys had resaddled, Dude said, "Brother Kyle, we also agreed to check what the riders are carrying. Want to do that now or after the parade to post?"

Shrugging, Kyle stepped down from the saddle and ambled over to Coyote.

"You savvy English?"

"Fairly well," the Comanche replied, smiling from the teeth. "I was graduated head of my class from Carlisle Indian

School, which as you know is in the state of Pennsylvania. My major interest was the works of the Bard of Stratford-on-Avon, one William Shakespeare, dramatist and poet as you know, and the sonnet form he perfected . . . composed of three quatrains and a terminal couplet with the rhyme pattern *abab cdcd efef gg* . . . retaining, however, the break or pause in theme that falls between the octave and sestet of earlier sonnet forms."

Kyle seemed to draw up and freeze. His craggy face reddened.

"As for those detractors who would ascribe the bard's works to Sir Francis Bacon because he was allegedly more cultured — fie, fie upon them, I say." Coyote Walking looked taller as he assumed haughty composure, indeed the look of a chief, Dude thought, relishing the scene as the Comanche continued, " 'To be or not to be: that is the question: Whether 'tis nobler in the mind to suffer the slings and arrows of outrageous fortune . . . or to take arms against a sea of troubles.' . . . Yes, fairly well, Mr. Kyle."

Dude made the sign for scalped. Uncle Billy curtsied.

Now Coyote handed the horse trader his Comanche quirt, brass tacks in patterns of horse tracks on the short wooden handle, streaks of blue and red between the tracks, the wrist strap and lashes of braided rawhide.

Kyle ran suspicious fingers over the brass tacks, weighed the quirt in the palm of his hand. He scowled as he tapped the handle with a forefinger, obviously searching for complaint. "What about these here brass tacks?"

"This is a medicine whip," Coyote intoned. "The tracks you see make patterns of horse tracks which symbolize the swiftness of a good horse. I do not strike my horse with the wooden handle. He would resent that, and thus break the power of the medicine. He understands when I hasten him with the rawhide — good horse that he is." Again the farcical pose. "Every man needs a good horse, as you know and as the king says in *Richard the Third*, act five, scene four, lines seven and thirteen, when his medicine breaks and the tide of battle goes against him: 'A horse! a horse! my kingdom for a horse!' "

Kyle, not amused, passed the whip back and grunted, "Let me see them moccasins." Coyote took them off and Kyle examined the heels and then the sides that would be next to a horse's flanks, his face rife with suspicion. After a deliberate moment, he handed them back and nodded approval to Clark.

He's nit-picking, Dude angered. Well, two can play the game. He stepped over to Gentry, who held out his leather whip for inspection. It was leaded, yet nothing you could complain about. Returning it, Dude said, "Careful you don't knock ol' Rattler off his feet with that billy. Now, I'd like to see what's inside your boots. Mind taking 'em off?"

Gentry started to protest. But at Kyle's nod, he pulled off the right one and hobbled about gingerly on his dirty-sock foot.

Dude looked it over carefully, his nose squinching. There was nothing inside the boot. "Now the other one," he insisted.

Gentry pulled on the right one and removed the left. Consuming needless time, Dude saw that it also was empty.

Kyle chuckled. "What'd you expect to find in there, good neighbor . . . snakes?"

"Just like everything to be four square, Brother Kyle."

"Laws alive, if you don't sound like a man that's afraid his horse is gonna eat dust."

"When we hear that brand of brag down Texas way, we always remember the old saying: 'An ounce of performance beats a pound of hot air.' "

Kyle's retort was more chuckles, and Dude, ignoring him, turned to Clark. "We're ready to run."

"All right, gentlemen," Clark announced, "we'll have the Parade to Post." A dry grin broke across his face. "Sorry our bugler didn't show up today."

Gentry mounted on his own, as nimble as a monkey, and Kyle, in the saddle, led Rattler down track. Although the Judge needed no pony horse to lead him past the crowd and back, that was part of the show and the crowd anticipated it and deserved it. Therefore, Dude mounted Blue Grass and led the gelding away.

The noisy mass became a lake of faces spilling along both sides of the course, concentrated midway and on to the finish. Bowman and Neale called and waved encouragement. Not unfriendly voices hooted at the half-naked Comanche. Coyote hooted back at them and grinned ferociously. A flurry of activity caught Dude's eyes. It was Hanley taking last-minute bets, surrounded by a knot of farmers.

Dude had a disturbing apprehension. Did Kyle & Company have yet another advantage than the one lost at the camp? What could it be? Gentry bumping the Judge at the break? Yet Rattler was no bigger than the Judge. That stratagem worked best with a third put-in horse. Gentry trying to carry the Judge to the outside? If so, he would have to be even or on the lead. Gentry roughing Coyote with his leaded whip? If so, everyone would be witnesses. And if that happened and the Judge lost, all hell would freeze over before bets were paid. No, Dude reasoned, those crude possibilities didn't fit Kyle's style. Kyle was slick.

Still uneasy, he turned the horses at the finish line to parade past the crowd again. But wasn't he always jumpy like this before a race? He was. Didn't Uncle say he was a worrier? He was — and sometimes it had paid off. He blocked the foreboding from his mind.

Onward about a hundred yards, where the crowd began to thin somewhat, his eyes went to a woman standing near the track's edge. Well-dressed, wearing a feathered hat, she was in close and earnest conversation with a man. They stood apart from the crowd.

Dude's recognition was sudden. The woman was Vicky Todd and the man was the red-shirted drunk who had spooked her horse in front of the camp. Except he didn't act drunk at all now. A large man, he towered over her while he listened intently and bobbed his head. Sober as a judge!

Past the main body of the restless crowd, Dude freed the lead rope. "Uncle Billy will be behind you at the break," he told Coyote. And then, prompted by his vague intuition, he said, "Gentry may try something, even though they think they've fixed our horse. Just imagine it's a hundred years ago, Coyote, and you're riding your buffalo runner on a big hunt. Good luck, my friend!"

"White father, you make this Comanche feel brave today, you do!" He rode on.

Dude cut back to wait and fret. Something, some instinct, some further distrust, drew him circling around and behind the Todd woman and the red-shirted big man. Tying his horse to a wagon, Dude strolled within a few steps of the pair. They had quit talking to watch the head of the track.

The crowd's din fell to a pulsing undertone.

Dude could see Kyle instructing Gentry, and Uncle Billy speaking brief words to Coyote and taking a last look at the Judge, and then Clark was waving the jockeys behind the line to get ready for the start. They walked their mounts back and turned, which placed the Judge in the opposite lane from Dude.

As he saw that, the Todd woman and the man suddenly crossed to the other side of the track flanking the Judge's lane. Dude followed, slipping into the jostling crowd behind them. When he looked again, both horses were behaving.

A prickling fear began to go up his back. Like the Judge, Rattler was a veteran campaigner. He knew what to do. He had run three-fifty in : 18-1/5. On the horses walked, swerving a little, dancing nervously, knowing what was coming, each horse keyed for the all-important break. Coyote was already low in the saddle, like one with his horse.

Dude froze. The horses looked as closely lapped as a team.

Clark's upraised arm struck downward, his shout faintly audible against the wind. They were off! A clean start. No bumping. Although the Judge took the break, Rattler was just one jump behind him.

Dude fisted his hands.

They were coming full bore now, full stride, the Judge out half a length. Both horses running straight and true. For the first hundred yards the margin between them stayed unchanged.

A screeching whoop sliced across the wind. Coyote was calling early on his horse to run faster, and he was stretching out, those fox ears laid back. Boy, was he coming! Dude could barely see Coyote's dark head, so low was he riding, naked legs high and snug, like coppery extensions of the flying horse.

Gentry held his whip high. He began beating Rattler in rhythm, every time the gelding hit the ground. Rattler came on. He was game. He surged to the Judge's shoulder, and seemed to lodge there.

Coyote whooped again. Nothing changed. They ran as if locked. Coyote whooped twice. His horse, rushing faster, slowly pulled away. Now Rattler ran at the Judge's tail. Now there was daylight.

The horses were coming like a thundering storm, when suddenly before him Dude saw the Todd woman punch the red-shirted man's arm. In Dude's concentration on the race, he had forgotten them.

Startled, he saw the man begin weaving like a drunk and stagger to the rim of the track and rake off his hat, shouting and making a show. He also seemed to ready himself, to spring.

Meaning crashed through Dude. If the man just stepped out on the track and waved his hat in the Judge's face, that would cause the horse to break stride, possibly send him flying into the crowd.

Dude hurled himself between two bystanders and pounced, feeling the ropy muscles under the red shirt. The horses were quite near, everybody jumping up and down and hollering. With all his strength, Dude bearhugged the man's arms to his sides and wrestled him away from the track, aware of the horses rushing past, aware that he was rudely knocking people aside. For a frozen interval the two danced in awkward quickstep, this way and that, Dude unable to throw the man, the other unable to free himself.

Furious, Dude suddenly shifted his hold and heaved. The man sprawled, only to scramble up and disappear into the crowd, milling and shifting like a wave toward the finish line. By the ebbing sounds Dude knew that the race was over. Did he dare look that way?

Swinging about, he encountered the Todd woman's damning eyes on him. Her mouth was a slash, her features file-hard and much older. Her eyes raked him once more, and slowly, very slowly, with growing unwillingness, she went heavily over to Hanley coming from the finish line.

The gambler was slumped, arms hanging, his face pale and shocked. Seeing her, he shuffled and stopped. His eyes shot accusations. He spread his hands — a gesture of disbelief, of how did it go wrong?

Watching them, Dude understood everything. *So that's it. That was it all along. The two of them with Kyle. Her trying to pump me. The race a double fix. First, the laudanum cubes. If that failed and Rattler fell behind, they pulled the desperate stunt at the track.*

A hurrying man bumped into him. It was Neale and he shouted, "Your horse won it by daylight! I'm goin' for my money from Hanley." Anger rippled across his face. "Cat's outa the bag about Kyle's sugar pills. He's next!" He was gone with the threat.

After a satisfying victory like this, you could afford to relax, to collect your bet without the pressure of sudden departure as in the past, keyed for challenge or fisticuffs or gunplay. Sometimes you had to chase the loser down. So Dude mused while he strolled over to stakeholder Alf Tinker for his money.

Tinker, wearing an indignant scowl, muttered as he handed him the winnings. "Reed Neale told me how Kyle tried to fix your horse with those doped sugar pills same as he fixed Pardner."

"That's not all," Dude said, getting hot again, and related what had almost happened in the race, telling it all.

Tinker gave an outraged jerk. "I'm getting a committee together to call on Kyle. I'll include Tug Rankin. Understand he's expected in town this afternoon to do some handshakin' and babykissin'."

"Rankin?" Dude said over, feeling his breath go.

"Yes — the sheriff."

"He'll be here . . . in town?"

"Why not? We're in his county. He's up for re-election. Want to go along with us when we call on Kyle?"

So they were still in Rankin's county! "Much obliged, Alf, but I have to see about my horse. He seemed to drag around this morning."

Tinker's eyebrows flew up. "If he was, he sure didn't show it a while ago. I'll wait on you."

"Go ahead. I always have Dr. Lockhart look him over right after he runs. See you later." He was in motion as he finished, dodging through the crowd to his horse. Mounted, he looked across where he had last seen Hanley and the woman. They weren't there, nowhere that he could see.

He found a swarm of well-wishers around

Coyote and the Judge.

"Texas Jack ran like a different horse today," a man said loudly, while Dude wigwagged futilely to get the Comanche's attention. Other voices broke in,

"Guess nobody can ride like an Injun."

"Don't believe he went to the whip once — just whooped."

"Yeah. It was the whoops that did it."

"Tell us how you won it, young Injun. Was it the whoops?"

Coyote's response was his even-toothed smile. Then, "Me no savvy much white-man talk. Me Comanche."

"Listen to that! He can speak *some* English."

Coyote lifted one shoulder. "*¿Quién sabe?*"

"That's Spanish. What's it mean? Anybody here speak Spanish?"

Nobody answered.

"Tell us, Injun. Tell us how you won it!"

Deliberately, Coyote lifted his head and gazed far off, playing to his audience. His chief's look, Dude saw impatiently. Blamed if he wasn't getting as taken with being the center of attention as Uncle Billy was.

Coyote spoke ceremoniously, at the same time making the sign for talk: tip of forefinger closed against the thumb, snapping the wrist. "Me tell you how. Horse him run — Comanche him ride." At last, he caught Dude's frantic signaling. Pounding his chest and jabbing heels to the Judge's flanks, he left with a whoop to the crowd's noisy delight.

Dude was waiting. "That mean sheriff's due in town any minute. We've got to break camp fast. Let's find Uncle Billy."

They rode to the starting line. Uncle Billy wasn't there. Neither was Van Clark.

"Bet I know where he is," Dude fretted. "At the Union for a little toddy. Of all the times!"

They raised dust on the road, at times delayed by wagons and buggies and pedestrians. A jubilant Danny met them at the edge of camp. "Hear we won? I let Swink go."

"We did," Dude said. "You bet we did. Have you seen Uncle Billy?"

"He rode by awhile ago with Mr. Clark."

Dude groaned. "Sheriff Rankin may be in town now. You and Coyote get everything ready to leave."

Traffic thickened as Dude reined for town, forcing him to walk his horse. Looking ahead, he saw the east-bound stage pulled up in front of the Blue Front Hotel. There also a thick-set man was shaking hands and greeting people. He swept off his

187

big hat, bowed and spoke to a farm woman holding a baby, bent and kissed the baby, bowed and spoke again to the woman.

Rankin — Tug Rankin.

Then Dude saw Reed Neale step up and shake Rankin's hand and speak.

The Union Saloon's hitching rail was full, so Dude had to tie up half a block away. More lost time, he worried, moving along the crowded boardwalk. By now Rankin would have heard all about the race and the Indian riding the winner. Coming to the saloon's entrance, he faced an ingoing current three men deep.

Pushing in, craning to see, he worked across to the bar and looked up and down it. No Uncle Billy. He turned to survey the smoky room, table by table. No Uncle Billy. Neither, it occurred to him, was Hanley at his accustomed place.

"Looking for an old gent with a white beard?"

Van Clark stood at his shoulder.

"Sure am. Where'd he go?"

"Where horses are, you might know. Had his toddy and went to the auction grounds to look over a smooth saddle horse some farmer bought this morning." He grinned. "Seems the horse has developed the heaves."

Dude barged through to the street,

hotfooted to his horse, and swung up. Rankin was still holding forth at the Blue Front. Tinker and Bowman had arrived. With Neale, they were presenting their complaints, talking jaw to jaw and gesturing angrily.

Dude reined away from them, galloped to the end of the street, and cut for the auction grounds, a cluster of board corrals, pens, and chutes. Uncle Billy and a man were studying a gray horse in a holding pen.

As Dude rode up, he caught the tail end of the old man's instructive voice, ". . . and mix that in four quarts of spring water . . . give one pint twice a day. That should bring him out of it. Not a cure — but good to trade on through today and early tomorrow — just as the other fella traded him off to you."

At the sound of Dude's horse, Uncle Billy turned alertly. He came right out.

Dude said, "We better make far-away tracks. Sheriff Rankin's in town."

"He's here?"

"In the flesh. We're still in his county."

"And I was certain we were out of his jurisdiction. Let's go!"

By now three quarters of an hour had passed since the race. The outfit had the sorrels hitched, the camp gear in the wagon,

and the Judge and Texas Jack on halters behind the wagon, when Dude saw them
coming.

Three men. His muscles loosened as he
recognized Neale, Bowman, Tinker. Where
was Rankin?

"What's the hurry here?" Neale sang out.

"Thought we'd mosey on south to Indian
Territory," Dude replied, straining for plau-
sibility. "Coyote's homesick to see his father
the chief and his kinfolks, and Dr. Lockhart
believes the change will help his catarrh.
They say it's much drier down there."

Uncle Billy coughed and hawked in his
throat.

"Hate to see you go," Neale said earnestly.

"We all do," Bowman said, and Tinker
nodded the same.

"Well," Neale began, "Sugar Kyle got
away from us. Slipped out of town right
after the race. Hightailed it north with both
wagons. Got away after all the tricks he
pulled. And Rattler wasn't lame. That story
was just to whet the betting on Texas Jack."

"What about Hanley and his wife?"

"*Wife?* You mean his girl friend. The one
you told Alf about that you said called herself Vicky Todd. They caught the east-
bound stage little while ago. But not before
Hanley paid off. They'd worked the game

before with Kyle. Kyle would come in first and set the stage. Hanley's job was to ramrod the betting. He told us everything on the condition he could leave town."

Dude could feel his face reddening, because other than what had been attempted at the track, he had told Uncle Billy nothing.

"Where's Sheriff Rankin?" Dude asked, trying to sound casual.

"Why, we sent him after Kyle. Had him issue a warrant on his own, accusing Kyle of cruelty to animals and public fraud. You see, Rankin is not the most popular man in the county. Hews too close to the letter of the law instead of the spirit. He's up against a tough opponent this time, and he knows it. He'd serve a warrant on a mule if he thought it would get him a few more votes."

Neale's words brought a sense of release to Dude. They could clear out now before Rankin returned. Yet, he felt, something was left unsaid.

The silence dragged on. Neale was eyeballing the haltered lookalike horses. Bowman hitched at his belt. Tinker lit a cigar, snapping the match on his thumbnail.

Dude went cold. They'd slipped up this once. The watchful night, capped by the would-be fixer's attempt near dawn, had caused the outfit to forget to paint a blaze on Texas Jack's face.

"Have to say," Neale said at last, "that I never saw a horse break like Texas Jack did today, or run, either. And never saw a horse improve so much in such a short time."

"Oh, he can run a little bit sometimes when he feels like it," Dude stuck in, on the modest side. "Now that he's over the colic."

Neale's gaze swung back to the horses. "Whatever happened to that blaze-faced gelding you had?"

"You mean that ol' packhorse we called Buck. Man came through here headed for Colorado. Was gonna prospect for gold. Needed a good packhorse. So we swapped that ol' Buck horse for his brown-faced horse, the one on the far side there, and some boot. We sure did."

"Reason I asked," Neale said, drawing out his words, "Sheriff Rankin told us he was on the lookout for a bush-track outfit that carried a real fast blaze-faced horse and an Indian jockey. One fellow rode a claybank gelding, and there was a white-bearded old gent."

"Well . . . that is interesting."

"Seems Rankin matched his horse against this outfit's brown-faced horse. Now this is hard to believe. . . . You see, it had started to rain hard. Doggoned, if that brown-faced horse wasn't a blaze-faced horse by the time he crossed the finish line ahead of Rankin's horse."

"Now *that* is interesting."

"It is — very. But keep in mind that Rankin is known to stretch the blanket at times. You know how politicians are?"

"Indeed I do, comin' from the Lone Star State."

"Man couldn't quite swallow that, could he?"

"Sounds more like the sheriff was a poor loser."

"Exactly. So guess what we told him?"

"That would be interesting, friend Reed."

"We told Rankin that he was wasting his time around Lost Creek. There was no such outfit. And we'd sure know if anybody did."

"You would."

Neale was looking straight at Coyote Walking, who had donned his white man's clothes. "Furthermore," Neale said, "seems to me it's getting harder and harder to tell an Indian from a white man these days. Take right now. I don't see anybody dressed up like an Indian. I sure don't see a blaze-faced horse or a claybank, and the woods are full of kind old gents with white beards." A smile cracked across his face, widening by the moment. "Good luck. And thanks. Come back someday."

The three of them turned for town.

Uncle Billy shook out the reins and the sorrels took the wagon away at a smart trot. As Lost Creek fell behind, he studied Dude, riding alongside the wagon. The worldly old eyes held more than mild inquiry.

"Dude, pardner, how come you knew so much about that woman?"

"What woman?" Dude said, eyes front.

"Mile-High Hanley's woman."

"Oh, that woman."

"Yes, that saddle-blanket gambler's woman."

"Wouldn't pry, would you, Uncle?"

"Just wondered how you happened to know her name, is all."

"Did I say? If I mentioned Bohemia, would that mean I'd been there?"

Chapter 10

Dude McQuinn could hear cattle bawling their unrest long before the outfit topped the grassy rise that afternoon and saw the town like something flung without thought on the bluestem prairie. A dusty pall hung over its eastern edge where the stockyards massed. The snake of a rail line slithered out of the wooded hills up to the little depot and on to a sprawling maze of stock pens and chutes.

"So there's Wagon Mound," Uncle Billy mused. "From the looks of things guess it's all that cowboy claimed it is. A border town with the hair on. Bad place to have your gun stick — and racehorse crazy."

Dude said, "You didn't hear all that cowboy had to say. They got a slick way of getting around Kansas quarantine regulations. Since it's against the law to drive tick-infested cattle over the state line, cattle shipped here from Texas are driven under the state line."

"Whoa, now. Run that one by me again."

"Yes — *under.* They drive 'em under the state line bridge south of town into pens on the Osage Reservation side in Indian Territory. Later they move 'em to pasture. In the fall they're brought in at round-up time and shipped from Wagon Mound to Kansas City. Slick, eh?"

"Only an Alamo Texan could think up that technicality."

"Just hope the town's not as slick at match racing."

Uncle Billy kept swinging his gaze back and forth. "Have you noticed anything unusual down there besides the size of the yards?"

Dude, after staring a moment, shook his head. "What is it?"

An indignant snort, and, "You say *I'm* the one that needs glasses! I don't see one church steeple. There's not one church in the whole shebang."

"Now that you mention it, I don't see anything that looks like a schoolhouse, either. Or a race track."

They went on, traveling slower as they entered town, Uncle Billy and Danny on the wagon seat, Coyote Walking dangling his legs over the tailgate, Dude bringing up the rear, leading the packhorse-looking Judge

Blair, while Texas Jack, curried and brushed until his dark bay coat gleamed, trailed prominently behind the wagon. Like Rebel of old, he always looked smooth, especially at a distance.

Loafers in the shade of the Wagon Mound Mercantile, which bore the words, EVERYTHING FROM THE CRADLE TO THE GRAVE, ceased whittling and talking and spitting to follow the gelding's passage. Several blanketed Indians, backs to the wall of the store, looked but did not turn their heads. A barber, scissors at the ready, stopped cutting hair to watch. A cowboy leaving the Osage Saddlery & Harness halted to gape. Passers-by on the board-walks paused to stare, perhaps to conjecture. A sign across the unpainted face of a two-story, box-shaped frame building, proclaimed: HOUSE OF LORDS. Dude smiled at the cow-town pretension.

He counted three saloons on the broad street, the most elaborate the two-story Royal Flush, which occupied about a fifty-foot front in the heart of town next to the mercantile, and was the noisiest and evidently the most popular. It was while passing here that Texas Jack attracted his largest audience. Every idling cowboy set eyes on the parading gelding, appraising his conformation, his seemingly spirited step.

Onward, past the Osage Hills Livery, past a drugstore and bakery and Big Jim's Pool Hall & Domino Parlor, past the post office and wagonyard, the outfit came shortly to a broad stream bottom, unhitched and prepared camp among the cool sycamores, elms, cottonwoods, and walnut trees. A spring meandered down between low limestone hills.

They watered the horses, unsaddled, hung the harness on the wagon tongue, set up the camp chairs and wash bench, laid the bedrolls under the wagon, gathered firewood — and waited.

"It won't be long," Uncle Billy predicted.

"I've heard that before," Dude said.

Within the hour, a shining black carriage drew up, the likes of which Dude had not seen. Neither buckboard nor buggy, but a roofed carriage, drawn by two high-stepping matched grays with blinders. Dude guessed it either a landau or a brougham.

The burly driver, showing a noncommittal face, occupied a seat outside the vehicle. As he looped the reins around the whip socket and stepped down over the wheel and shuffled to the door, Dude saw heraldic bearings blazoned thereon: two gold-painted shields, flanked by an upright lion and unicorn, a horn spiraling from the latter's head. Over the shields rested a crown.

The coachman opened the door, stood aside, and a tall man got out, visibly accustomed to such preferred status. In fact, Dude thought, he did not step down — he *descended*. He inclined his head as he came forward and spoke, the coachman trailing at a shuffling gait. "I am Commodore Weir, proprietor of the Royal Flush, which you no doubt observed as you passed through town. This is my business associate, Mr. Sweetwater Smith."

This Commodore Weir, Dude sensed immediately, was a different brand of *hombre* from what the outfit usually encountered. He had a patrician profile, a noble brow, a mien of aristocratic aloofness. Elegant in appearance, he wore a Homburg hat and bench-made ankle shoes, a black broadcloth frock coat and vest to match, plus a heavy gold watch chain that looked stout enough for a harness trace. A watch key and a small gold knife dangled from the chain. His shirt looked linen. His celluloid collar was turned down, and a black silk cravat sat bow-tie fashion under the tips of the collar. His brown goatee was carefully trimmed, his face lean, the gray eyes deep set, the mouth pencil-line thin. Even out here in the open he emitted the scent of toilet water.

Sweetwater Smith? That first handle was at odds with the flattened nose and ears and lopsided mouth. He appeared to have no neck. His head was perched on his blocky torso like a bowling ball, nothing in between. His hands, hooked in an extra large leather belt, hung like sledges on the short handles of his thick arms. His eyes, too small for his battered face, peered out from puffy sockets beneath scarred brows. He wore a rumpled brown suit and a rusty-brown hat, the brim pulled low, and dusty-brown boots — in all, as unkempt as Weir was fastidious.

Shaking hands, Dude decided to play a fairly straight role after his quick size-up of the callers. Any necessary improvisations could come later, once he had a line on these two, who undoubtedly were here for a purpose other than welcoming strangers to their fair city. "This is my uncle, Dr. William T. Lockhart . . . Coyote Walking . . . Danny Featherstone."

Shaking Coyote's hand, Weir said, "Judging by your size and leanness, I ascertain that you are not a member of the Osage tribe, our area aborigines. The Osages are quite large."

"I am Comanche," Coyote said, proud of it. "We used to fight the Osages."

"A noble race, the Comanche," Weir said, "noted for their breeding of fine horses." His manner of speaking was clipped.

"Buffalo runners," Coyote replied succinctly.

Following Weir, Smith shook hands laxly with each one of the outfit. He stood somewhat pigeon-toed, balanced on the balls of his booted feet.

"I could not help but notice," Weir continued, turning to Dude, "that you carry a running horse."

Ah, Dude thought, here we are. He scratched the back of his neck and looked down. "Sometimes Texas Jack acts like a racehorse, sometimes not."

"Would you consider matching him, Mr. McQuinn?"

"To tell you the truth, sir, we're just travelin' around . . . campin' out . . . mainly for my uncle's health. The dry Southwest, y'know."

"Bully! A wise choice. This section is noted for its salubrious climate."

"Nothing catching. It's his catarrh. He's on the mend."

"I am delighted to hear that." He nodded

toward Uncle Billy. "Meantime, you might consider running at us. In addition, I should like for you gentlemen, all of you, to drop by the Royal Flush for refreshments on the house early this evening."

"Thank you, sir. We might just do that, if Uncle feels up to it."

"I shall look forward to seeing you." Inclining his head, Weir turned to the carriage. Sweetwater Smith opened the door for him, stood stiffly aside, closed the door securely, mounted to his seat, unlooped the reins, shook them, and drove away.

"What do you make of 'em, Uncle?"

"First off, quit making me out so poorly."

"Don't take it personal. It was just conversation so we wouldn't seem eager."

"Conversation or not, a man comes to his place by the f'ar soon enough."

Dude stabbed him a look of surprise and concern, conscious that maybe he had been tactless, that he had overdone it. Uncle Billy really meant that. He sounded forlorn and put upon. "I didn't mean it," Dude said. "That's the last time you'll hear that from me. Now tell us what your size-up is of those two."

Gradually, the old man perked up, his hurt expression ebbing. (Sometimes, Dude thought, he's like a child.) "I'd say they figure they got the advantage over any brought-in horse," Uncle Billy began, in his element again, his eyes lively. "Probably cleaned up on everything around here."

"Did you catch that insignia on the door?"

"I did. Looks like a coat of arms. More important, did you sight that Weir fella's shirt cuffs? Starched stiff and extra wide — gambler's cuffs. He could hide a mail-order catalogue up his sleeve."

"I missed that," Dude confessed.

"After all I've schooled you!" He broke into a jubilant grin, his momentary mood forgotten, his voice projecting the familiar tetchiness. "What say, this evening let's take Weir up on his invite and see what he's got up that starched sleeve?"

"We'll do that."

"Meanwhile, think I'll have me a little cat nap." Starting for the wagon, he wheeled suddenly. "But don't get the idy I'm tard. It's just to ponder on this a bit." He displayed contempt. "That's the trouble with so many old fellas — they sleep too damn much."

Coyote and Danny left for town to fill a list of grocery needs.

Some minutes later, when Dude chanced

to glance toward the wagon, Uncle was flat on his back, head against his bedroll, tiredly snoring and chuffing away.

Understanding wound through Dude. Uncle Billy was getting old, a certainty he would never admit. Yet he always carried a man's full load, never asked for quarter. A pang of guilt caught at Dude. A man had the right to guard his past without being guyed about it. The realization came anew that Uncle Billy's whole life was tied to horses, caring for them, seeing that they performed up to their potential. He had no kin — his family was the little outfit of unlike characters. Well, Dude vowed, from now on he was going to see that life was made easier for William Tecumseh Lockhart, if that was really his name.

He tiptoed over to a chair and sat down to wait while the old man finished his nap.

Uncle Billy was up and rattling bottles in his medicine chest, as spry as a March horse colt, when Coyote and Danny arrived from town with a sack of supplies.

"Quite a rodeo going on behind the livery," Danny said. "Some cowboys riding broncs. They got one they can't seem to handle. Can't saddle him."

A look passed between Dude and Uncle Billy. "Believe it's time," said the latter, "for a little demonstration of Professor Gleason's Eureka Bridle. Fetch your rope, Dude, pardner."

He stepped to the rear of the wagon, leaned in, was there a moment, and when he turned he had a length of stout cord with a slip noose in one end.

"On second thought," Dude said, "believe I'd better saddle the Judge in case we need extra savvy and muscle."

They could hear the whooping and hollering and guffawing as they neared the livery and went around behind. Cowboys perched atop the corral yelled bantering advice to two men struggling on a rope tied to the neck of a stout sorrel gelding. A third man danced about, holding a hackamore. Saddle and blanket lay nearby. As the sorrel fought the rope, the two men were jerked this way and that.

The problem, Dude saw, was the lack of a snubbing post.

Uncle Billy opened the corral gate and slipped inside. "Mind if we give you a hand?" he called to the hackamore holder.

The man cut him his belittlement, as if to say, "What can you do, old man?"

"Glad to," the old man said, before the puncher could refuse, and held the gate wide for Dude to ride through.

Shaking out a loop, Dude reined behind the sorrel. He cast for the right hind foot, giving the noose an inward twist to flip it against the cannon, ready for the catch. The loop fell just right, but the fast-moving bronc stepped in and out before Dude could yank up the slack — all to the jeering delight of the corral railbirds.

Grinning, he retrieved unhurriedly and fashioned a somewhat smaller loop. Just as he tossed, the gelding bolted and the loop fell short.

That raised a second storm of hoots.

Doffing his hat, giving them his arena smile, Dude made another loop and gently touched heels to his horse. He cast again. The loop hit the dust and flipped, and the bronc stepped in, caught, kicking. Judge Blair, knowing what to do, backed up quickly, dug in with hind feet and held the rope taut.

"Not too tight, now," Dude heard Uncle Billy call. "Don't want to jerk him down."

The two helpers worked along the rope to the head of the sorrel, which fought powerfully. The two shortened holds and advanced closer. The hackamore man, jumping from side to side, couldn't make connection. He dropped his frustrated hands, goaded by the chorus of hoots from the top rails.

"Get on the rope!" Uncle Billy barked at him. "Let me in there!"

The puncher was startled, but obeyed. As the three of them slowly fought the bronc's head down, Uncle Billy eased forward.

"Careful — Uncle!" Dude shouted. All he could see at that moment was a frail-looking little man, the thinnest of ropes in his hands, opposing a thousand pounds of wild horse-flesh.

Murmuring unintelligible soft talk, Uncle Billy edged closer. He maneuvered his hands gradually, no sudden movements. Nearer now, much nearer. The bronc was wall-eyed, blowing through distended nostrils. Gently, very gently, Uncle Billy slipped the noose over the horse's face and ears and neck. Still murmuring, he drew the cord through the mouth over the tongue from the off side. Swiftly next, his hands blurring, through the noose on the near side, and a firm forward pull. Next, over the head just behind the ears from the near side, then under the upper lip, above the upper jaw from the off side, thus passing through a second cord, and, finally, a firm tie.

When the sorrel fought to toss and rear, Uncle Billy pulled and the horse came down. "Now saddle him!" the old man yelled. "Hold tight over there, Dude!"

Quickly, the punchers slammed on blanket and saddle and cinched up.

"Mount up!" Uncle Billy yelled. He drew the neck rope free over the bridle.

The puncher climbed aboard and the old man handed him the ends of the cord. "Let him walk out of it, Dude. Slack up!" Dude gave slack and as the bronc snaked out of it, the old man shrilled, "He's all yours!" and backstepped clear.

For a couple of counts the bronc stood still, not realizing his freedom. And then, bogging his head between his forelegs, he broke bucking. The puncher hung on without pulling leather. He could ride. The horse was an honest pitcher: close-to-the-ground bucks, and gut-twisting, cloud-hunting tricks, but the puncher stayed with him, spurs raking every jump, finding the sorrel's rhythm. They circled the corral in that violent display, while the railbirds whooped and hollered.

"Pull 'im up!" Uncle Billy yelled.

The rider pulled and the sorrel's head came up. He quit pitching and went to crow-hopping, just arching his back and stiffening his knees.

"If you want 'im to buck, give 'im rein! When you don't, pull up!"

The puncher gave rein and the horse

bucked, slower this time, for he was tiring. When the rider pulled up, the horse quit.

"Now," Uncle Billy instructed, "just ride him around and cool him down. He'll handle quite nicely. You could probably lead him on a string."

Around the corral again and again, until the sorrel broke into a tired trot. The bronc twister reined to a halt. Uncle Billy came out and held the horse during the unsaddling, talking that soothing nonsense to him. Untying the knot, he slipped the cord free and released the horse.

"Is that all that is," a voice drawled in his ear, "a little bitty piece of cord?"

It was the bronc rider: angular of body, level ash-gray eyes that tended to crinkle at the corners from wind and sun, a weathered face both reckless and easy-going.

"It's far more than that, young man. It's a bridle."

The twister continued to stare at the cord, as if his eyes might delve up some concealed contrivance. "A bridle?" he repeated.

"A bridle," Uncle Billy echoed, withholding explanation until the railbirds had come down and drifted across.

Dude's mouth curled in a grin. *Timing.* Another wrinkle he had learned from Uncle — *timing.* Why waste your main spiel on a lone cowboy when, by delaying, you could build an audience, and possibly make friends, and thereby glean the lay of the land?

"This cord's a bridle," the cowboy marveled, turning to the others.

"Professor Gleason's Eureka Bridle," the old man said, explicit about it. "In use for years in the eastern horse states. First time in this part of the country . . . as you have just seen demonstrated — the most successful bridle ever devised for the management of vicious horses, or for the purpose of doctoring the eyes or making surgical operations. This bridle will hold any horse under any circumstances."

"It works," the cowboy said, impressed. "Except it looks mighty complicated, the way you tied it."

"Let me show you again . . . this time on a gentle horse."

Dude rode forward. The gawking railbirds crowded closer.

"First," Uncle Billy lectured, "the slip noose." Step by step, he went through the passes to the tie. "Now you try it."

The cowboy slipped the noose around the Judge's neck, passed the cord through the mouth over the tongue from the off side, through the noose on the near side and pulled. Gaining confidence, he took the cord over the head behind the ears, started downward and through the mouth —

"Stop there! Just under the upper lip — always just under the upper lip against the upper jaw. That's where the leverage counts most. . . . You've got it! Now pass through and make your knot. . . . Young man, you have just tied the Eureka Bridle!"

After the railbirds had bunched closer to see, Uncle Billy untied the cord. With an air of official bestowment, he presented the cord to the first cowboy. "Yours," he said formally, "for being the first man in Wagon Mound to master these intricate weavings devised so long ago by Professor Gleason."

The pleased recipient hung his head. "Say, I'm sure much obliged to you, Mr. . . . ah . . ."

"Dr. William T. Lockhart of the Blue Grass Region of Kentucky."

"I'm Slim Overmire, from the LX outfit on the Osage Reservation."

"Very glad to know you, Slim."

They shook hands energetically, and Uncle Billy said, "The ugly gent on the horse there is Dude McQuinn. He can't help it if he scares people the way he looks."

Paying the old man a stiff look, Dude dismounted and shook Overmire's hand. In another moment he and Uncle Billy were shaking hands all around.

"This Professor Gleason," Overmire then inquired. "Who's he?"

"The *late* Professor Gleason, I regret to say . . . an old colleague of mine . . . founder of the Kentucky Academy of Science and longtime consultant to various jockey clubs, including that of New York state and the Old Dominion of Virginia, which is a veritable fountainhead of racing blood. Weary of watching the mishandling of spirited horses, he invented the Eureka Bridle after years of trial and error. The Eureka," he stressed, "is also the bridle that subdued the immortal Himyar."

"Himyar?"

"Himyar sired the Kentucky Derby winner, Plaudit. Now that takes me back. Let's see. Himyar was . . ." He turned. "Dude, when was Himyar foaled?"

"Seventy-four, I think. I believe it's in your latest work, the *Official American Stud Book*." He screwed up his face, concentrating. "Or maybe it was in seventy-five, though I wouldn't bet my saddle on it."

"You're right — it was seventy-five." Back to Overmire: "As a young stud, Himyar was kind of on the rank side. High-spirited. Tremendous girth and immense stifle. So fractious they considered altering him. Just about that time Professor Gleason developed the Eureka, which enabled Himyar's trainer to control him and school him and thus pass on his speed and heart and conformation, prominent to this day in bloodlines on the American turf. Which calls to mind, do you fellas ever race horses hereabouts?"

Overmire's face became wry. "We've brought some pretty fast cow horses in here, but Commodore Weir — he runs the Royal Flush — always takes us."

"I've met Mr. Weir. Where do you race? I've seen no track."

"We run right down Main Street. Finish in front of the Royal Flush."

"What's Weir got that is so fast?"

"A stud called Sir James. Supposed to be imported from England, bought in Maryland."

Uncle Billy sniffed. "They have some tol'able good racing blood there. What distance have you been matching Weir?"

"Long — too long, it seems. Last time it was six furlongs and Sir James daylighted our filly, Osage Girl, by five lengths. Weir wouldn't match us at the quarter mile or under."

"Young man, you must always make the match at your horse's best distance. Never too short, never too long."

"Reckon we know that now. We got too eager to run at him. Before that he took us twice at five furlongs. Right now we're fresh out of runnin' horses." He brightened. "Saw that dark bay tied to your wagon when you came in. Sure looked smooth. He a race-horse?"

Uncle Billy gazed off toward the stock-yards where the cattle bawled incessantly. "At times."

"Was hoping, after all the dust we've had to eat. Like to kick some at the Commodore for a batch of reasons. All us cowboys would."

"Why?"

"One thing, Weir sure can rub it in on a man when he wins. It's that way he's got, like he's too good for ranch folks. Goes around with his nose stuck up in the air. Even claims he's a descendent of the Duke of Newmarket, whoever that *hombre* was."

"Hhmmnn. What else?"

"Well, the whiskey at the Royal Flush is watered. We know that, but we can't prove it. The games are crooked, too, but we can't prove that, either."

"Young man, don't you know by now that all games in saloons are crooked? Remember that old song? 'You play with a gambler who's got a marked pack; you walk back to camp with your saddle on your back.' Best advice a cowboy ever had — and the least heeded."

"Man's got to have a little fun."

"Why not patronize another saloon? I believe Wagon Mound boasts two others."

"Weir owns 'em all — the Bull's Head, the Red Eye. That's not all — he owns the Wagon Mound Mercantile. Might say, he owns the town. Everything but the bakery. Likewise, Weir has cut the girls down to a fifteen-cent take on each drink they get the boys to buy, when in Wichita it's twenty-five cents."

"What would you expect of a monopoly, the absence of free American enterprise? It's take it or leave it."

"Reckon we'll have to take it." A hopefulness strengthened his voice. "You aim to match Weir or not?"

"Young man, I refer you to a saying of Mark Twain's. Ever read him?"

"Not unless it was a Bull Durham sack."

"Well, Mr. Twain wrote, and I quote him verbatim — which is from the Latin word *verbum* — 'It is difference of opinion that makes horse races.' " Abruptly, he exited for the corral gate. One, two, three, four steps and he glanced over his right shoulder.

"Slim, you rode that bronc purty and slick."

Timing, Dude thought. Timing.

They left the corral and circled around to the street. There Dude said, "What was that back there about me bein' ugly? Sure fails to tally with what the girls say when they paw over me."

"Don't take it personal. Just conversation so we wouldn't seem uppity to all them ugly cowboys."

Chapter 11

At seven o'clock the slicked-up outfit trailed into the Royal Flush to the accompaniment of off-key music, the click of chips at the gaming tables, the tinkle of glasses, the jangle of spurs, the raucous laughter and whoops of dancing cowboys and girls going hippity-hop, arms swinging like pump handles.

Dude got a compound of smells, yet each distinct — raw whiskey, spilled beer, sweat, strong tobacco, kerosene-fed lamps, sawdust, and perfume of not the most delicate scent.

Commodore Weir was waiting. He left his station by the bar and inclined his head, that gesture of proper civility. "Evening, gentlemen. I have a table reserved for you," and he led them across. Once they were seated, he raised a beckoning finger and a red-faced bartender hustled over, wiping wet hands on his greasy apron, which Weir eyed critically. "Change that before the next shift," he snapped, aside.

"Sure will, Mr. Weir. Been kinda busy."

"Now, gentlemen," said Weir, "may I offer you the best of the house this Saturday evening. Mr. O'Fallon will take your orders. I shall join you later." He left them to go to an office at the rear of the long room near the stairs.

"What'll it be?" O'Fallon asked, perceptibly relieved at Weir's departure, waiting first on Uncle Billy.

"He," Dude spoke up, thinking of the old horseman's well-being, "will have a soda water."

"I," declared Uncle Billy, "will have an Old Green River. Double shot."

"The same for me," Dude sighed, thinking that was the thanks you got for trying to look out for the old codger.

O'Fallon turned next to an uncomfortable Coyote Walking, who said uncertainly, "A strawberry soda water, please."

"That we ain't got. How about a beer?"

"Beer, then, if you please."

Bug-eyed at such manners, O'Fallon swallowed and switched to Danny, who said, "Irish whiskey."

"That also we ain't got. How about Old Green River?"

"It's not the same," Danny differed mildly.

"It is here," O'Fallon said and left.

Coyote's attention was on the toiling musicians and the hippity-hop dancers. He said, "How strange the white man's ways, to dance without drums." He looked boyish and somewhat scholarly in his Carlisle School clothes, which he kept carefully stored in his parfleche, taken out only on special occasions: the dark-as-doom suit, wrinkled and tight through the shoulders, the sleeves reaching inches above his wrists. A black four-in-hand tie formed a choking knot at the throat of his gray flannel shirt. The brim of his black hat, as oversize as his outgrown suit was undersize, rode atop his ears, making his dark eyes as those of a beaver peering out from under a stream bank; and the crown of the hat, rising like a chimney pot, stood him a foot taller.

"That's not dancin', anyway," Dude said. "That's cow-town wrestlin'."

O'Fallon brought the drinks and skedaddled. He wore a clean apron.

Dude looked around. The long bar had polished brass fixtures and rails. On the wall behind the bar giant mirrors reflected the brightly labeled bottles. Above the center mirror hung an enlarged painting of the lion and unicorn and the shields and crown seen on Weir's carriage door. On other walls were paintings of overfleshed nudes reclining on couches and strumming harps beside misty waterfalls.

The green gaming tables, watched over by an unsmiling Sweetwater Smith, took more space than the crowded dance floor. The busy gamblers affected black suits with fine white stripes, as proper as Weir himself. The musicians, at piano, banjo, and fiddle, labored in evening dress from a seated recess below the purple-curtained stage.

Just then a slim, dapper man, also in evening dress, his plastered-down black hair parted in the middle, stepped out between the curtains and the music ceased. Reluctantly, the hippity-hop dancers stopped and sought chairs at tables. Raising a strident voice that Dude figured could be heard to the stockyards, the master of ceremonies bellowed:

"Lay-dees and gen-tul-men . . . the management of the Royal Flush . . . by popular demand and at great expense . . . continuing Mr. Commodore Weir's policy of always bringing you the finest of entertainment . . . now presents the feature of the evening — the celebrated English Songbird — direct from London's famous

Drury Lane — Lady Jane Penrose!"

Backing off stage, he whapped his hands while the orchestra struck up a rapid-fire introduction. From the opposite wing of the stage a full-bosomed figured glided out.

She wore a low-necked, tight-fitting blue dress on which gold-colored spangles gleamed and shook, adding a constant swaying to the sinuous movements of her rather stout body. Stormy applause and whistling broke. She jiggled her head until her red curls danced, summoned an indulgent smile, batted her eyes, and waved a glittering hand. She had a round, full face, more than amply powdered, and her mouth was an enormous cupid's bow. When the clapping and whistling subsided, she looked down at the musicians. "Perfessor," she called, "let's take a little ride up 'The Old Chisholm Trail.' " Whereupon, the professor ran the keys, the banjo and bass fiddle players joined as madly, and after a moment as the music slowed for the opening, she commenced singing:

> *Come along, boys, and listen to my tale;*
> *I'll tell you of my troubles*
> *   on the Old Chisholm Trail.*
> *Come a ti yi yippy, yippy yay, yippy yay,*
> *Come a ti yi yippy, yippy yay.*

She wasn't bad, Dude decided, and she wasn't good, as her tired voice strained at the familiar notes; but she was loud and bouncy and that suited the entertainment-starved cow crowd. The song over, she bowed to applause and took a teasing turn as if to leave, at which the cowboys whooped for more, the loudest, Dude saw, being Slim Overmire. Turning bit by bit to tantalize the crowd, she nodded, finally, to the professor, who swung into "Sam Bass," and she sang how traitor Jim had sold out Sam at Round Rock, Texas, that fatal day when the Rangers waited. The song, Dude remembered, was one of the best at quieting a herd during a thunderstorm.

Presently, when the song ended, and Lady Jane exited to another gale of clapping and whooping and whistling, Overmire stopped at the outfit's table.

"How'd you boys like Lady Jane's warblin'?"

"Mighty fine," Dude said. "Makes me homesick for Texas."

Overmire leaned down, his voice guarded. "Mighty fine — even if she used to be Talcum Annie of Wichita. I been closer to Drury Lane than she has. . . . You matched that horse race yet?"

"It's a little early. Right now the Commodore is plying us with drink."

"Better hold on to your riggin'."

The orchestra struck up a lively dance tune and Overmire, with a hurried wave, shot away and grabbed himself a partner, whom he swung clear of the floor for an entire circle and into the dance. Hippity-hop. Hippity-hop.

O'Fallon materialized out of the milling with more drinks for the outfit.

Suddenly, above the racy music and the stomping and hopping, Dude heard voices clash, followed by two distinct blows. He turned. Two cowboys were whaling away at each other.

From nowhere, it seemed, a figure burst. It was Sweetwater Smith. He grabbed the foremost fighter, spun him like a top to the floor. As the second one stared at him, momentarily dumbfounded, Smith seized him by the nape of the neck and the seat of his Levi's and rushed him toward the door. There he threw the man headlong into the street.

The dance hall stilled.

That done, Smith clumped deliberately to the tables to watch the gaming. The gamblers had not even glanced up at the swift commotion. The leftover cowboy picked himself up, grabbed a girl, and resumed dancing.

"Believe Slim Overmire would have contested Sweetwater Smith better'n that," Dude observed.

"I wouldn't bet on it," Uncle Billy contradicted him, looking at his empty glass. "This place has more aliases than an outlaw's hangout. *Business Associate Smith* is an ex-pug, probably off the New York waterfront. Lady Jane Penrose is Talcum Annie from Wichita. My whiskey is not Old Green River. Whatever it is, it's half water. I think I've seen that coat of arms somewhere on a Scotch whiskey bottle. And if Commodore Weir is the Duke of Newmarket, I'm chief of all the Comanches."

"You would make a good chief, Grandfather," Coyote Walking said, nodding. "You are very wise."

"Thank you, Coyote, but don't call me Grandfather."

The music raced to a still faster tempo and the tireless dancers, not to be outdone, whirled faster. Hippity-hop. Hippity-hop. Overmire and his girl, cavorting near the bar, happened to kick a brass cuspidor, which wobbled precariously, then righted itself.

"Hey — look!" Dude cried, pointing. "Self-rightin' spittoons. Never saw that before. You can't say this is not a classy dive, Uncle."

Weir came to the table, the considerate host. "Hope you gentlemen are enjoying yourselves?"

"Couldn't be better," Dude boomed.

"Another round of drinks?"

Dude's impulse was to decline, for a stranger's free drinks invariably concealed a catch for the unwary horseman, but Uncle Billy coughed and said, "Believe I'll have another toddy," and coughed again.

Instantly, Weir signaled, and instantly O'Fallon was there.

Drawing up a chair, Weir sat and drew a long cigar from the breast pocket of the broadcloth coat, snipped the end with the gold knife on the gold watch chain, laid the cigar between even teeth, and leaned back. He could be pompous, Dude saw, and he was now. Weir said, "I do not wish to intrude upon the province of your privacy, Mr. McQuinn, but if I may say so, your drawl is reminiscent of my favorite American city — San Antonio, Texas."

Ah, Dude thought, it's starting. He drawled, "I am a Texan, though not of San Antone."

"I have ranch holdings in the vicinity of San Antonio," Weir clipped. "Once a year I journey there to check on matters. It was there that I witnessed a most exciting event, one I shall not forget."

"How many got shot?"

"No gunfight — a horse race. A most memorable horse race. I saw the quarter mile covered in the ramarkable time of twenty-two seconds flat, as you say in Texas — furthermore, against the wind. And you know how the wind blows in Texas?"

"Do I? Can't sleep without it. Been music to my ears since cradle days, high and low. I suppose this was a stud?"

"A gelding. A blaze-faced bay gelding." Weir shook his head at the memory. "Twenty-two seconds."

"That is goin' some. A blaze-faced gelding, you say?"

"With four white-sock feet. A dark bay gelding."

Dude groaned to himself. "Seems I recall a split-breeze gelding named Ranger that took the slack out of every horse around there."

"Mr. McQuinn! I'm surprised at you, a Texan. The horse in question was known as Judge Blair. I remember the name because of the judicial appellation."

There goes our chance, Dude moaned inwardly, of running the Judge under his true name and true colors. "You're right. A man wouldn't forget that name."

"Without being too biased, I believe Sir James, my stallion, could equal that time at the quarter mile — or even surpass it — if given competition."

Dude whistled softly. "You don't say! Then your horse has to come from quality folks."

Weir pulled out his watch, which was gold, inserted the watch key and wound with an imperious clicking. "Sir James," he said, "was foaled in England on the estate of the late Duke of Newmarket, a maternal uncle of mine . . . an estate, I regret to say, which has since passed from family hands due to the whims of fortune."

How this Weir *hombre* could heap it on! "Gosh," Dude sympathized, "that's too bad. I remember when steers hit ten cents in Fort Worth, and we lost the old homeplace on the Salt Fork of the Brazos. For a long time after that it was just biscuits and sow belly, I tell you." He smiled at Weir. "So you fell heir to Sir James?"

"Were it only so, Mr. McQuinn." Sadness enveloped the saloonman's disciplined face.

"Just call me Dude."

"When the estate was broken up, all the blood stock was sold to satisfy the creditors and Sir James was afterward shipped to

Maryland as a yearling. By the most fortu-
itous of happenings . . . being a long-time
member of the Maryland Jockey Club . . . I
was at Pimlico, where I had a string of
horses running. I bought the colt on the
spot . . . sentiment, you understand. He
looked terribly ill-used. Only later did I
learn that he could run."

"Sometimes Lady Luck smiles."

"That was a bully day, I assure you."

"How was he bred?" Dude asked courteously, set for the vaunting.

It came like a flourish of trumpets, "Sir
James is by King James, out of Queen's
Rule. An excellent nick or cross, as they say
in Kentucky." Weir slid the watch into the
vest pocket and smoothed the pocket.

Dude thought, Why this bird's got more
lip than a muley cow, and said genially, "A
scorpion, eh?"

"Both short and long, Mr. McQuinn."

"You booger me when you talk like that."

"I beg your pardon?" Weir said, lifting an
eyebrow.

"I mean you scare me off."

"I trust not. May I inquire as to the
breeding of your ah — gelding, Texas Jack? I
ask, since I am rather keen on ancestry, as
you have gathered."

"Texas Jack is just an ol' cow pony that

can run a little when the wind's at his tail. Came out of a cow outfit's remuda. Good cuttin' horse. His sire was a range stud of unknown folks, his dam a range mare of Spanish blood."

"Spanish blood? That's bully! Perhaps, then, he stems from the hot blood that bore the conquistadors across the Americas?"

"Mr. Weir, I figure you hit it right on the head."

"And you say he can run a little?"

"At times."

"Come, Mr. McQuinn, Texas Jack must be a goer, else you would not match him."

"You make a man hunt for a bigger size hat," Dude answered, laughing outright, "way you brag about his horse. We're just a little ol' outfit on the travel. We trade some, we race some. Don't figure Texas Jack is in the same class with your Sir James."

"There are many factors in a race."

"You can say that again — and the main one is speed."

"Speed, and the ability to hold it. A stayer."

"If we do match you, we'll have to have odds."

Weir looked startled. "I never give odds."

"But your Sir James would be the big favorite, him bein' imported and all that royal breeding behind him. Don't you see?"

"Not necessarily. A fast horse is a fast horse, whether of noble or commoner blood."

Dude spread his hands. "Oh, we might take a look at your stud. Always like to see a good horse."

"At your convenience, Mr. McQuinn."

So, Dude reckoned, they were getting down to taw. "Tomorrow?"

"Tomorrow at nine, say?"

"Where?"

"If you gentlemen will oblige me by assembling here, we can canter out to my ranch north of town."

Dude held out his hand. "We'll be here."

Weir shook hands and stood. "O'Fallon, another round for these gentlemen."

After Weir had taken leave, Uncle Billy complained, "Didn't think you two'd ever dally your tongues. Was just ready to put on my hip boots if the tide got any higher."

"What do you think?" Dude asked seriously.

"What do I think?" He waited until O'Fallon had set down the drinks and gone. "He's as cagey as a bunkhouse rat. Most horsemen wouldn't hot air their horse the way he did, for fear they'd scare off the other side. He went sky high, laid it on. We're up against a new wrinkle. But I keep coming back to those wide cuffs of his — he's a gambler, I figure, with acquired airs."

When Dude and Uncle Billy rode up to the Royal Flush at nine o'clock, two horses, one bearing a hornless English saddle, tail-switched flies at the rail. Sweetwater Smith was posted at the doorway like a tireless brown watchdog in his rumpled suit. He nodded, without expression, which was as close as Dude had yet to see him speak. At this Sunday hour the saloon, like the silent street, seemed to be sleeping off the night's carousal, expelling its fetid breath through the batwing doors.

Smith went inside at his shuffling gait. He came out behind Weir, who carried a riding crop and favored riding livery today: close-fitting tan breeches, gleaming long boots that reached to his knees, a red-and-white checkered vest under his long-tailed blue coat, and red-billed riding cap. Dude took the get-up for a fox-hunting outfit. After a civil "good morning," Weir mounted the English saddle.

Dude fell in beside him as they followed the north road, saddling across prairie into gently rolling, lush-green hills, here and there outcroppings of limestone and sandstone against the carpet of bluestem. The cool breeze smelled of sweat grass. Fat whitefaces grazed the flats and hills, filled themselves at mirrorlike pods. Red-tailed hawks rode the sky.

As they journeyed along, Weir would point to an expanse and comment, "I have all that leased to yonder ridge," or "I expect to come into possession of that within the year."

Not long afterward, they reached a wire gate. Beyond stood a modest frame ranch house, and a busy windmill, its wheel a disk of spinning sunlight, and barn and sheds and corrals, and a neat orchard and a broad hay meadow and rolling pasture — a well-kept little ranch. Here, however, Dude saw few cattle.

While Smith swung down to open the gate, Weir trailed his eyes back and forth, from meadow to ranch house, from ranch house to meadow. "This will soon be mine," he confided to Dude. "I shall move here from town. As it is, I stable my horse here." His anticipation swelled, "Initially, I shall enlarge the house. I will dig a well in the meadow and plant alfalfa. By irrigating, I believe I can get two cuttings annually."

"Nice little place," Dude answered, wondering how the change of ownership had come about.

Riding by the house, where varicolored hollyhocks and daisies curtsied in the wind, Dude saw an elderly couple rocking on the porch. Weir tendered them his curt recognition. Something, a sense a wrongness, plucked at Dude as they rode on. The old people back there hadn't smiled welcome. Was that numbed shock he had read on their plain faces?

He forgot them when Weir halted at the corrals and began hot airing his horse again. ". . . and you will see that Sir James is everything I've described to you . . . an outstanding individual . . . plenty of bone and muscle. If you gentlemen will excuse me, I shall now go to collect Sir James."

Smith opened the heavy corral gate and followed Weir's polished heels into the high-peaked red barn.

Shortly, Weir emerged leading a snorty-acting gray stud.

Uncle Billy stared hard for a space and spoke low to Dude, "A distance horse. Match him as short as you can."

Weir halted in the center of the corral, and Dude and Uncle Billy, coming over, began a circling look-see. The gray was rangy, built a good deal along the lines of Blue Grass —

straight of leg, long of back, high at the withers, an excellent head, a racy-looking animal.

"What is your judgment?" Weir's tone said that he expected praise.

"Mighty smooth," Dude answered. "Such legs. Must have a twenty-six-foot stride. Looks like a Thoroughbred, Commodore."

"He is that through and through, bred to the purple."

They had beaten around the bush long enough, Dude decided suddenly. He looked straight at Weir. "Give us two-to-one odds and we'll scamper you three hundred and fifty yards."

"I never give odds." Weir had an antagonizing manner of tilting his head and looking down at you, a lordly air. He did so now. "However, I might agree to even money at six furlongs."

There it was, the distance that had been too much for Osage Girl. Dude went to whistling "Dixie" and looking off. "You're way past me there, Commodore."

"And you are considerably short, Mr. McQuinn."

"Why, if I matched my little ol' cow pony that far, he'd never speak to me again."

Weir smiled thinly. "Less than that would scarcely be a warm-up for Sir James."

"Looks like if we match this go, you'll have to come down and I'll have to come up — say to four hundred yards."

Weir's reply was to lead his horse back into the barn. Coming out, he wore a condescending expression. "Shall we ponder on this awhile, Mr. McQuinn?"

Dude pretended indifference. "There's no hurry. Fair enough, Commodore."

"Bully, Mr. McQuinn! You strike me as a true sportsman of the turf. Possibly we can yet match this race."

"Just call me Dude."

Passing the house, Dude saw that the porch was empty. The old couple stayed in his mind all the way to town, though he said nothing. After a drink at Weir's invitation, he and Uncle Billy left.

"Well, Uncle?"

He did not answer at once. A distant look stood in the clear blue eyes. He seemed far away, preoccupied. Dude recognized the signs. Uncle Billy was visualizing the match. Then he said, "Sir James is an obvious distance horse, which is why Weir won't match him short. I would do the same, use my advantage. These young cowboys were fools to match him long. They know better now." He paused and Dude waited. The cagey voice spoke again:

"Weir will expect us to try to match him short next time we talk. We're forgetting that the Judge can go five or six furlongs at full speed, maybe seven, if he has to. However, we haven't matched him over the quarter mile since we cleaned up on the Nebraska plow-chasers."

"Can he go half a mile now?"

"Can with some long breezes under his belt."

"You've got me thinking, Uncle."

"Before we make any moves in that direction, we need time to ready him over the longer distances. I want to clock him. Problem is, where?"

"There's the whole Osage Reservation just south of the state line."

Chapter 12

After the noon meal, the two horsemen rode south of Wagon Mound, following a broad trail that plunged into the rounded hills and flowing prairies of the Osage Nation. Dude inhaled earth scents and the breeze carried the voices of meadowlarks and mourning doves. The town was well out of sight when Uncle Billy pulled up on a long stretch over which he sent measuring eyes, back and forth.

"This will do," he said.

"Hope you're a better judge of distance than I am," Dude said, dismounting to mark the starting line.

"I can come within three feet of estimating one furlong," was the testy reply. Dude didn't argue. Uncle Billy's arthritis was bothering him today.

The old man rode off at a concentrating trot. Down the trail he dismounted and scratched a line with the toe of his boot to mark the first furlong. Three more times he halted, then trotted back. Together they rode over the course, picking up troublesome rocks. The center of the trail was the cleanest. On the last half of the stretch a gentle rise lifted gradually toward the timber-shaggy hills.

"I've purposely figured this a long half mile," the old man said, "so the Judge will be running upgrade a good deal of the way. It never pays to pamper a runnin' horse, same as a human. Ease makes a horse fat and slow, a man slow on the draw."

The rest of the afternoon and the whole of the evening passed without change.

"The Commodore is waiting us out," Uncle Billy said.

"And we are waiting him out, Uncle."

First light was half an hour distant when the outfit slipped away from camp. At the state-line bridge, Dude said, "Hold up. Let's see if we're being followed." They watched and listened, seeing only formless shadows back there and no sounds.

They rode quietly on.

Before many minutes they reached the long stretch on the beaten trail. Fawn light was breaking, pinking the tops of the furry hills. The pungent grass began to glitter dew. Dude found his little mound of rocks that marked the starting line.

Uncle Billy told Coyote, "School him on the swinging start and gallop hard the full distance to me — I want him to sweat," and rode to the finish line.

When Uncle Billy was waiting downtrack, Coyote walked Judge Blair to the getaway line and turned him slightly. Dude dropped his arm downward and shouted "Go!" Coyote jumped the horse out, galloping hard. Against the half light, jockey and horse could be spectral shapes, so rapidly did they diminish, the beat of their passage growing fainter and fainter, hushed at the finish.

Watching keenly, Dude saw Coyote ease the Judge off and slowly bring him around. The two riders trotted back.

"He wants to run, this horse," Coyote exulted to Dude.

"Good. We'll clock him before long."

The day spent itself with only one caller, a cowboy wanting to talk horses. The next afternoon, while Uncle Billy napped under the wagon, Dude walked to the Royal Flush. Taking bottle and glasses from a weary-eyed O'Fallon, he chose a table near Weir's office.

Directly, Sweetwater Smith clumped down the stairs and rapped on the office door. A curt voice answered. Smith went in. By and by, he and Weir came out, Smith taking a position at the end of the bar. An unusual affability broke through the crust of Weir's reserve as he discovered Dude.

"Why, good afternoon, Mr. McQuinn."

"It's plain Dude, remember? Have a drink with me, Commodore." Dude had noticed that the man responded to the title.

"You are generous, Mr. McQuinn, but I insist that you permit me the honor." He called O'Fallon. "A bottle of my private stock," and when O'Fallon hustled it over, Weir poured liberally and raised his glass. "Here's hoping you've reconsidered and lengthened the distance."

Dude, lifting his glass, "And here's hoping you've taken up the slack, Commodore." He tossed down the drink, expecting the usual bar belly-wash. Instead, it was surprisingly smooth.

Weir twirled his empty glass. "I might come down to five furlongs."

"As a sporting gesture," Dude replied, "I might go up to the full quarter mile."

Weir's reply was a clipped laugh. "Still too short, Mr. McQuinn."

They sat a bit in silence, like two antagonists across a checkerboard deliberating the next move. Dude said, "I'll put it this way —

your horse would be heavily favored. I'd have to have odds, and I'd have to have a distance my ol' cow pony can run. You're a horseman. You can see that, Commodore."

Weir rose, his manner coolly rejecting, yet not final. "I never give odds. We'll have to ponder further. Meanwhile, enjoy yourself, Mr. McQuinn."

"Commodore, you are a judge of good whiskey."

When Dude turned his head, thinking of another drink, the bottle of private stock had vanished, and so had O'Fallon.

He was still sitting there, still amused at the brevity of Weir's hospitality, when rustling skirts pulled his eyes to the stairs.

Lady Jane Penrose was coming down, spangled for the evening, this time in shimmery green. He saw her heavy-lidded eyes go questioningly from him to Smith at the bar; if some understanding passed between them, Dude didn't catch it. Hardly pausing, she swayed over to Dude's table, her costume rustling and shivering, while she favored him her full-lipped smile.

"I believe you're Dude McQuinn, the horseman. Word gets around, you know." She arched an eyebrow.

He stood immediately, sweeping off his hat and bowing from the waist. "I am, indeed, and you are *The* Lady Jane Penrose of stage and song."

Accustomed as she no doubt was to the coarse flattery of the lusty cow crowd, the pink of her blush surfaced through the thickness of powder and paint. "I believe you're a gentleman, too," she said.

"Just an ol' country boy that wandered into town, got lost, and never found his way out again — that's all."

"Also modest, I believe," she said, looking him up and down.

"Just on my manners around a purty lady. Won't you have some refreshments?"

"It's too early for a drink, but I'll sit and visit awhile."

He drew out a chair and seated her, his courtesy exaggeratedly gallant. She looked up at him. "And you claim you're no gentleman?"

"Just something I learned at country pie suppers."

"And where might that have been?"

"Down in Texas where the live oaks grow."

He seated himself across from her. She was pushing thirty-five if she was a day, and her voice was worn and she was picking up tallow around the middle. There were bags under her eyes and wrinkles here and there which no amount of powder and rouge could disguise. Even so, the even mold of her face was attractive, though growing fleshy, and her eyes were large and dark, which long lashes accented, and there was a hearty liveliness about her that did not escape him.

"Whereabouts in Texas?"

"Along the Salt Fork of the Brazos, out where the hoot owls holler. You sure made me homesick the other evening when you sang 'The Old Chisholm Trail.' That took me back, I tell you."

She leaned in, resting powdered elbows on the table. "You've been up the trail?"

"Just once, when I was a boy." Now why had he said that?

"You don't look that old."

"How you do talk, fair lady. But it makes me feel younger."

"I hear you own a fast horse."

"Oh, I've got this ol' cow pony that can run a lick or two."

"How fast a lick?"

"Maybe a furlong, when he's not all boogered up and his feet don't hurt."

"How fast a furlong?"

There it was again, trying to get a line on a man's horse. "I'll put it this way — he looks fast when he wins, slow when he loses."

"You're quite a joker."

"It beats bragging."

"Don't all horsemen brag?"

"Brags don't win horse races."

"He must be fast, if you won't say."

"Or he could be slow and I'm on the cover-up."

Her laughter brushed ridicule. "You'd better get serious if you match Sir James."

"I didn't say how slow. Some folks bet the jockey, not the horse."

"I've heard of that."

"A Comanche Indian rides for us. He's half panther, half west wind."

She fluttered her dark eyes, simulating fear. "You make me want to bet your jockey."

"That's not all," he continued, thinking there was more than one way to penetrate the enemy's camp. "There's a young Irish lad with us who can sing and dance and play the harmonica like you never heard before. This boy has trod the boards at the Palace in Denver."

"Send him around late some afternoon. Maybe he can sing for his supper. We're open seven days a week. I get tired of doing the same old songs, and the cowboys get tired of hearing them."

"That's not the way I got it the other evening. They hollered and stomped for more."

She touched his hand. "That was nice. I didn't like you at first, showin' off your fancy manners." She studied him, seemingly with more than casual interest. "I'm having a little soiree in my suite after the midnight show. We shut off the fun early on week nights. Like to come up?"

"Lady Jane," he said, controlling his surprise, "I'll be there with my hair parted in the middle. And just where might your suite be?"

"Upstairs, down the hall. Last door on your left."

"Let's see," he said, moving his hands up and down. "Hayfoot, strawfoot. I've got it."

She bore that patiently, half-smiling her tolerance.

The musicians, dressed as usual, their faces puffy from daytime sleep, were coming in. She sighed and turned to him. She had been speaking in an assertive voice; it lessened, softening, as she flicked her eyes on the office door. "I hate to see my cowboys lose every time they race. They're the best friends a girl could have." She rose, Dude with her. She said wearily, "Time to go. Time to decide whether to sing 'The Old Chisholm Trail' first or second." She laid that heavy-lidded look on him. "Don't forget now, Mr. McQuinn.

Right after the midnight show."

"Lady Jane, you can count me in your tally!"

Two strange saddle horses were tied at the wagon when Dude reached camp. Slim Overmire and an old man were shaking hands with the outfit.

"Want you to meet Bud Potter," Overmire said, when Dude came in. "I used to ride for him. . . . Dude McQuinn, here, is mighty slick with a rope. Never misses on the third try."

Potter was in the neighborhood of Uncle Billy's age, of stocky build, his legs bowed, his hair long and still dark, his rugged face as brown as an Indian's. There was a worry about his gray eyes; it faded as he shook hands and said, "Glad to know you, Dude. Don't let this mail-order cowboy get under your skin. When he rode for me, he had to have his milk toast every morning an' was so scared of the dark I had to buy a bulldog to sleep with 'im. He made a right good bronc twister after a time, though. Broke both my little Shetlands to lead."

The funning preliminaries over, they all sat around and smoked and exchanged comments about the cattle market, the weather, and range conditions. Dude sensed a purpose behind the visitors' coming.

246

Presently, Overmire said, "I was just tellin' Bud that you all might match Weir. Right away he wanted to meet you. Weir keeps his stud at Bud's place north of town."

Dude got it then: The old couple on the porch.

"That is," Porter said, kind of lamely, "it's mine for a while yet. I came out to wish you luck."

"Nothing's been decided," Dude said. "We can't agree on distance or money. Mr. Potter, just how good a horse is Sir James?"

"Well, he's dusted everything around here. Guess Slim told you. If Sir James has a weakness as a runnin' horse, I don't know what it is." A wry smile. "I don't like the idea of Weir keepin' his horse at my place . . . Weir's reputation being what it is . . . but don't see how I can turn him down after what happened." The worry gripped his face. "You might as well tell 'em the whole story, Slim. I would, but it makes me sick."

"Bud had some tough luck," Overmire said reluctantly. "Got in a crooked poker game at the Royal Flush. Ended up with his ranch mortgaged to Weir."

"I played the fool," Potter admitted, his voice heavy with misery. "Whiskey and cards don't mix. Nobody's fault but my own."

Dude shook his head in sympathy. "Sure hate to hear that, Mr. Potter."

"Can't you get Weir to extend the mortgage?" Uncle Billy spoke up.

"Him? He won't — not one month, not one week, not one day. I've talked to him more than once. He's got me over a barrel and he figures to keep me there."

"Another reason," said Overmire, "why the Commodore is about as popular as a skunk in the bunkhouse. Why us cowboys hope you've got a good horse. We aim to get back at him for what he pulled on Bud."

"No —" Potter objected. "I don't want you boys in this. This is my worry. I won't impose on my friends. No sirree!"

How often Dude had heard just that while growing up. *Never impose on your friends.* But it was all right for your friends to impose on you! He was thinking hard and fast. "Mr. Potter, I don't mean to horn in on your business, but may I ask the amount of the mortgage?"

Potter looked down. "Two thousand dollars."

"That's not chicken feed."

"It is not."

"Guess you've tried to borrow the money elsewhere?"

"I've been west to Wellington and east to

Coffeyville. They don't know me — I don't know them. Land's cheap right now. There's not a bank in Kansas that would lend me fifty dollars."

"And your friends?"

His rugged face creased into a weak grin. "My friends are just old mossy-horns like me, hangin' on best they can. Besides, a man ought to carry his own load."

"Could you sell off some cattle?"

"Just run a few mother cows."

Their talk drifted away to the common-place, dwindled, ran out, and shortly Overmire and Potter got up to leave. "If you match the race," the cowboy said, "get Otto Unger, the stationmaster, for starter. He's fair as they come. Everybody respects him."

"Thanks, Slim," Dude said. "We'll remember that."

"What a shame," Uncle Billy gritted, as the two saddled off for town. "Man losing his little ranch just when he's ready for his place by the f'ar." He took several pulls on his beard. "Reminds me of something I been meanin' to do. Mind if I borrow Blue Grass?"

"Of course not. I'll saddle him for you."

"Since when," the old man retorted, taking instant affront, "did I get so feeble I couldn't saddle my own horse!"

"Didn't mean you couldn't. Just wanted to oblige."

"Well, don't pamper me!"

Dude said no more, deciding that Uncle's arthritis must be acting up something fierce today.

Saddled and mounted, Uncle Billy reined over, a sheepish apology upon him. "Kinda expected you to ask where I'm headed."

Dude cast him a poking laugh. "Would I dare?"

"I'm not forgetting we're pardners. It's to the depot to send a telegram."

"A telegram?"

"To an old friend that used to be a member of the Maryland Jockey Club. Hope he's still around Pimlico. Want him to take a look-see into the records there on his royal highness — this duke fella, this Commodore Weir — on him and his horse."

Dude could not desist from seizing the opening, puckering up his mouth and whistling keenly. "So you belonged to the Maryland Jockey Club? That's quality folks."

Wearily, "Now, Dude, did I say that? What I said was that my friend was, and just because I mentioned Maryland —"

"I know — *don't mean you've been there.*"

"Exactly."

Flashing an enigmatic smile, he swung the

gelding away into that smooth running walk.

After supper, Dude bathed at the creek, shaved carefully, rubbed on bay rum, changed clothes, dusted off his boots, and crimped his hat.

Uncle Billy raised an eyebrow. "What are you fixin' to do?"

"Lady Jane Penrose invited me to a little get-together after the last show. A soiree, she called it, in her suite."

"Lady Jane? You mean Talcum Annie."

"Slim Overmire could be wrong. She strikes me as quite a lady."

"A lady? After all I've schooled you and you fall for that?"

"She might let something drop about Weir. Same as you're trying to dig up at the other end. And we always need a better line on the other man's horse."

"Sir James is a distance horse. Everybody knows that."

Coyote Walking interrupted mildly. "There is a saying, Grandfather, 'What is past I know, but what is to come I know not.' "

Dude snapped his fingers. "That's it, Coyote. I was just about to say that, but not in those words."

"Just remember," Uncle Billy grunted, "we clock the Judge first thing in the morning."

By the time Dude was ready to leave, Uncle Billy had retired to his blankets, Coyote was reading by lanternlight, and Danny was softly playing the harmonica, making it moan, the notes rising and falling.

Dude remembered then. "I bragged on your act to Lady Jane. She said if you're interested, to come by the saloon late some afternoon."

"Did you tell her I've trod the boards at the Palace?"

"That I did."

"I'll see her tomorrow."

"And keep your ears open."

"That I will."

To kill time, Dude went first to the Red Eye Saloon, which was nearly empty, and struck up a conversation with the bartender. The long-winded exchange proved unproductive from the start. Not only was the man not interested in running horses, he longed for the Irish section of Kansas City, his hometown, and was catching the next train back. At the Bull's Head, Dude played two drawn-out games of dominoes with a lonely cowboy, lost, bought the puncher a drink each time and shot the breeze.

At eleven thirty o'clock he walked across to the Royal Flush. Here a handful of cowboys and girls danced hippity-hop to the energetic strains of "Dinah Had a Wooden Leg," while the idle gamblers played solitaire. Weir wasn't around. Over all this Sweetwater Smith stood watch. When the number ended, the dancers moved to the bar for drinks and, chatting noisily, drifted back to the tables.

A lull and the dapper master of ceremonies slipped onstage to present Lady Jane, who came out swaying. She sang "The Dying Cowboy," and, sure enough, "The Old Chisholm Trail," and bowed off to a smattering of applause. On that signal the musicians put away their instruments, the cowboys bade amorous farewells to their partners, and one by one the girls trailed upstairs, followed by the bass fiddler.

Awhile longer, and Dude climbed the stairs. Turning down the hall, he could hear giggles and the klink of glassware. The last door on the left was open. He removed his hat and took a step inside.

"About time you showed up," Lady Jane scolded him, possessing his arm, simultaneously kindling a tide of powder and perfume. Dude smothered a desire to sneeze. Loudly she announced, "This here is Dude

McQuinn, the new horseman in town. He thinks his little ol' cow pony can beat Sir James." Everybody grinned. "This is Maude and this is Gracie," Lady Jane continued, with a careless wave, and never mind their last names, Dude thought. "This gent is Philo, our stage manager . . . and that over there is Pinky, our mad bass fiddler," and never mind last handles, either.

Both girls looked sixteen, but in other ways a lot older: Maude — pale and intense, straw-colored hair, powdered up like a country girl who had just tipped over the flour bin. Gracie — slender and olive-skinned, a thin little face and lonely hazel eyes, both girls made up to ape the older woman.

"Hello," Philo said tonelessly. He shook hands and sat down, a lithe, pinch-featured man whose movements were feline. He seemed poured into his dark suit, and his plastered-down black hair, cut short, gleamed like a dipping vat at high noon.

Pinky waved languidly and half rose to give Dude a limp handshake, and sank back, a gangling young man, all bones and sharp edges, his long blond hair a tangled mass framing a bored face.

"My, never saw such purty girls!" Dude said, picking a footstool on which to sit.

Lady Jane's "suite," he saw, was merely a bedroom and curtained closet. A small table served as the bar.

"What did I tell you," Lady Jane crowed, her worn voice self-congratulatory. "He's got manners."

"I kinda like that," Gracie said, her eyes growing warm.

"Me, too," Maude seconded.

Almost immediately Dude found a glass in his hand and Lady Jane warmly sharing the narrow footstool with him. He was about to sneeze again.

"So you have a racehorse?" Philo opened the conversation.

"We match him now and then," Dude said vaguely.

"What's his best distance?"

"Shorter he goes, faster he runs."

Philo's amused grin showed between gapped teeth. "I thought it was the other way around — farther they go, faster they run."

"Texas Jack does everything opposite. You rein right, he goes left. You rein left, he goes right. . . . Oh, sure, he can scoot the quarter mile some, and sometimes he can manage a shade farther, if he don't fall down. Of course, he's gettin' on in years and his teeth are just about wore out. Why I have

to grind his feed. No roastin' ears for him."
Dude was commencing to have a feeling
about this Philo: his lightweight size, the
way he talked, his strong-looking hands, his
somewhat weathered face, his direct eyes.

Philo threw down his drink and stared at
his glass. "Have you sounded out Mr.
Weir?" Also, his voice; it sounded clipped,
like the Commodore's.

"Talked. That's all."

Philo's voice trailed down to a confidential level. "I'll let you in on something . . .
he'll never match you at the quarter mile."

"Son of a gun, I appreciate that, Philo.
Looks like I been on the wrong slant to get
him to go short when he wants to go long.
He sure sticks to his advantage."

"About what does your horse cover the
quarter mile in, Mr. McQuinn?"

This outfit sure had a bad case of the *mis-
ters,* and a worse case of the queries! Dude
drawled, "Depends which way the wind's
blowin', with him or against him."

He lost Philo's return expression as Lady
Jane rose to fill his glass again. As she did,
Gracie pre-empted her place on the footstool. She leaned down and massaged her
slippered foot. "My dogs are killin' me.
You'd think cowboys would know feet are
made for dancin', not stompin'."

He looked down at her, thinking that she was a likable kid, and lonely. At her age she ought to be back on the farm practicing her biscuits, suitors so thick her mama couldn't throw out a pan of dishwater without soaking one of the boys. He said, "That's all a cowboy knows, stomp, whoop, and holler."

She giggled. "An' pinch an' hug. I noticed you didn't dance tonight. How come?"

"Got there late. Wasn't warmed up."

Lady Jane sang out, "He claims he's just an ol' country boy, but no ol' country boy has manners that fancy." Her voice sharpened. "Now, Gracie, you get back over there where you belong and homestead with Pinky before he falls asleep."

Gracie flipped up and flounced down beside the lackadaisical Pinky. Lady Jane promptly and possessively plopped beside Dude. For Gracie's benefit, to break the strained silence, Dude said genially, "Lady Jane, I gave your message to Danny Featherstone. He'll see you tomorrow."

"Might work him in, if he's what you say."

"Good-lookin' boy, too," Dude said, "with extra nice manners," and winked at Gracie.

Not long after that Dude sensed there was a bug under the chip, as a suspicious cowboy might say, when all at once, as if a prearranged signal had been passed, the girls and the men got up to leave. As Gracie went out last, she left the door ajar and Lady Jane yelled, "Shut the door — Arkansas!" Gracie came back and closed it, not without glancing at Dude.

"These kids!" Lady Jane groused. "After all you've done for 'em. No bringin' up, no appreciation." Her voice had thickened. She handed Dude another drink, draping herself against him, and an uncomfortable feeling came over him, heightened as once again he got the stifling closeness of her powder and perfume.

"Philo," he said, now on the edge of the footstool, "reminds me of a jockey somehow."

"He should — he rides for the Commodore. Been on the big tracks back East."

"Makin's for a hard boot are back there. Why would he leave it for this?"

"You'll have to ask Philo."

"If you won't answer me that, maybe you'll tell me where the Commodore got his title?"

She jiggled her head in that tantalizing way she displayed on the stage. "Maybe his mother gave it to him."

"Or maybe it's self-bestowed?"

"For an ol' country boy you sure are nosy, my fancy-mannered friend."

"Just curious. The Commodore is a mighty interesting fellow."

"Well, Philo was steering you right when he told you how you'd have to match the Commodore."

"Why should I believe the jock who'd be riding against me?"

"You must be suspicious by nature?"

"I got that way gettin' outslicked on race tracks."

Dude's glass was empty. She filled it and nuzzled even closer against him.

"Much obliged, Annie," he said, the slip of the tongue gone before he realized it.

"Annie?" She jerked upright, her fleshy face darkening.

He was quick. "You remind me of a girl named Annie I used to know back home. Boy, was she purty!" That last drink had done it. He'd better watch himself.

Her face smoothed at the flattery. She said, "Just a little ol' country girl, I reckon?" imitating his drawl.

"You bet she was. Annie — her name was Annie Blossom — was about the purtiest girl around there. They grow some humdingers down along the Salt Fork, I tell you."

She seemed to cotton to that. Still mimicking him; "Out where the hoot owls holler?"

"And a cowboy smells just like his horse."

That touched off her laughter. "You're more fun than a barrel of monkeys. You know how to treat a woman . . . how to talk to her, how to make her laugh. You don't paw her. Tell me more about your little ol' country-boy self." By now she had that drawl down slick, and he wished he hadn't come here.

She was, he suspected, leading up to something. He made a show of modesty and began. "Oh, I've cowboyed around mostly. Learned three things early — never argue with the cook, a skunk, or a mule. Did some horse tradin' along the way . . . got skinned mostly till I learned how to tell a horse's age by his teeth and not how he looks when curried and brushed. . . . Even planted some cotton once, but it all washed out. That cured me of farmin'. . . . Then my life changed for better or worse. Won Texas Jack in a poor-man's poker game. Raced him. Won some, lost some. Here I am, come full circle. On my way back to Texas."

"You left out when you went up the trail as a boy."

"So I did. Don't like to brag. I was only a

horse wrangler." He patted her hand. "Now why don't you tell me all about Drury Lane?"

As unabashed as he, she began. "I was just a girl and they said my voice had an operatic quality, rich and clear. A true soprano, everybody said. Then this man — this older man, this rich American — came into my life. I was only seventeen. He promised me a career on the New York stage." She looked down at her empty glass. "He even promised me marriage, if . . . well, when we got to New York, he left me stranded."

"The dirty devil! Go on."

"I didn't let that get me down. A girl has to start somewhere. I started singing and dancing in the variety halls — New York, Buffalo, Chicago, Philadelphia, and the nation's capital. . . . A senator from Mississippi took a special liking to me, only I couldn't stand those long, black cigars. . . . One day, years later, I happened to go out to Pimlico. There I chanced to meet the Commodore. He was coming out West to go into business. He was looking for someone to . . . ah — run the entertainment end of his enterprises. So here I am." Something in his expression must have given him away, because she asked suddenly, "Don't you believe me?"

"Every word, Lady Jane."

"Just call me Jane."

"And me Dude."

"If there is one truth I've learned since leaving Drury Lane," she said, her tone so earnest it was hard not to believe her, "it is the value of lasting friendships. A girl never had stauncher friends than these cowboys, rough and uncouth may they be. They have hearts of gold, and lo! be the fate of him who insults one of us."

"You can say that again."

"Which is why it hurts me so when I see them lose every time they bring in a horse to run at the Commodore. They bet everything, even their boots and spurs."

"That's a cowboy for you, loyal down to his last pair of socks."

She started to take his glass, but he restrained her hand gently. His head was spinning. "This ol' country boy will have to pass this round. He can't keep up with you Drury Lane girls." As he spoke, it dawned on him that although he had seen her filling his glass, he had not seen her filling hers.

"You're a good sport, Dude, like all the cowboys." She glanced at the door, as if to be certain it was closed, and in a low-pitched voice said, "I'm going to tell you something, and if you breathe one little word of it Lady Jane will have to hightail it for the tules." Again she glanced apprehensively toward the door.

"For a Drury Lane girl, you do speak the lingo. What is it?"

"Can your horse go four furlongs?"

"Maybe, with a downhill pull."

"Be serious now. Can he?"

"I'll put it this way: It's not his best distance."

"Well . . ." she whispered, leaning in, "neither is it Sir James'. He's really a six-furlong horse."

"You mean?"

"Match the Commodore at four furlongs if you can, and if your horse is fast. Sir James won't hit his stride till he's gone five. He sorta pokes along till then."

"Why would the Commodore match me at four if that's not the distance his horse likes?"

She touched a silencing forefinger to her overpainted lips and whispered, "He might . . . if he thinks your horse is strictly a short goer . . . and if the cowboys bet heavy on your horse, which they will. They don't like the Commodore."

"I gathered as much." He rubbed his forehead. "You cause me to ponder, fair lady."

"You see," she reasoned, "he's always

matched the cowboys at five or six. Never at the half mile."

So Slim Overmire had said. "But where," he came back, "did they get the notion they could beat him long?"

"There's no fool like a fool cowboy." Before he could stop her she took his glass and had it and her own filled and was swaying back and handing him his. She downed hers. Of a sudden she broke into "The Old Chisholm Trail," singing it heartily, off key, verse after verse, in a voice that had become surprisingly slurred only these past few moments.

She was still singing when he heard a loud knock at the door. She shushed at once. The knock sounded again, then a series of peremptory knocks. With evident anger, she put down her glass and went to the door and opened it.

Sweetwater Smith bulked there. He muttered, "Quiet down — you're keeping the Commodore awake," at the same time nailing Dude his raw dislike.

Dude stood, his feeling mutual.

"Just havin' us a little ol' country fun," she answered Smith, her slurred voice indignant.

He looked around. "Where's Gracie?"

"She left with Pinky."

"Well, keep it quiet."

"Now you jus' go back and tend to your knittin' and I'll tend to mine." She slammed the door in his face and came to stand in the center of the room, her face working, wrinkling the mask of powder and paint. "Jus' cause he drives the Commodore aroun', you'd think he was the Duke of Newmarket."

"It's late," Dude said, "I'd better saddle along."

"Aw, stay awhile." Her tone, however, did not quite fit her invitation, which he discovered he did not mind; besides, an itinerant horseman always knew when it was time to move camp.

He found his hat, hurrying a little.

She touched her lips again, whispered, "Four furlongs, if you can, for all my cowboy friends," and plopped him a smeary, powder-smelling kiss on the mouth.

He went out.

Somehow it was wrong back there, all wrong, but he didn't know why.

Well, hippity-hop.

Chapter 13

They were clocking the Judge this morning.

So Uncle Billy had reminded him an instant ago, his merciless voice hissing, "Rise and shine, you night owl!"

Dude groaned and shut his eyes against thunderous throbbing as he threw back the blanket and sat up, immobile for a suspended moment. Wincing, he pulled on shirt, pants, boots and crawled out from under the wagon. He had a head big enough for a horse and a taste as if he'd had supper with a coyote.

Finally saddled, he rode through the pallid darkness with Uncle Billy and Coyote Walking. They halted at the state line as usual, listening, watching for a while, seeing the outscatter of Wagon Mound, silent and orderless, an overlapping of high and low shadows, and rode on.

At the marking rocks on the broad trail they stopped. Rose-pink light pierced the eastern sky, peeling back the cloak of murk. The breeze purring over the bluestem grass felt moist on Dude's face.

"We want a close clocking," the old man said gruffly, and trotted on to the finish line. There he turned, waiting.

As Coyote brought the horse even with him, Dude dropped his hand and shouted and the Judge shot away, horse and jockey as one, running straight.

"Forty-seven seconds," Uncle Billy said, coming back, neither pleased nor displeased. "Not bad for the half mile, on a rough track and upslope part of the distance. Win you some, lose you some. I want this horse faster than that."

Returning, they made a cautious swing to the west so as to place the camp between them and the town as they rode in. Danny had breakfast going. Afterward, they galloped Texas Jack back and forth across the creek bottom.

The day dragged on, unchanged. Wagon Mound appeared deserted. Only the continuous bawling from the cattle pens and the chuffing of a train broke the torpidity of the hot afternoon. Danny, dressed in his Denver best — yellow plaid suit, red suspenders, flowing cravat, blond hair slicked down — left for his audition at the Royal Flush.

When four o'clock passed and Weir had not come, Uncle Billy concluded, "Maybe this is one race we won't match, Dude, pardner."

"Last Weir said was he might come down to five furlongs," Dude said. "I said I might go up to the quarter mile. We left it there."

"Gamblers don't really gamble. They play a sure thing."

"I'm about ready to drift on down into Indian Territory."

Coyote Walking looked up from his copy of *Don Quixote*. He said, "Cervantes wrote, 'One swallow never makes a summer,' and likewise, long time ago, there was gambler white man who came to town near pony soldiers' house at Medicine Bluff called Fort Sill." He laid down the book and stood, folded his arms, his tobacco-brown eyes mirroring a far-away look — ceremonious signs, Dude recognized, that presaged a speech. Dude said no word, having learned early that you never hurried a Comanche.

Now: "This gambler white man had brown racehorse. My father, the chief, had spotted racehorse, which white men call pinto. In those days Comanches did not train racehorses like white man. After race was agreed, we tied racehorse to stake or tree. If racehorse was fat, we starved him down, giving him only water. If racehorse was drawn down lean, we led him to grass and in evening ran him over the course. At night we staked this horse, leaving him alone near camp."

He let sink in what he had spoken. Then: "Now my father, the chief, did this old-time thing, leaving spotted racehorse staked alone near camp, knowing gambler white man would see, which gambler white man did, concluding, 'Ah, these heathen Indians watch their racehorse do not. And Indians always sleep with eyes shut, especially just before daylight? Yes.' So gambler white man led spotted racehorse away. Out on prairie he ran spotted racehorse against brown racehorse. To his great joy, his brown horse easily outran spotted horse. When he led spotted horse back and staked him, Comanche camp still quiet, very quiet, Comanches still sleeping."

He gazed up at the sky, beginning to smile. Then: "What gambler white man did not know was that my father, the chief, had another spotted racehorse. A much-alike full brother to the first spotted racehorse — and much faster — which he was training other side of mountains. So fast this horse that when my father, the chief, was standing by track and horse ran by, he said there was sound as of great wind rushing over prairie. No other horse of Comanches made this sound, said my father, the chief." He left off, as if his listeners must relish that further. "Day of race, friends of gambler white man come, even white men from Texas, which as you know we Comanches once owned and where to this day Comanche braves their ghosts crying they are in our Texas there, hearing them I am still."

"You're gettin' off the subject," Dude guyed him.

"Race is distance race. Horses will run two miles to post, turn and come back. Horses ready. Gambler white man's brown horse looks smooth. Mean-looking white man rides him. Every hair has been rubbed and brushed into place. He arches his neck. But he is very nervous. Poor spotted horse of my father the chief hangs his head. His hair is rough. He stands hipshot."

He looked away again.

"But just as race is about to start spotted horse is transformed. His head comes up. He stamps his feet, like this. His eyes burn like mesquite coals, like this. His muscles quiver. Little Indian boy rides him bareback, with hair rope for bridle."

Suddenly, Coyote clapped his hands. "They're off! Spotted horse jumps out, takes lead. Horses grow smaller and smaller." Pantomiming, he handshaded his eyes. "Little Indian boy whoops. Spotted horse runs faster. Suddenly, there is much daylight between horses. When little Indian boy comes to post, he turns spotted horse slowly and looks back, waiting for brown horse to catch up. Again little Indian boy whoops and spotted horse takes off. They are waiting beside finish line when brown horse comes in.

"Gambler white man stomps on nice new hat. How can spotted horse he led out on prairie which his brown horse beat with ease, today run off and leave brown horse? Afterward, my father, the chief, tells gambler white man; 'You just did not know how to make Comanche horse run that night.' "

Having spoken, Coyote Walking sat down.

"One thing about Coyote's stories," Dude commented, his face wry, "the Indian always wins and the white men are always mean."

"Not all white men," Coyote protested. "Just mean white men."

"And *little Indian boy whoops*. That sounds familiar somehow. Could it be that . . . ?"

A creeping smile of admission. "Yes,

white father — little Indian boy whoops was I."

Uncle Billy, sitting in a camp chair, was obviously not thinking of the humor of the recitation. He snapped to his feet. "It might work for us."

"It's a long shot."

"We have to keep this in mind — Weir, like all so-called gamblers, is looking for the sure thing."

"Gambler white man did not take spotted horse first night," Coyote reminded.

Dude shook his head. "If I know the Commodore, he won't take the bait. He's too slick."

"Yet," the old man deliberated, "he knows nothing about our horse. He can't tell by the way we gallop Texas Jack."

"If he fails to bite in a few days, we can light a shuck for Indian Territory."

An hour before dusk, Coyote Walking led Texas Jack well beyond the wagon on the grassy creek bottom and placed him on picket, within eyesight of the Royal Flush.

Danny dashed in, full of excitement, booked for Saturday evening, when the cowboy trade reached its peak at the Royal Flush.

The outfit cooked supper, sat around, decided on a system of watches, with Uncle

Billy taking the first this time, Dude the last.

Nothing happened.

"It's a little early in the game," Uncle Billy said at breakfast.

"Remember, Grandfather," Coyote said, "long time ago gambler white man did not take spotted racehorse first night."

"At least we've got a full moon," Dude stuck in doubtfully.

"Tell you what," Uncle Billy said, warming to the stratagem, "let's change the wrinkle to attract more attention. Let's gallop Texas Jack up to the edge of town and back in the morning, about the time the Royal Flush is opening, then again in the evening before we cool him down and stake him out. That'll catch their eye. Meanwhile, we'll work the Judge every other morning. He's legging up pretty good."

They did.

Once again nothing happened during the night.

After supper next evening while they sat around camp, a hoot owl *hoomed* from the creek timber. Immediately Coyote Walking jumped up and waved his arms. "Good sign! Owl Person has spoken! Gambler white man will come tonight for Texas Jack."

"I've been hearing hoot owl music every

night," Dude scoffed. "They sing bass for the coyotes."

"Not Owl Person."

"How can you tell?"

"Only Comanches know," Coyote replied, looking mysterious.

It was past three o'clock when Danny woke Dude and he slipped out where he could watch Texas Jack. Insects droned in the grass. Dude ducked when a nighthawk swooped low over the grassy bottom, crying shrill *peenks* as it chased bugs. A coyote raised its high voice from a moon-bathed ridge. Far off, another answered, both accompanied by the hoot owl chorus. Dude yawned. Now how could Coyote distinguish any Owl Person in that gibberish?

He crouched down, seeing Texas Jack's indistinct grazing shape, feeling the humid breath of the creek enveloping him, thinking this was a waste of time, when a man needed to be in his blankets. Well, they would wait out today, and possibly another day, before they broke camp.

Off and on, he dozed.

At some vague time he detected faint movements, and suddenly more distinct sounds registered fully upon his dull senses: the unbroken scuffing of feet through the thick grass. He flattened down.

One figure materialized through the gloom. Now two. One large man, one small man. They were almost to the horse. Texas Jack snorted. The pair froze. Was the gelding going to make such a racket he would scare them away?

Texas Jack resumed grazing.

The two reached the horse. Within moments they were leading the gelding toward town. Dude rose and followed a way. A short while and he heard hoofbeats leaving the vicinity of the Royal Flush.

He retraced his steps and settled down to wait.

In less than an hour, he heard horses shuffling quietly into town from the east. The hoofbeats faded out. Soon the sound of a single horse walking reached him. He could make out bobbing movements through the moonglow: two men leading the horse. They left the road and came across the grass, walking fast. They picketed Texas Jack as before and vanished.

Daylight wasn't many minutes away.

To make certain of this night, Dude went over and felt of the gelding's back. It was wet with sweat, so they had run him in a speed trial.

Yawning, he made for camp. As he walked to the wagon, Coyote Walking sat up. "Owl

Person was right," Dude whispered. "They came."

The morning ran its course without change, while Dude curbed his impatience. What was delaying Weir? He could not possibly have discovered that Texas Jack was faster than Sir James. A new and disturbing line of thought occurred. Or was the gelding so slow that Weir suspected something?

Near midafternoon the roofed carriage was observed drawing up to the Royal Flush and leaving, the Commodore aboard, Sweetwater Smith on the box, the matched grays stepping lively. When Weir descended, he seemed more civil than that first day.

"I have pondered at length on the race," he said, courteously addressing both Dude and Uncle Billy, "and have decided to propose we go five furlongs."

"That is mighty considerate of you, Commodore," Dude fenced, his tone as courteous as a hat-tipping Texas sheriff on election day. "We have pondered as well, knowing in advance that you are a true horseman, and have decided to go up to the full quarter mile."

Weir knotted his eyebrows. "We are still

far apart. Would you be amenable to four furlongs?"

"Might to three."

"A bully proposition, Mr. McQuinn, but I cannot come down to that distance."

Dude said, "As the bard Cervantes once penned, 'One swaller won't last all summer,'" and saw Coyote flinch. "By the same token, one proposition don't scratch a horse race."

"I agree wholeheartedly, Mr. McQuinn," Weir replied, his smile leaking. "Possibly you have a counter proposal?"

"Tell you what, Commodore. You say you will go four furlongs, which is fair. You are a man to ride the river with. We will run you four furlongs for three-to-one odds."

Weir seemed to stagger as from a blow to the jaw. "You are bold, Mr. McQuinn."

"I beg to differ. Foolhardy is the word — I'm foolhardy to match my ol' cow pony at any distance against a Thoroughbred of Sir James' class. That's why I have to have odds."

"As you are aware, I never give odds."

"There's always a first time when it's fair, Commodore."

"I cannot, I will not, hazard three-to-one odds," Weir clipped, "even though my horse is the favorite."

As the saloonman's finely hewn brow clouded and his lean face stiffened, Dude thought, He's already made up his mind or he wouldn't be here. But I don't want to scare him off. He said, "Would you listen to some two-to-one talk at four furlongs, Commodore?" making a play on the title.

Suddenly Weir smiled and said, "As a sportsman, I would consider that. How much do you want to wager?"

"Say . . . ah . . . a hundred dollars."

"*One hundred dollars!*" Weir actually sneered. "I refuse to run my horse for that insignificant wager."

"Two hundred?"

"Mr. McQuinn, we are discussing a bona fide race between sporting gentlemen. Not some mere frolic between two drifting cowboys to see who buys the drinks."

"Reckon I could scrape up three, maybe four, hundred, but I sure don't aim to put up my saddle, which my Grandpa gave me."

Weir's unyielding expression, more angry than not, did not alter. Neither did he speak.

"Well," Dude jockeyed, "how much would you run your horse for?"

"One thousand dollars."

Dude fell to whistling "Dixie" and scratching behind his ear. "Commodore," he said, "you kind of put me between a rock and the hard place. But guess I've made my brag." He turned in appeal. "Uncle, could you back me a little?"

Uncle Billy coughed, and instead of his usual gruffness, his voice came through that of an oldster, strengthless and cautious. "Bein' as you're my only sister's only boy, how can I say no? Just hope you don't bite off more'n you can chew. Maybe the boys will chip in, too?"

When Coyote and Danny nodded, Dude swallowed and said, "A thousand it is, Commodore. At four furlongs."

"Bully, Mr. McQuinn. Bully!"

"And you put up two thousand?"

"Agreed."

"Payable right after the race?"

"Correct." Weir held out his hand. They shook. He asked, "When would you like to run?"

"You name the day, Commodore."

"I like to run on Saturday as a drawing card to attract more people into town for trade. But tomorrow is Saturday and that is too soon for either of us, I judge, and too early for news of the race to reach the forks of the creek, as they say hereabouts. Would a week from Saturday at three o'clock be agreeable?"

"It is."

"Rain or shine?"

Dude did not need Uncle Billy's warning eye to say, "I'll have to back off on a rainy-day go, Commodore. Happens my ol' cow pony is all turtle when it comes to mud."

Weir, laughing, "Agreed. Rain is hardly a problem this time of year, anyway. You have a starter in mind?"

"I hear tell this Otto Unger is a fair man."

"He is. Agreed."

A bush-track caution rang in Dude's mind. When a horseman was so agreeable, without even one counter, look out. And before Dude could speak again, Weir was saying, "It's customary here for each side to choose one judge and to draw for the third, each side putting in a name. Is that agreeable?"

"Sounds fair and square. Uncle Billy will be my judge."

"Sweetwater Smith will be mine. We can meet at the Royal Flush tomorrow morning to decide the third person, then go over the track and discuss other conditions."

"All right, Commodore."

"Until tomorrow morning then, Mr. McQuinn. Say around ten o'clock?"

"Fine."

Sweetwater Smith was waiting, holding the emblazoned door open. Weir ascended, Smith carefully closed the door and climbed to the box, unwrapped reins from whip socket and sent the high-stepping grays away, the wheels of the carriage spinning dust.

"I would say," Dude remarked, pleased with himself, "that we have just matched ourselves a little ol' horse race."

Coyote and Danny nodded, but the old man was silent, absorbed in thought. As if he had not heard, he brooded, "Still no word from my telegram."

"So what? The Commodore don't know the Judge can burn the breeze at the half mile."

"Neither do we know what Sir James can do at that distance."

"Lady Jane told me he tends to loaf the first four furlongs."

The old man cocked a doubting eyebrow. "Though he's never been matched that short around here? Mark my words, this whole shebang will come full circle when we get that telegram — if we get it." He stalked over to the medicine chest and started moving bottles and jars and cans, a sure sign that his mind was elsewhere. A minute or more of that and he came back. "Let's pay Unger a call, Dude. I want him to understand how we start our horse, and I want to check on that telegram."

They found Otto Unger at the depot counter, talking to a dusty cowman upset over the shortage of cattle cars. After the placated rancher left, Unger remarked to his callers, "Putting together a cattle train for tomorrow afternoon. Sometimes you have to be more peacemaker than stationmaster." He was a strapping, open-faced man of about fifty. A mane of wolf-gray hair swept back from his great dome of a forehead. He had about him the air of an efficient, even-tempered individual, capable of handling the pressures of schedules and complaints. His rumbling, cheerful voice retained a trace of old-country accent.

"This is my pardner, Dude McQuinn," Uncle Billy told him. "We've matched a race with Commodore Weir a week from tomorrow. Both sides have agreed we want you to start it."

Unger shook hands and grinned. "Didn't think I'd refuse, did you? That's my one recreation. Some nights I have to sleep here. What time that Saturday?"

"Three o'clock, if that fits for you?"

"It will. My cattle train won't pull out for Kansas City till four o'clock."

"We appreciate that. Also want to tell you in advance how our horse Texas Jack starts. Different from most. He turns just a little and swings into it. Takes that short step to get off on. It's a peculiarity he has."

Unger thrust out his lower lip, nodding. "I'll remember. Shouldn't be any problem. All I look for at the break is to make certain they're evenly lapped. What is your horse?"

"A dark bay gelding. He behaves well."

"That will help get 'em off. Sir James can be fractious."

"We're goin' half a mile," Dude said. "Just hope that's not too long for our ol' pony."

The telegraph started chattering and Unger hurried over to the sounder.

Uncle Billy gave a start. "Maybe that's our telegram."

Unger was writing on a pad. When the message ended, he continued to write for another moment, then put down his pencil and spiked the message.

"Was hoping that was the answer to my telegram to Baltimore," Uncle Billy said.

"Sorry, Dr. Lockhart."

At ten o'clock the following morning, Weir was waiting for Dude like an old friend meeting the train, hand outstretched. After a startling slap on the back, Dude was escorted to a table where Weir called for his private stock. A liberal drink and the saloonman asked genially, "How shall we decide the third judge, Mr. McQuinn? Draw or flip?"

"Let's flip," Dude said, seeing less chance for trickery, and having Bud Potter in mind. "And call me Dude."

"All right, Dude. You toss the coin and I'll call."

Taking a silver dollar, Dude joggled it in both hands, covered it on his thumbnail and flipped. As the coin started downward, Weir called, "Heads," and Dude slapped it on the back of his left hand and looked. "Heads, you win, Commodore."

"Lady Jane will be the third judge," Weir said.

"Lady Jane?"

"A woman can pick the winner as well as a man."

True, Dude thought, shrugging, yet a little unusual.

"Shall we go over the track now."

They rode toward the cattle-bawling stockyards, Weir chatting as they went. A flag would mark each furlong, he said, which was customary, and townsmen would be posted to keep the crowd out of the way, and the horses would finish in front of the Royal Flush.

The road, Dude saw, was broad and straight, dusty and hard, cupped from the passage of wagons, yet not excessively, and free of rocks. In all, rougher than some tracks on which the Judge had run, and better than others. Coming to where the starting line would be, Dude saw no advantage in either lane, and when Weir suggested they flip for sides, Dude said it mattered not, whereupon Weir said let the jockeys decide.

"Now," Weir went on in that uncharacteristic obliging tone, "do you prefer the lap-and-tap start or chutes?"

"I won't start my horse out of a chute. Too many throw a fit and hurt themselves. That's what happened to ol' Steel Dust, down in Texas years ago, when he was matched against Shiloh. He reared up, broke a board, ran a piece into his shoulder. Had to forfeit. It's far safer to have them walk up to the line and the starter to tap them off by dropping his hand or hat when they're lapped."

"Very well, we shall lap-and-tap." Weir's voice turned clipped, patronizing. "Ah, yes, the Steel Dust horse. I *have* heard of him. Also that he was not cleanly bred."

Now, fumed Dude, he's back to bein' his true, natural, stuck-up self. "Steel Dust was a big-jawed quarter horse that could run like hell and gone," Dude stated. "His sire,

Harry Bluff, was out of a Thoroughbred mare, though that didn't slow him down any."

"I see," said Weir, his uppity air unchanged, "that you are quick to defend horses native to the Lone Star State."

"I'll put it this way, Commodore: A fast horse is a fast horse, regardless of what side of the tracks he's from."

Weir spread his lips in that thin-line way of his that got under Dude's skin. "Can you think of any other condition we need to consider, Mr. McQuinn."

So they were back on that *mister* formality. Dude shook his head.

"Bully, Mr. McQuinn!"

They parted back at the Royal Flush.

Dude had no more than reined away when realization jarred him — the weights! He had plumb forgotten, so accustomed was he to quick matches on bush tracks, the set-to with Sugar Kyle excepted. Sir James was the heavy favorite; by rights, he ought to carry top weight. Dude should have jockeyed for that advantage. But would Weir have agreed? Not a chance.

When he told the outfit about his omission, the old man merely smiled. "Weir wouldn't handicap his own horse when he didn't have to. Only reason Sugar Kyle agreed to even weights was to lead us on to the advantage he thought he had." His eyes narrowed. His saintly features switched ever so slightly, giving way to the caginess that served as an omen of surprise for somebody. "I'll guarantee you this duke fella's horse will pack more weight than the Judge."

"How?"

"I'm thinking," Uncle Billy said, and slanted an eye at Coyote Walking.

Chapter 14

Nothing, Dude McQuinn told himself, drew people like a horse race or the promise of one. Even the gentle womenfolk, who abhorred fisticuffs and the companion racing evils of gambling and whiskey-drinking and cursing, adored fast horses.

A four-seater open carriage of bonneted Wagon Mound ladies was slowly drawing past the camp, all eyes on the meticulously groomed Texas Jack, handsome bay coat glistening, picketed for all the world to see, and where he would be picketed tonight. *Consistency.* That was important at this stage of the game. If the gelding was picketed there before the race was matched, there he must stand after the race was matched. Also keeping up the visible workouts. *Consistency.*

Now the ladies were waving wee handkerchiefs.

Smiling broadly, Dude took off his white

hat, holding it high — his rodeo arena pose — until the ladies took notice, and when they did, sweeping it off with a grand flourish and bowing from the waist.

They tittered and drove on.

He glanced at the sun, seeing the time had come to pony Texas Jack to the edge of town and back for his matinee performance. While he saddled Blue Grass, Coyote Walking cinched the light racing saddle on Texas Jack. They mounted. Out on the road, Dude positioned Blue Grass on the gelding's left, took the lead rope, and they trotted off.

A pony horse must exhibit steadfastness at all times, indifferent to the capers of the high-spirited racer he is escorting. All this the reliable Blue Grass was. Seeing the usual collection of loafers gathered in the elm shade at the edge of town, and that Texas Jack was acting too much like a pony horse instead of a frolicsome speed merchant pent-up to run, Dude said low, "Goose him a little, Coyote. Make him prance like a racehorse."

They were within yards of the watchers when Coyote jabbed Texas Jack's flank with his left moccasined heel, hidden from view of the audience.

Suddenly everything went wrong. Texas

Jack spooked right and bogged his head, humping his back to pitch. Coyote dug for leather, flapping about on the saddle. Dude yanked on the lead rope to bring the gelding's head up. He could not. They were heading straight for the elm trees. Beneath him Dude sensed even Blue Grass' desire to pitch. The onlookers scattered like a covey of quail. By then Dude had settled the saddler. At the edge of the road he brought Texas Jack under control and Coyote located his seat.

Well, this might as well be played to the limit. So deciding, Dude laid on the spurs and took the horses into a dust-raising, eye-catching circle, as if Texas Jack might yet break away, and came around tightly.

The loafers were warily reassembling, their cautious attention fixed on this spirited runner. Coming by them again, holding the wall-eyed Texas Jack on short lead, his head high, Dude called, "I believe he's ready!" and the onlookers nodded to that for certain.

Dude ponied on to camp. There, for the further gratification of the idlers, Coyote galloped Texas Jack across the grassy bottom and back.

This happened on Wednesday.

Come daylight Thursday, Judge Blair

breezed one half mile on the cattle trail, his last workout before Saturday's showdown.

By Friday morning the town was beginning to bulge. Drummers staying over for the big race. Full-blood Osages and mixed-blood families from the reservation. Cowboys drifting in. The wagonyard was jammed. Din from the three saloons could be heard in the camp. Danny Featherstone, now appearing twice nightly at the Royal Flush, dancing and singing as the "Irish Troubadour," brought word that the House of Lords was "booked to the rafters" and the flat between town and the stockyards "looked like a tent city." And the enterprising proprietor of Big Jim's Pool Hall & Domino Parlor was selling sleeping reservations on the billiard tables at one dollar a head, provided you removed your spurs.

"Miss Gracie is kind of stuck on you," Danny said, grinning at Dude. "She keeps asking me why you don't come back."

"Tell 'er I'm bashful, but I'll buy her a great big drink tonight."

Visitors trailed out to the camp to view Texas Jack, staked on the grass, Slim Overmire among them. "How's our runnin' hoss shapin' up?" he asked Dude.

"Why, if he ran any faster he'd be illegal."

"Glad to hear that. Bud Potter don't know

it, but a big bunch of us boys has formed a pool and bet the whole wad for Bud at two-to-one odds. The gamblers are coverin' anything we can rake up. Some of the boys have bet their saddles. Either we'll all be ridin' high or busted when this is over and friend Bud will have the mortgage paid off or livin' with kinfolks."

"Bud in town?"

"Haven't seen him. He rode down our way few days ago. Said Weir works his horse on the ranch road." Worry lines creased the sunburned face. "That stud looks fast."

"Does he tend to loaf the first half mile?"

"Loaf? He led our filly by a length at the first furlong." He gave Dude's face a curious search. "Where'd you get that?"

"Something I heard," Dude said, feeling the tap of a vague but growing unease. "How did he do on the break?"

"He took the break, which surprised me, because that little filly's no slouch."

"Did anybody happen to clock the quarter or the half mile?"

"Nobody did. But I know it was fast."

Fast, Dude scowled. Had they matched themselves a scorpion? Forcibly he cleared himself of doubt. "Mind covering some of that two-to-one money for us, Slim?"

"Glad to, podner."

Dude peeled off five one-hundred-dollar bills. "I'd place it myself, but I want the Commodore to keep on thinkin' we're just a shirt-tail outfit," he said, wishing he felt as confident as he sounded.

Staying busy, he led the Judge out of sight behind the wagon and trimmed his feet and reset the lightweight racing shoes.

Eight o'clock had come when Dude took off for the Royal Flush, leaving Coyote Walking reading by lantern light and Uncle Billy retiring early in preparation for to-morrow. As a precaution on the eve of the race, Judge Blair was tied at the wagon with Blue Grass and the sorrels. First thing in the morning, the old horseman would cover up the Judge's blaze and paint one on Texas Jack.

Lady Jane was winding up her hearty rendition of "The Old Chisholm Trail" and bowing off to the tinkling piano, the strumming banjo and the scraping bass fiddle, when Dude squeezed into the packed saloon. The cowboys stomped and hollered, Lady Jane swayed out and took her bow.

Then Philo stepped out from the purple curtain and raised his hand. The hum of voices ebbed. His strident voice rose:

"Lay-dees and gen-tul-men . . . the management of the Royal Flush . . . with great pride and at no little expense . . . presents the one and only Irish Troubadour — fresh off the boat from Dublin — Danny Featherstone!"

He exited clapping and this time there was no holding back as the crowd joined him.

Danny emerged from the opposite end of the stage, clad as Dude had not seen before: striped britches of blue and white, red coat buttoned at his slim waist, light-blue vest, a scarf of deep blue at his throat. His yellow hair, parted on the side, hung in ringlets. He looked boyish and handsomely devil-may-care.

Danny smiled at the applauding crowd and looked down at the musicians, and Dude heard him say, "Intro, please, Perfessor, for 'Danny Boy.' "

Ever so slowly and softly, the orchestra moved into the tender notes, the professor really laying on the tinkling melody, the banjo and bass fiddle furnishing background. And then, as Danny began singing, *"Oh, Danny boy . . . the pipes are calling . . . from glen to glen . . . and down the mountain-side . . ."* a hush settled over the cow-town crowd, broken only by the faint *ping* of glassware or the scrape of a boot.

Dude was touched as he could not re-

294

member, for Danny sang from the heart, and his tenor voice, so absolutely clear and full of feeling, raked up memories of faraway home and long-ago young love.

"The summer's gone . . . and all the roses falling . . ."

A burly freighter choked up, tears rolling like giant raindrops down the whiskered slopes of his rough face.

A cowboy, suddenly affected, took off his hat.

Somebody sniffed.

O'Fallon, behind the bar, wiped one eye with a dirty towel. As Danny reached the finale, *"If you must go and I must bye . . . oh, Danny boy . . . I love you so . . ."* and the music faded for intermission, the freighter leaped atop the bar and roared, "Free drinks for ever'body! Come on!"

A girl who had paused near Dude when Danny began singing suddenly broke into tears. She kept crying uncontrollably.

He could not suppress the instinct to place a comforting arm around her thin shoulders and guide her out of the ensuing stampede to the bar and across to a vacated table. Their eyes met and he saw that it was Gracie.

"Dude!" she said gratefully, those big hazel eyes luminous with tears. "Danny said you'd come tonight."

"Never break my word to a purty girl. Came to buy you that big drink."

"Let's just talk, if you don't mind," she said, looking distraught. "Danny's song got to me tonight."

Dude could read her like a book. If she was sixteen, she was just barely, and a long way from home. She was about to cry some more. He said, "Hey, now. Perk up. It's all right."

She regarded him through glistening eyes, trying to brace up. When she sniffed, he swiped clumsily at her nose with his red bandanna as he would have a child.

"You're a little homesick, is all," he said. "We all are tonight. I'm homesick for Texas, myself. Where you from, Gracie?"

"Springdale, Kansas," she replied, showing reticence. "It's northwest of Kansas City," the last thrown in as if nearness to a big city improved its status.

"Springdale, Kansas," he repeated, becoming enthusiastic. "Why, that sounds like a regular metropolis compared to my hometown."

"Where?" she brightened. She had a mighty nice smile.

"Little place called Live Oak, way down on the Salt Fork of the Brazos."

"Bet it's bigger than Springdale."

"Couldn't be — just one store and a water trough, and it leaks. Guess you have folks in Springdale?"

She skipped that. "There's a boy there I used to know. He keeps writing me. Had a letter from him today."

"You kinda like him?"

She blushed prettily. "I write him, too."

"Can you make biscuits?"

Her thin face quickened. "You bet I can. I make good biscuits."

He decided to take the bull by the horns. "North-bound stage pulls out at noon tomorrow. Why don't you be on it?"

He saw conflicting emotions shuttle across her face — eagerness, apprehension? He couldn't tell which was the stronger.

"But it leaves from in front of the Mercantile," she said uncertainly. "There'd be trouble. Big trouble."

So that was it — she was afraid of something.

"I can't," she finished, "even if I could."

He figured he saw through that as well: money. Reaching impulsively, keeping his hands under the table, he peeled off a greenback, folded it and slipped it into the palm of her hand almost before she knew it.

"Better yet," he encouraged her, "there's

a trainload of cattle leavin' here at four o'clock tomorrow afternoon for the Kansas City market. You can ride the caboose. From Kansas City you can take the stage, arrive in style . . . get off with your head held high."

Her large eyes kept growing larger. "How can I repay you?"

"Oh, you can bake me a cherry pie sometime."

"I wish I could."

"You just be on that caboose. Tell Otto Unger you want to go home. Meanwhile, I'll put a bug in his ear."

He saw her start to speak, saw her catch herself and tighten her lips, her face freezing as Sweetwater Smith shuffled over to the table. He said to her, "Believe you'd better circulate around instead of visiting all night."

She didn't reply. She seemed to grow smaller before Dude's eyes.

Something twisted inside Dude. This unspoken rub between Smith and himself had to come to a head sooner or later, and now was as good a time as any. But as he came to his feet he realized that he and Gracie hadn't finished their say, and he had a curb bit on himself when he said, "The Commodore hasn't lost a dime on my outfit tonight.

No doubt you heard Danny Featherstone sing?"

"That kid!" Smith snorted disdain.

"*That kid* just sold enough watered-down whiskey with his song to float this two-bit joint plumb to the Indian Territory line."

At that moment the orchestra struck up "Sweet Betsy from Pike" and Dude turned to her. "Come on, Gracie. Let's burn a hole in the wind on this one, then have us another drink." Taking her arm, he whirled her out to the dance floor, already filling with whooping, stomping dancers. He could feel her tenseness as they went hippity-hop. On the other side of the floor, he spoke into her ear, "What time do you come on?"

"Four o'clock."

"Good. The horse race is at three o'clock. Soon as it's over you be in the alley, ready to ride. I'll be there as fast as I can. May be a little while." He could foresee collection problems looming if they won. "I'll have your ticket."

"But you already gave me money."

"You'll need that up the line. Buy yourself some new clothes."

She drew back, her eyes troubled. "I wish you'd stay out of this, Dude. That man is meaner than you think. I know . . . I tried to leave once before. He thinks he's in love with me. He's kind of — well, crazy. He scares me."

She looked so young. He said, "I'm gonna get you out of here."

"I can take care of myself," she said, flouncing one shoulder. "Been on my own since I was fourteen. Ran away from home."

"You're goin' to Springdale."

"What if they won't let a girl on the caboose? It's just for the train crew and cowmen taking cattle to market."

"I've thought of that. You be dressed like a boy. Will you be there, now?"

They stomped and hopped and pumped through several turns. Dude laid back his head and whooped like the others and let go a rollicking "Ah . . . hah" for effect, thinking, She's not going. She's afraid.

"I will," she said forthwith, her mouth firm. "I'll go. I'll be there. Only be careful, Dude. So very careful."

"Springdale — here we come!"

Chapter 15

Dude could hear the chatter of the telegraph as he entered the depot next morning. Unger, who was taking down the message, glanced up and nodded when Dude came to the counter, his boots clomping on the wooden floor.

The sounder's gossipy voice snapped off, suddenly spent. Unger wrote on for additional moments; finished, he folded the message, inserted it into an envelope, rose and handed it to Dude. "Here's Dr. Lockhart's answer. Finally got it."

"Mighty fine. He'll be glad to get this."

Unger volunteered no hint of its contents, but his eyes seemed to reflect a possibly differing opinion.

"What I'm here for, Mr. Unger," Dude opened, "is to ask your help for a young lady."

"Young lady?"

Having broken the ice, Dude plunged into

Gracie's story, stressing her longing for home and her fear of Sweetwater Smith. "She's been on her own since she was fourteen," he added. "Ran away. Now she's homesick, and I want to buy her a ticket to Kansas City. She can take the stage from there to Springdale."

"It's strictly against Santa Fe regulations for a woman to ride the caboose."

"Can't you make an exception just this one time?"

Unger chewed his lower lip. "I'm 'fraid not."

"She wouldn't be any trouble. A little slip of a thing like her. She's a mighty nice kid."

"That's not the point. It's against regulations."

"I understand your position, Mr. Unger. But let's say a young boy shows up here after the horse race. Nobody could claim you let a girl board the caboose, now could they?"

Unger's stern front did not change one whit.

Dude thought of bribery, but a cooler judgment whispered that Unger would get mad and not take it. He said earnestly,

"If you will sell me a ticket, it will prevent the sure killing of one Dude McQuinn, the slowest draw in Texas. Only thing I ever shot when I was a kid was a cottontail, which made me sick to my stomach."

Unger's brow wrinkled. No more.

"I know Smith's ringey enough with his fists," Dude kept on, desperation hollowing his voice. "On top of that, they tell me he's one bolt of lightning with a gun. Shot two cowboys over at Wichita before they could clear their holsters." He gazed down, as Uncle Billy had schooled him when circling around to match a race at odds. "Be another dyin' cowboy for sure there in the dust outside the Mercantile." His voice trailed off. "Shot tryin' to save a young girl from goin' on down the road of sin. . . . Her lookin' down at him, blaming herself, 'cause she longed to see her ol' daddy and mother just one more time . . . them both poorly and way up in years . . . not to mention that country boy she's pinin' her heart out to marry."

Unger threw up both hands. "Cut it out, McQuinn!" He reached for the ticket pad on the counter. "Just make damn certain *that boy looks like a boy.* Get me?"

"Mr. Unger, you're straight as a wagon tongue!"

Reaching camp, Dude saw that the usual precautions had been taken during his absence: bedrolls and cooking utensils loaded into the wagon, the sorrel team brushed and curried, ready for harnessing later, tied with Texas Jack, now the spittin' image of Judge Blair, and the Judge, his blaze painted to fit Texas Jack's markings, standing in pre-race seclusion behind the wagon. It paid to be ready if trouble developed, which it did more times than not.

"Got it!" Dude called, waving the envelope.

Uncle Billy darted over. He tore at the envelope and unfolded the message, holding it at arm's length, his squinting eyes devouring the written lines.

The seconds seemed endless.

He let his hands fall, his cherry-red mouth forming an *O* that spelled surprise and concern.

"Well, what is it?" Dude asked.

"Commodore Weir," the old man said, "left Maryland three years ago, permanently banned from state tracks for fixing other men's horses. Philo was suspended again and again for rough riding." He squinted through the message again. "Sir James ran at Pimlico as a two-year-old. True, he was foaled in England and shipped to this country, but nothing is known about any Duke of Newmarket." His keen eyes moved in an arc from Dude to the younger men and back to Dude. "Now, listen to this: Sir James still holds the Pimlico record for four furlongs — forty-six seconds flat! Weir has pulled a slick one on us. He's matched his horse at his best distance. We're up against a sprinting Thoroughbred champion!"

Dude felt his throat muscles pull tight. Lady Jane's words tolled through his mind: *"Four furlongs . . . for all my cowboy friends."*

He shook his head in pain. "It's my fault. Lady Jane took me. Oh, how she took me. That old saying was never more true about you can take the boy out of the country, but you can't take the country out of the boy."

"My friend was out of town," Uncle Billy said. "Otherwise, we'd had the telegram before we made the match. But don't blame yourself, Dude. We all know that a horseman is the only animal that can be skinned more than once."

Head bent, Uncle Billy strolled over to the wagon tongue and started fooling with the light racing saddle draped there. His hand suddenly froze on the right stirrup leather. He looked down, his eyes widening. He roared, "Come over here!"

Dude ran over with the others.

"Look at this!" The old man held out the

stirrup leather for them to see, his hands shaking with rage.

It was partly severed, more than half way, Dude saw, his anger swelling. "If Coyote stood up in the irons, he could be hurt or even killed."

Uncle Billy was puzzled. "How'd they get in here?"

"Three of us took horses to water, remember?" Coyote said, "while white father was at depot. Been people coming by all morning."

Wrathy as the old man was, a light seemed to break across his face. "We'll just turn this little dido around," he said, the blue eyes glinting, "and give the Judge a weight advantage."

"How?" Dude asked.

"Have Coyote ride bareback, way he used to on the reservation for his father, the chief. But this duke fella won't know it till we take our horse to the starting line. . . . There's another wrinkle we can use. Coyote, when Unger tells you jockeys to walk up to the line, I want you to jump your horse off early — before the horses can be lapped enough for the break. That should draw Sir James off. He's high strung. Maybe he'll run off down there a hundred yards or so . . . use himself up. But hold the Judge back. Don't let him go far, just enough to set Sir James off. Likely, Unger won't let you get by with this a second time. You'll have to use your own judgment on that." He affected restraint. "Naturally, I don't like to stoop to such extreme measures unless the other fella tries to take unfair advantage, such as we see in this slashed stirrup."

"Naturally," Dude echoed.

"Be that as it may," Uncle Billy said, sobering, "I see Sir James as the toughest horse the Judge has ever been up against. If he wins this, and I believe he can, he will be the fastest half-mile horse in America — bar none." He turned fond eyes on Coyote. "Be prepared for Philo to try some rough riding. He's what you call a mean white man."

"Watch, this Comanche will, Grandfather."

"And don't call me —" He made a gesture of futility. "Aw, forget it."

The morning passed much too slowly for Dude. Still, the curious rode and drove by, eyes on the camp. At noon the outfit ate a cold lunch. At one-thirty all hands joined to give the Judge a rubdown from head to tail. Afterward, Uncle Billy opened a can of greenish-looking ointment and rubbed some in the gelding's nostrils.

"What's that stuff?" Dude puzzled.

"Just petroleum jelly, camphor, and menthol — to open him up. He'll need every breath he can pull in today."

"No doubt one of Professor Gleason's conditioners?"

"Happens it is not. It is Dr. Hood's Magic Balm, the Celebrated English Cure, once sold as a positive guarantee for all respiratory ailments."

"Bet that was fun, travelin' with a medicine show?"

He cocked an eye at Dude, his trackless face letting in that unfathomable saintliness. "Now, did I say? Happened the good doctor generously presented me this sample after I cured his buggy horse of the thumps. An odd thing, too. I found out the balm works as well on horses as it does on humans."

He returned the can to the medicine chest.

Post time.

Except that today it was different, unlike any other race the outfit had matched. Something sensed. An underlying premonition of trouble. An extra tenseness. Uncle Billy's observation that gamblers played only a sure thing kept running through Dude's mind as he saddled Blue Grass. Earlier, the sorrels had been harnessed, the last of the camping equipment packed, including the water bucket, should sudden departure be prudent after the race.

The hum of the waiting, restless crowd had a tonic effect on Dude. Sounds like bees swarming, he thought. Mounting, he rode around the wagon to pony the Judge to the starting line.

There he halted to view the old man's "new wrinkle." Coyote was riding bareback and naked to the waist as usual, his lean body shining like copper. Today he carried a switch instead of the Comanche quirt. Furthermore, he wore no moccasins, and furthermore the Judge, in lieu of bridle, had a hair rope on his lower jaw. As Dude watched, Uncle Billy handed Coyote a bright red blanket, which he drew over his shoulders and let fall over the Judge's back and withers. An eagle feather fluttered from the Judge's forelock like a guidon.

"Want that duke fella to wonder and worry when he sees us come on the track," the old man informed Dude. "I figure we'll be four or five pounds lighter than the other horse. Coyote says be sure to look after his red blanket, which his father, the chief, gave him long ago."

"I will."

Ready, now. Uncle Billy and Danny

climbed to the wagon seat, and the old man, chirruping to the team, drove for town, Dude trailing, leading the Judge. At the edge of town Uncle Billy parked the wagon under the trees where Texas Jack had routed the idlers that day.

"I won't be far away when they cross the finish line," Dude told him, and ponied on toward the shifting mass of humanity that thronged both sides of the street. Slim Overmire waved and let go a whoop. Applause rippled through the crowd, growing as the cowboy contingent voiced its choice.

Lady Jane — all bustle and bows and ruffles and cinched up like a racehorse — stood in the judges' box and smiled at Dude beneath the flapping wings of her flowered hat.

Dude ignored her.

Now down the road pranced Sir James, tossing his handsome head, dancing sideways as he reacted to the noise of the crowd. Commodore Weir wearing his fox-hunting getup, led the long-legged gray stud.

But the bantam Philo was the eye-catcher: blue cap, red jacket, white pants encased in polished black boots. Sir James tossed his head again, revealing a silver-mounted bridle.

The Commodore nodded formally as the horses passed.

Dude glanced at his watch. Three-fourteen. It was going to be a late start. The tooting of the cattle train reminded him anew of its four o'clock departure.

Riding to the starting line, he released his horse and spoke to Unger. Back there the saloonman was just now at the Royal Flush. He was deliberately walking Sir James.

Dude glowered. Was Weir making him wait, playing that old game to raise the other horse's nervousness? "He's sure takin' his time," Dude said to Unger.

"Is . . . but he's coming along now."

Weir was, pumping up and down. As he reached the starting line, Coyote chose that moment to undrape the blanket and toss it to Dude, who laid it across the pommel of his saddle.

Weir's eyes bugged on Coyote. Without comment, he freed Sir James of the lead rope and motioned, a peremptory command; promptly, a man ran out and sponged the stallion's mouth.

Now that's cute, Dude thought. Is it water or something to make a horse run faster?

"All right, gentlemen," Unger said in a take-charge voice. "You will walk your horses up to the starting line. When you're fairly lapped, I'll drop my hand and shout go. Not before. This track's plenty wide. I

311

want room between you — no bumping at the break. Any questions?"

Neither jockey spoke. Therefore, at Unger's signal, they turned and rode back a short distance and turned again. Philo, the veteran reinsman, moved aggressively, careful not to let Coyote get the edge. When Sir James lunged and reared, eager to run, Philo held him in.

The horses were nearing Unger, fairly lapped, when suddenly Judge Blair, to all appearances, broke out of control. Sir James broke after him, plunging hard, Philo unable to stop him. A short distance and Coyote held up his horse, while Sir James tore on down the track. He covered nearly a hundred yards, fighting the bit, resenting it, before Philo could slow and turn him. Sweat was pouring off the gray horse.

"That was a deliberate false start," Weir protested to Unger.

Dude said, "My ol' cow pony's just eager to run."

Unger, watching the horses, said nothing. But when Coyote came up, he warned him, "No more of that, young man."

"Horse him run, Injun no hold 'im," Coyote shrugged.

Weir rode out and spoke something curt to Philo. The jockey scowled in Coyote's direction and nodded.

Dude, giving Coyote a good-luck wave, galloped downtrack, looking back as he rode. When he saw the horses approach the line again, he reined off behind the crowd.

This time Sir James broke early, bolting fifty yards before Philo could yank him down. Coyote merely turned the Judge about and waited, the print of boredom on his high-boned face.

Again, Weir hurried out to confer with his jockey.

Again, the jockeys walked the horses back and turned.

Again, the horses looked fairly lapped.

Unger raised his hand.

Dude grew tense. *Pull his head a little more, Coyote. Swing him. That's it.*

Unger's hand dropped.

A roar went up from the crowd as the horses got away. The Judge had the break, winging a length in front. When the horses hit racing stride, the stud began to shorten the distance, bit by bit, until he reached the Judge's withers. They ran with that difference, seemingly fixed, to the one-furlong stake. At the quarter mile Dude's horse yet had the edge. Dude whooped. So the Judge would have beaten Sir James at that distance!

Philo was laying on the whip now. The gray horse shot away and drew even, then gradually forged out front — a head, a neck. The outcome, Dude knew, was being decided right here. He waited for Coyote's whoop.

It burst. More drawn-out screech than whoop, an urgency that chilled the blood, that seemed to call: *Run faster, horse. Run like buffalo horse. Run, horse, run.*

Judge Blair moved up, full of run, full of heart.

Dude whooped. Boy, he was comin' now!

And then he saw it happen. Philo's arm whipping up and Philo lashing the charging Judge Blair across the face. The gelding checked instinctively, falling back until he trailed by a length.

The horses flashed by the third-furlong stake.

Dude groaned and braced himself. Just one furlong left. He knotted within, waiting.

Coyote's screech sounded high above the pounding hoofs. Another screech. Another. Judge Blair was coming again. All at once he surged to the gray's tail. Hearing that thunder, Philo sneaked a backward glance. But just as he came up again with the whip, Coyote screeched louder and took his horse to the outside.

Philo's swing missed.

Indian and horse pulled away. They passed. As they swept on, Coyote twisted around and held the switch aloft for Philo to see and brought it down: the Plains Indian sign for Finished. Done.

Thereafter, the scene became all dust and bay and gray horseflesh charging past the Royal Flush.

Dude whooped and started riding through the crowd rushing out on the road. Cowboys were yelling. More people pressed forward. A horseman bulled past, shouting for clearance. It was Weir, his face raging.

Dude had to stop or trample somebody; for moments his way was blocked. Ahead, he could see Uncle Billy and Danny in the crush around the finish line. The old man waved. Danny was jumping up and down and waving, too. When Dude finally barged through, Uncle Billy hollered:

"Fastest half-mile horse in America! By a length!"

Beyond this vortex of people, the Judge was still galloping, still wanting to run. Philo had pulled up and was circling wide to avoid the crowd.

Dude swung down and tied up at the finish pole; together he and Uncle Billy and Danny marched inside the Royal Flush.

Boy, was it quiet in here! Long-faced gamblers paying off jubilant cowboys. Slim Overmire's crowing laugh.

No sign of Weir, who had time to get here. Only Sweetwater Smith, standing at the end of the bar near the stairway. And, Dude figured, where Smith was the Commodore should be near. Like a bird dog and its master.

Dude slowed step. At that uneasy instant Weir hurried in from the rear. Ignoring Dude, he turned quickly for his office.

"Hold on," Dude called. As he stepped toward Weir, stealthy movements down the stairs registered on the rim of his vision . . . a slim boy carrying a canvas suitcase. The "boy" was Gracie. Smith spotted her a second after, but shifted his attention back to Dude when Dude kept going to intercept Weir.

"Commodore," Dude called, louder, "we've come for our money."

Weir's lean face was ashen with shock, as gray as the dust on his long-tailed blue coat. "There will be no pay-off. Your horse is a ringer. Get out!"

"Ringer! Yours holds the half-mile record at Pimlico. For an even surer thing, you had our stirrup leather cut. We want our money now, Commodore. We aim to collect it!"

Weir blinked but had no reply, strangely unconcerned.

Hearing a scuffle behind him, Dude found Smith holding Uncle Billy with one arm while he poked a six-shooter at Dude.

"You heard what the Commodore said," Smith muttered. "Get out or the old man goes bye-bye."

Dude had never been so angry. He said, "Touch one hair on Uncle Billy's head and you're a goner," and his voice came to him like a jar. He held his ground, emotion overpowering his reason. Danny? Where was Danny? With the flash of the question, he saw Danny slipping in behind Smith.

Weir yelled a warning. But when Smith jerked to see, Danny ducked low, and Dude lunged and shoved. Uncle Billy and Smith fell backward over Danny's back.

Dude moved fast to stomp Smith's gun hand. The six-gun plopped free and Dude scooped it up. As Smith reared up to get at him, Dude laid the barrel across the bowling-ball head. Blood flew like racetrack mud. Smith sank to the floor, dazed but not out.

"That was all for nothing, McQuinn."

Dude spun around to look into the snout of Weir's handgun.

"Drop the gun, McQuinn."

Before he quite realized what he was doing, Dude said, "Here," and pitched the weapon straight at Weir. When Weir dodged, Dude charged him. He aimed the point of his shoulder for the middle button of the blue coat and heard Weir gasp for wind. Weir's handgun went off in Dude's ear, but he felt no pain. Furious, he wrenched about, grabbed, caught, and twisted Weir's arm. The handgun *thunked* in the sawdust. Dude got it.

"Now," he snarled, "our money." A glance showed Uncle Billy covering Smith, up on one knee, nursing his head, and Slim Overmire, gun in hand, holding O'Fallon and the gamblers at bay.

"Our money," Dude said again. "Dig!"

"Don't have it on me."

"Your money belt bulges like a well rope. Dig, Commodore!"

Weir dawdled at pulling up his shirt.

"Faster!"

Weir opened a pocket on his money belt, removed some bills, counting as he did so, and inched them across.

Dude counted rapidly. "You're just short five hundred. Dig, Commodore!"

With a look of pain, Weir removed five bills and passed them to Dude. He counted five hundred dollars.

318

Weir shook his head, baffled. He said, "Your horse . . . I don't understand how he ran that fast."

"You just didn't know how to make my ol' cow pony run when you tried him out that night," Dude said, folding the greenbacks with satisfaction. "You see, Commodore, it takes an Indian. A particular kind of Indian — a Comanche — the son of a chief."

In the distance a train whistle hooted.

"Let's go!" Dude said. Wheeling, he met the brunt of Smith's everlasting enmity.

They ran out into a milling, curious crowd, the cowboys following. Overmire caught Dude's arm. "Here's your money, podner. We'll keep an eye out till you clear town. That Osage country is mighty pretty this time of year, if you know what I mean?"

Dude slapped him on the back and yelled at Uncle Billy, "Wait for me at the state line."

"What's up?"

"No time to tell you. Go on!"

Dude hit the saddle and galloped downstreet to the first opening. He still had Weir's handgun, which he dropped as he cut for the alley. Turning there, he raced for the rear of the Royal Flush.

He didn't see her.

The train hooted again. He could hear it chuffing.

At once two figures filled the narrow doorway leading into the saloon. Two women struggling. Lady Jane wrestling to hold Gracie. The girl swung the canvas suitcase with a sidearm motion that took the older woman across the side of her head. The flowered hat sailed like a wind-blown leaf. Lady Jane went down, cussing and yelling for Sweetwater Smith.

Gracie broke on top, swinging the suitcase. Dude pulled her up behind him and heeled Blue Grass away. Tearing along the alley, Dude saw Smith run out the back door, look, spot them, and sprint toward saddle horses tied behind the Wagon Mound Mercantile.

The alley ended and Dude rushed out on the road, the saddler bounding full stride, Gracie holding onto Dude's waist with one arm, the suitcase bouncing on the other side. Departing wagons and buggies fell behind them. Ahead, Dude saw the cattle-train engine puffing steam, yet not in motion. He looked behind.

Smith was coming fast. Dude thought of Weir's handgun, which he had foolishly dropped back there.

Time seemed to stand still before they

raced up to the depot, but Dude knew little time had passed, for the old gelding could eat up ground.

Gracie slipped down and Dude, after her, dropped the reins and pressed the ticket into her hand. About fifty yards downtrack sat the caboose on the tail end of cars of bawling cattle. A brakeman signaled. The engine's bell clanged. The train jerked convulsively, the cars shuddering and banging.

"Run!" Dude hurried her.

She hesitated. "Oh, Dude, I'm so afraid for you."

A horse was coming. Whipping around, Dude saw Smith storming off the horse and tearing on at a shuffling run.

Dude drove his voice at her. "Run, Gracie — run!"

She threw him a heartfelt look and ran.

Dude, bracing himself, threw a bear hug around the oncoming barrel-shaped body. It was like wrestling a side of hung beef. Smith broke the hold easily; on balanced feet, he smashed his right fist into Dude's lower ribs, a professional's punch of astonishing power that brought shivers of pain and shortened breath. Dude felt himself going down. He gulped for wind.

But Smith had to gloat a moment before giving chase, the jungle fighter used to standing over his opponent to make certain he stayed down. When he hastened to go, Dude stuck out one foot. Smith tripped. On hands and knees, Dude sprang upon him. They rolled over and over, punching, kicking. Dude was quicker, but Smith was stronger, his loglike body unaffected by Dude's blows. The blue sky was spinning crazily for Dude. A blow to his face blotted out even that.

Smith stood over him, hacking, "You and your fancy manners." His hand slid inside his coat. Dude recoiled at sight of the blackjack. Smith hefted it with relish.

It was now or never, Dude knew. When Smith stepped in, Dude kicked with all his strength. His bootheels caught Smith fully in the groin. He screamed and buckled, rumping down, his thick legs like collapsing stanchions, hands clutching himself low.

Hearing the train gathering speed, Dude pushed up. He grimaced at the pain in his ribs and wondered if they were broken. His left eye was half shut. The cattle cars were passing, clicking faster and faster. Now the caboose. Had she made it?

Gracie stood on the rear platform. She waved and threw him a kiss.

Dude, pressing his ribs with one hand, waved his hat and held it high and managed a weak facsimile of his arena smile. It came to him that some lucky cuss back in Springdale was going to get himself a mighty good little biscuit shooter.

Otto Unger came running out of the depot. He looked at Smith writhing on the ground and said, "First civic improvement we've had around here."

"He's all yours now," Dude said and reeled to his horse and pulled himself to the saddle. Smith was getting to his feet, but he made no effort to follow.

Dude swung wide of the town and the outfit was waiting at the state line.

"What took you so long?" Uncle Billy asked.

"A little matter."

The old man's wise eyes read Dude's face. "Couldn't have been a girl, could it?"

"Now, Uncle, did I say?"

Chapter 16

Cracked ribs do not a rider make; hence, on this third day after the race at Wagon Mound, the outfit still tarried within the Osage Reservation, which proved as appealing as Slim Overmire said it was: deep-running creeks and sweet-water springs, and emerald waves of grass so high it tickled a tall horse's belly.

"Believe I can ride this morning," Dude said, gingerly exploring his rib cage.

"What's your notion?" Uncle Billy asked.

"I keep thinking of Texas."

"If we move on southeast we can pick up the old Texas Road. It runs on down through eastern Indian Territory to Red River. How does that strike you?" He had never been more obliging, more genial. Dude could see that Judge Blair's victory had fed fresh gratification into the horseman's soul of William Tecumseh Lockhart.

"Anything with Texas in it sounds good to me, Uncle."

"Might even match a race or two along the way."

"Never get tard, do you?"

"When that day comes, I'll be in my rocker by the f'ar."

"That day is a long way off," Dude assured him. "Let's move camp."

"I'm ready."

"Wonder if there's a likely town we could head for?"

Uncle Billy dwelled on that. "Come to think of it," he said, with an odd little smile, "there might be. I've heard tell of a place called Cherokee Gap that was salty back in the early days. Understand outlaws used to ride in from the hills to trade there and race horses and throw their money around like chicken feed."

"Think you'll recognize it after all these years?" Dude slipped in, narrowing his eyes.

With that never-failing guardedness; "Dude, I do believe you're hard of hearing, which is unfortunate at your age. Did I say I'd been there? What I said was *I'd heard tell.*"

"Oh, sure."

Cherokee Gap.

Peering off through the glassy brightness of morning, Dude saw beyond the church-

325

steepled town a broad gap that opened into a disarray of tumbling hills. It looked rough as a cob in there, timbered, rocky, broken, forbidding, a haven for outlaws and ambuscade.

Like actors coming on stage in the opening of a melodrama performed many times, the outfit dragged along Main Street. Heading the cast, Uncle Billy, a patriarch at the reins of the sorrels, and young Danny beside him like a fresh-faced schoolboy. As if ad libbing, Coyote Walking rode Texas Jack bareback. Now and then the Comanche would surreptitiously nudge heel to flank and the gelding would swerve and caper. And Dude, leading packhorse Judge Blair on Blue Grass, would call out; "Hold him up there! Don't let 'im bolt on you! Keep his head up! He's rarin' to run!" And Coyote would saw on the reins and bounce around.

Even so, when heads turned they showed merely mild interest.

Now that's strange, Dude frowned. What kind of burg is this? If there was anything unusual about the town that he could see, it was the opera house, the Isis, which you wouldn't find in Wagon Mound or Lost Creek or Kiowa Peak. There was, moreover, another difference here, a subtle one, an air of decorum and respectability as the residents went about their affairs. He sensed that. And almost every store front, including that of the Citizen's Bank and the one general store, wore faces of new paint. He rode on, scanning both sides of the street.

Meaning struck him like the kick of a mule. There was something missing. No saloons! And no pool halls!

They chose a camping place at the edge of town, unpacked and set up to await the first eager horseman, making certain that Texas Jack occupied a conspicuous spot.

Three o'clock passed. Four o'clock.

"Quietest town I've ever been in," Dude fretted to Uncle Billy.

"Some horseman will show up. Be patient," he replied carefully.

In contradiction, the afternoon and evening elapsed without a visitor. So did the next morning.

"This town is inhabited, I believe," Dude observed, waxing sarcastic. "I'd swear I saw people as we came in and I believe I see some now. And there's a man on a horse, a real, live horse. What do you make of it, Uncle?"

The old man tucked in his cherry-red lips and folded his arms. A pinpoint of thought seemed to bob to the surface of his seraphic features, growing, speeding, until it formed, complete for utterance. He said, "When the bees don't come to the honey, you take the honey to the bees."

"Sorta like we did in Nocona that time, when the preachers had folks too boogered to match a race?"

"Ah, you remember."

"Think I'd forget?"

"It pleases me, Dude, when I see that you haven't forgotten *everything* I've schooled you in."

After a bit, they moseyed uptown. In front of the bank, Dude inquired of a well-padded gentleman. "Pardon me, sir. Will you kindly tell me the proprietor of the general store?"

"Mr. Tobias Appleman, sir. He's also the mayor."

"Thank you, sir."

"You are welcome, sir." He drew himself up and held out a pale hand. "I am P. T. Purcell, president of the bank. Welcome to Cherokee Gap."

"Thank you, sir. I am Dude McQuinn, and this is Dr. William Lockhart. Your friendly greeting inspires us to linger longer in your fair city."

They entered the store and when Dude asked for Appleman, a clerk directed them to an inner office. The man there, bent over account ledgers, glanced up only after Dude coughed discreetly.

"Mr. Appleman, sir?"

A tired nod.

Striding in, flourishing his outstretched hand: "My name is Dude McQuinn, of Live Oak, Texas, better known as the Little Houston on the Salt Fork of the Brazos. . . . I am pleased to present my uncle, Dr. William Tecumseh Lockhart, of Lexington, Kentucky . . . Saratoga, New York . . . and the Old Dominion of Virginia." Just mention *doctor* or Kentucky or New York or Virginia, Dude thought, any place that was far away, and these yokels were impressed.

Appleman nodded tiredly. His handshakes were listless, though his face was round and pleasant. He wore his hair cut short and greased down, parted in the middle, and his waxed mustache curled at the ends. Over his white shirt he favored a black alpaca vest, its leftside pocket sprouting a forest of pencils sharpened to fine points. As yet, he had said no word.

"Dr. Lockhart represents the Kentucky Humane Society," Dude went on importantly. "His territory is west of the Mississippi and his mission is to demonstrate Professor Gleason's Eureka Bridle, developed after years of trial and error for the prevention of cruelty to horses and for the safety of mankind."

Appleman did not look impressed, across his face the weary tolerance of having suffered all kinds of grandiose spiels from fast-talking drummers, along with back-slapping anecdotes and odorous "twofer" cigars.

"No doubt, sir," Dude carried on, "as a captain of enterprise, you are familiar with the Eureka Bridle?"

"Sorry to say I am not," Appleman said finally, flatly, his expression further retreating, his voice conveying a backing-off tone. "And I've just put in an order for bridles from Shipley of Kansas City."

Raising protesting hands, Dude soothed, "You've got us all wrong, sir. We're not peddling one little thing. All we ask is permission to demonstrate Professor Gleason's Eureka Bridle in front of your store come Saturday morning. You could call it a demonstration in community safety for man, woman, and child." Catching Appleman's frown, he added, "Your store should sell a lot of cord that day."

"Cord? Sell?" Although confused, Appleman perked up.

Uncle Billy seized the opening with,

"Yes — cord — lengths of stout cord," and casting Duke his rebuke, "I apologize for my nephew, who in his enthusiasm for the efficacy of the Eureka Bridle, neglected to explain its surprising simplicity. I use cord instead of leather." Upon which, dressed for the occasion — frock coat, white shirt, string tie, flat-topped hat, ebony boots shined — he laid on the clincher, "I shall be delighted to give you a private demonstration, sir, of this remarkable device."

"I'm busy right now."

"Is there a horse tied behind the store?"

"Well — yes, there is. My own saddler."

"It will take about three minutes, Mr. Appleman, I promise you I shall require no more of your time than that, aware as I am of your unremitting adherence to serve the public."

"Well . . ." Appleman said, not interested; then, perchance reasoning the quickest way to rid himself of the two; "All right. Let's get it over with."

"So you have a saddler," Uncle Billy said, his tone comradely. He turned to Dude. "Any copies left in the wagon of my latest two-volume work, *The American Saddler, Man's Pride and Joy*? I should like to autograph same and present to Mr. Appleman as an expression of the Society's appreciation."

"That horseman in Sedalia bought the last ones."

"I'd forgotten. What about the book that just came off the press in Philadelphia, *The Spell of Saddling*?

"The shipment we ordered failed to reach us in time at St. Louis. Remember?"

"There must be one copy left of *Lockhart's Horse and Horsemanship*." Impatience sharpened his voice.

"Sorry, Uncle. It's sold out."

Uncle Billy shook his head in abject apology. "From now on," he told Dude, not without asperity, "I wish you would let me know when these tomes are no longer available. This is embarrassing."

Without delay, Appleman led them to a shed behind the store where a plain-looking brown horse stood dejectedly at halter.

Uncle Billy stopped to look. "Ah . . . a splendid animal, Mr. Appleman. I congratulate you, sir. I can see at first glance that you care well for him. His glossy coat alone tells me that."

"He's been poorly of late. Had a touch of the heaves."

The old man took the cue immediately, whipping out his memorandum book and scribbling decisively. "Doctor him with this," he said, tearing out a leaf. "I believe you will find it quite salutary when given as directed." He raised a warning finger. "And don't forget the lobelia. Two ounces, mind you — no more."

"Say —" Appleman broke into a first-time smile. "I'm obliged to you. Is there a charge, Dr. Lockhart?"

"None a-tall. Absolutely free. Part of my missionary work, such as demonstrating Professor Gleason's Eureka Bridle." He removed his hat and as a magician would pull out a rabbit, he drew from it a length of cord which he dangled auspiciously. "If you will remove the halter, Mr. Appleman, I shall demonstrate the Eureka."

The merchant did so, intrigued, and the old man slipped the noose over the saddler's head, and slowly went through the passes, ending with the tie, explaining as he went. "There," he said. "Now, Dude, give me a leg up."

Mounted bareback, Uncle Billy heeled the horse in a circle, reining left and right, the saddler answering each pull of the reins, then halting.

"By golly, it works," Appleman said, convinced, scratching the part in his hair.

"Would you like to tie it?" the old man suggested, sliding nimbly down.

"You'd better show me again."

"Gladly." Which Uncle Billy did, step by step. Untying, leaving only the loop around the saddler's neck, he handed the cord to Appleman, who lost himself in tangles, but on the second try completed the tie, as excited as a boy solving a puzzle.

"You did it! It's all a matter of leverage against the upper lip, which is quite sensitive. Proven in the field as the most successful bridle ever devised for the management of unruly horses and for the safety of the rider." Untying the cord, he bowed graciously and presented it to Appleman.

"You're sure there's no charge now?" the storekeeper asked, some of his early suspicion returning.

"There's no joker in this deck, friend Appleman. Our one desire is permission to demonstrate the Eureka's efficacy for the public good."

"You have it."

"Thank you, friend Appleman. You are generous, a public benefactor. Based on past demonstrations across the country, I can assure you in advance that this will serve the store as a gesture of good will for years to come."

Appleman flung him a keen look. "And a way to whet up more cash trade. We need that, with all that's out on the books. Let's go back to the office and visit on this." When everyone was seated, he said, "You wanted Saturday morning. Why not two o'clock? That will give folks time to come in from the country. Let's see . . . this is Wednesday," he calculated, warming to his subject. "Just right to have handbills printed and circulated." Suddenly he pounded the desk, eyes flashing. "Best advertising in the world. Community service! Good will! Glad I thought of that!"

Uncle Billy did not turn a hair at the appropriation.

Appleman hardly paused. "What length of cord is this, Doctor?"

"Ten feet. You can make it longer, depending on how long you want the reins."

"I'll say twelve feet for good measure. What is the cord's diameter?"

"One eighth of an inch is sufficient. Any larger would be too cumbersome in the mouth."

Appleman made swift notations. "I will have a batch of these cut and labeled . . . placed on display in the front window with handbills. Two dollars should be a fair price." He almost chortled. "Every farmer has at least one mean mule and one jugheaded work horse." He leaned back, pleased. "It will work on mules, won't it?"

"Friend Appleman, it will work on a bull moose, provided you can get it over his antlers."

Roaring, Appleman reached behind a stack of thick ledgers and hauled up a full bottle of whiskey. None other, Dude saw, than Old Green River. Glancing at the doorway, Appleman uncorked and, still watching, handed the bottle to Uncle Billy, who drank until gurgles sounded, wiped the bottle clean with a handkerchief, and passed it to Appleman, who, still watching, handed it to Dude, who took a long pull, wiped it clean, and gave it to Appleman, who stepped out of the line of sight of anyone looking through the doorway and raised the bottle to his lips, high like a trumpet. He held it there, his throat muscles working. Dude gaped as the level within the bottle dropped.

Appleman finished with a drawn-out "Ahhh . . ." and sat the bottle behind his desk. He coughed and said, "I hope you gentlemen do not think I make a regular practice of this. You see, every year about this time, without fail, a dreadful cough comes upon me. Nothing else seems to help."

"Catarrh," Uncle Billy diagnosed positively, with outright sympathy. "Inflammation of the mucous membranes. A most annoying affliction. I myself am a fellow sufferer, friend Appleman. It is incurable, yet can be allayed as you have so ably demonstrated."

"In a town of this strait-laced nature," Appleman confided, "a man must drink on the sly, even when it's for medicinal purposes, such as mine. You never know when some preacher's gonna pop through the doorway on the bulge for another donation. As you've probably noticed, Cherokee Gap has no saloons and no pool halls."

"There is nothing like a clean town, friend Appleman."

Glancing again at the doorway, Appleman passed the bottle, and when it had completed its stops, he cleared his throat and said, "Neither do we allow horse races in town. They used to run 'em right down Main Street. People kept getting run over and banged into. Invariably, the races were staged on Saturday, our one good trade day, which helped bring folks in. But it also attracted gamblers from Fort Smith."

"Horse races and gamblers," Uncle Billy said, shaking his head. "The two seem to go together. I take it there are no racehorse men around here anymore?"

"A few come in on Saturday to race outside of town a piece. I don't mind. Wasn't always this way. Cherokee Gap was a rip-roarer years ago, they tell me. Ten saloons and as many pool halls. A brawl every ten minutes. Painted women and pie-anny music. It was that way till some gunfights thinned out the toughs and the preachers swamped us. As more law-abiding folks settled here, they built the Isis — that's our opera house. We allow some play-actors to come in, if the Uplift Society approves. Sometimes even a minstrel show. Sometimes we just have readings by the school children, such as 'The Face on the Barroom Floor.' Something with a strong moral lesson."

"That will pack 'em in every time," Uncle Billy approved, laying on the piety.

"On the contrary, such programs are often presented to a near-empty house, attended only by doting parents and moralizing preachers. You can tight-rein folks just so far. On the other hand, neither do we need the undesirable element that trades and loafs here."

"What element?"

"A family . . . goes back to the old outlaw days. Three young men, brothers. Thirty years ago they would be holding up stages, trains, banks. As it is, we know they make whiskey out in the hills and steal horses. So far, Marshal Moose Butler has kept them in line, but I feel it's just a matter of time till something breaks loose. When it does, trade will suffer."

Before Uncle Billy could frame another question, a clerk stepped into the doorway. "Excuse me, Mr. Appleman. A man wants to talk to you about some harness on the credit."

"Be there in a minute." Aside, Appleman groaned, "*On the credit.* That's why I'm gonna charge two dollars for two-bits worth of cord. Am I being unreasonable, Doctor?"

"The wheels of enterprise must be greased with a fair profit, else they will cease to turn, friend Appleman."

Appleman's round face, flushed by now, beamed pure plagiarism. "*Wheels of enterprise.* Hmmmnn. And *captain of enterprise.* Glad I thought of that! Gentlemen, I want to say that I am fully in accord with the high aims of the Society."

"Thank you, friend Appleman," Uncle Billy said. "I shall note same in my next report to the Society."

"And if we can be of any further service, sir," Dude followed through, "just give us a holler."

★ ★ ★

Saturday afternoon.

The drone of the trade-day crowd had been growing louder for the past hour.

Uncle Billy looked around. "Are we all set? Where's Danny?"

"He left thirty minutes ago to mingle with the crowd," Dude answered, dumbfounded. "Don't you remember?"

The old man gave a slight start. "Guess it slipped my mind. I was thinking about the demonstration. First, I figured we would put the Eureka on Texas Jack here; then we'd only have to take it off at the store and put it back on."

"Right, Grandfather," Coyote Walking said, not quite knowing what to make of that reasoning.

A resigned roll of the blue eyes, and, "Reckon I'll never break you of that, will I?"

"Right, Grandfather."

Dude said, "He respects his elders, is all. You gonna ride or walk?"

"Walk. I'll be there when you pony up Texas Jack. Now you two know what to do?"

"You hoot owl, you've told us three times."

Dude and Coyote shared worried looks as the old man walked away. "Grandfather

Billy," said the Comanche, "his mind is far off."

"Never saw him so forgetful. And he keeps watchin' the street."

When it was time to leave, Dude led Texas Jack out on the road, the gelding on his right, as docile as an ol' pet. They were approaching the crowd gathered in front of the store when Coyote nudged with his heel. The gelding pranced sideways and tossed his head and walled his eyes.

Dude overreacted on the lead rope, calling, "Hold 'im up! Hold 'im! He's gonna bolt!"

The crowd bent like a receding wave, womenfolk squealing, and Dude, halting the horses, heard Uncle Billy's calming voice, "There's no need to be concerned, folks. Boys, bring that horse in here!" Which they did, Dude holding Texas Jack's head high to make his eyes bug. When Dude dismounted to hold the lead rope up short and Coyote stood at his shoulder, "What you're going to see demonstrated, folks, is how Professor Gleason's Eureka Bridle can subdue this high-spirited, vicious horse. . . . Now hold 'im steady there, Dude. . . . Now take the rope off your saddle and dab a loop on 'im — that's good! Hold 'im tight, he's a booger. . . . Now remove the halter. Not too fast!" Facing the crowd, "Now you men watch carefully. . . . First, the slip noose as you see here. Next, pass the cord through the mouth over the tongue from the off side, like this. . . . firmly. . . . Now over the head — just behind the ears — from the near side. . . . Now from the off side, pass the cord under the upper lip above the upper jaw, and tie firmly as you see here. . . . Take off your rope, Dude. . . . All right, Coyote! Mount up!" When Coyote was mounted, "Now take him away. Show these folks how he reins and behaves."

Coyote took Texas Jack away, reining sharply left and right, halted, moved on, turned, rode back and drew up, the gelding standing quietly.

"See!" Uncle Billy sang out. "A vicious horse made a perfect gentleman. Would one of you men like to tie the bridle on your own horse?"

A man led his saddle horse forward, and Uncle Billy produced another length of cord and began schooling the rider, step by step, while others bunched in to watch, murmuring and nodding.

While glancing idly over the crowd, Dude noticed three young horsemen. Their manner suggested disdain, not only for the demonstration, but for the onlookers, who gave them a wide berth. There was a marked likeness about the trio: coarse-featured men from the same rough mold. At times they flung surly looks at a man watching them from the rim of the crowd. A large, formidable man. A star on his vest. What had Appleman called the marshal? Butler — Moose Butler. Yes.

Presently, at a nod from the oldest rider, the three rode off.

Soon afterward a canopy-topped phaeton came lightly along the street, a stylishly dressed woman at the reins, her attention on the demonstration mildly curious. As she watched, her interest became intent. She drove to the street's end and wheeled the phaeton to drive past again, coming slowly, her gaze fixed. Opposite the demonstration, she pulled up and took an even longer look; with a snap of the whip, she drove on, wheels churning dust.

"Now, folks," Uncle Billy was concluding, "you have just witnessed the remarkable simplicity of the famed Eureka Bridle, used exclusively in the East to subdue unruly horses and mules, often made that way through inept and cruel handling. I dare say there's no man or boy here today who cannot now tie the Eureka." He paused, a measured pause that spurred the crowd's eagerness.

343

"Mister," a young voice spoke up, "I'd like to buy the first one." It was Danny playing the shill, clad in bib overalls, blue flannel shirt and straw hat. "How much is it, sir?"

"Young man, contrary to what it may seem, I am not in the business of selling bridles. My mission is to demonstrate the Eureka for the safety of mankind and beasts of burden. But I believe Mr. Appleman can accommodate you within the store."

There was a rush up the steps and into the store. Danny held back, letting himself be jostled aside. He drifted away.

Uncle Billy meandered over to Texas Jack and pretended to examine the Eureka Bridle, waiting, Dude knew.

Before many moments a farmer sidled up to the old man, a droll slyness about his face. His jaws ground on a wad of tobacco the size of a goose egg.

Finally! Dude thought.

"This here a racehorse?" the farmer asked.

Uncle Billy shrugged. "Depends on what you call a racehorse."

"He looks like a racehorse."

"Better talk to my nephew over there."

Moving in on that cue, Dude said, "Good afternoon, sir. Hope you enjoyed the demonstration."

"Did. Inter-estin'. Was lookin' at your horse. Can he run a little?"

Dude laughed. "Little's about right. When he wins sometimes, I call him a racehorse. When he loses, he's just another horse."

"Well, I got an old bay mare."

"I see."

"Sidewalls of her feet are thin. Trouble keepin' shoes on 'er. But she's shod now and she's over the windgalls."

That's it, Dude thought, smiling. Play your horse down, old-timer. "Well," he said, "I might take a look at your mare."

"Where you camped?"

Dude pointed. "End of town."

"I'll bring her over." He stuck out a horny hand. "I'm Light Ledbetter. I farm south of here."

"Pleased to make your acquaintance. I'm Dude McQuinn. On my way to Texas."

Light Ledbetter's "old bay mare," as Dude expected, turned out to be a walking picture not a day over four years old, her teeth revealed, and he could not help commenting, "If she looks this smooth when she's old, wonder what she looked like when she was young?" and Ledbetter's reply was a possum grin. "What's the young lady's name, Mr. Ledbetter?"

"Betsy Lou."

"Purty name. That's Texas Jack over there. About how far you want to run?"

"I'm not hard to get along with."

"Neither am I. What say one furlong?"

"Sounds about right."

Dude looked at him. No dickering over distance? "You are what you say you are, sir. How much you want to bet?"

"Fifty dollars."

Dude didn't say anything.

"Is that a little too steep for you?" Ledbetter was an earthy, unpretentious man, awkward and friendly, sly in a likable way, a horseman who played the game for the game's sake. Dude said, "Oh, I was just thinkin' it's a long way to Texas. Fifty's fine. When can you run?"

"Have to be this afternoon. I just come to town on Saturday."

"I understand, Mr. Ledbetter."

"Call me Light."

"Who's a fair starter?"

"Believe I can get Appleman."

"Appleman?"

"Between you and me he likes horse races. So does Marshal Butler. I would like him for a judge."

"Dr. Lockhart will represent us. And, say, where's the track?"

"On down the road a piece from here."

★ ★ ★

The sun stood at midafternoon when all the principals gathered at the track, a stretch of level prairie so seldom used the lanes were overgrown with grass. Dude was surprised at the size of the crowd streaming out from town, and when he mentioned the turnout to Ledbetter while they paced off the 220 yards, the farmer grinned crookedly. "In a town as dull as Cherokee Gap, a game of marbles draws a crowd."

Walking back to the starting line, Dude caught sight of the three riders he had seen in town. They were talking to the woman in the phaeton midway along the track.

Appleman, evidently enjoying himself, instructed Coyote and the boy riding the mare. The usual walk-up start. When the horses were lapped, Appleman would drop a flag and holler big.

To Dude's pleasure, Texas Jack took the break. You could say that for him, he always broke fairly well. But the mare, although caught flat-footed, recovered fast and was making up ground before they had covered fifty yards. She had him at one hundred. After that it was all Betsy Lou. When they crossed the marker, there was enough daylight between them to drive two hay wagons.

Dude galloped to the line, and when

Ledbetter could break away from the back-slapping, Dude paid him. "My ol' horse just didn't have it today," he said loudly for any listener who might consider odds next time. "That's not taking anything away from your mare. She's plenty fast."

Ledbetter gazed down at the easy fifty in his hand. He seemed close to apology. "I'll say this, you pay off. Last time Betsy Lou won I had to chase the other feller almost to Arkansas. You aim to be here a spell?"

"Expect so, if we match another race."

"Come down and see me. Four miles south of town. Big red barn with a Brown's Mule Tobacco sign painted on it."

"May do that, Light. Thanks. Good luck with your mare."

The outfit mounted and left for camp. Riding on, Dude saw the phaeton still parked by the track. The three riders had gone. Uncle Billy and Coyote were discussing the race as they passed the phaeton. On the road to town, Dude happened to glance back. The phaeton was coming slowly among the last of the stragglers.

Coyote was rubbing down Texas Jack, Uncle Billy pawing through the medicine chest, Danny and Dude chopping wood for the supper fire, when the phaeton stopped.

Everybody turned to look.

348

A woman stepped down.

She wore a star-shaped, flowered hat of navy blue and a stylish plaid suit with a sailor collar and a white front. A tall, erect woman whose figure held the eye, whose face was hidden behind a veil, but which could not hide the contours of a comely face and the pools of deep brown eyes.

She hesitated, then went straight to the old man. "Billy!" she said.

He stared, open-mouthed.

She drew aside the veil. "Billy, don't you remember me?"

"Katy girl," he said, more astonished than Dude had ever seen him. "Kate Taggart."

She hugged and kissed him, all of which he accepted dazedly. Stepping back, she said, "You look mighty good, Billy boy."

He hemmed and hawed and pulled on his beard before he got out, "You look mighty good too, Katy girl." And to cover his confusion, he haltingly introduced the outfit.

She shook hands with each one, on her finger an enormous diamond ring, on her somewhat sharp-featured face enough war paint for the whole Comanche tribe, Dude thought. She was, he judged, fifty-five if she was a day, but she looked forty-five — a good-looking forty-five. He sensed a timelessness about her, an impression that she had outlasted her era, perhaps, and yet was still the same strong-willed person, unwilling to accept change.

"Well, Billy," she said, the deep brown eyes taking in the camp. "I see you still have a runnin' horse." She lifted a teasing eyebrow. "Except he didn't look so good today. All right on the break, but after that . . ."

"Texas Jack belongs to Dude. We shouldn't have run him today. He's out of condition. But he'll come back, give him a little while."

"Mean you'll match him again here?"

"Might, when he's ready."

Full-bodied, she strolled around Texas Jack, her experienced eyes sizing up, and from him to the other horses. "Now this," she said, eyeballing Judge Blair, "looks like a real runnin' horse. Good bone, good muscle, good balance."

"That old packhorse!" Uncle Billy hooted. "He couldn't outrun a hop toad. You've lost your judgment, Kate."

"That's one thing I've never lost." Her face hardened momentarily, then smoothed, teasing him again. "I could have told you not to match Light Ledbetter's mare. And that demonstration I saw! Couldn't believe it was you. What was that all about, anyway?"

"You called it right. A demonstration of Professor Gleason's Eureka Bridle. Ever hear of it?"

"Now, Billy. Must be some new wrinkle of yours?"

His shrug was enigmatic.

She laughed. "Same old Billy boy. Well — for old times' sake, how would you and the boys like to come to dinner at my place tomorrow evening?"

When Uncle Billy didn't answer, Dude spoke up, "Why, thank you, ma'am, we'd be pleased and honored," and saw the old man frown.

"Come out early," she said, "and the name is Kate. I want to show you the fastest hunk of horseflesh from here to Memphis — my stud Jackpot. I live past the gap. My name's on the gate." She strolled to the phaeton and turned, ridicule curling her red lips. "Watch out for the street cars when you go through town."

She drove away.

"*Katy girl* and *Billy boy*," Dude cooed sweetly. "Well . . . well."

"Shut up!"

Chapter 17

The four of them turned off the road by the wooden sign set in stone that read: KATE TAGGART'S RANCH — though Dude could see no cattle grazing the green pastures — and as if the stone were a harbinger, a two-story stone house rose over the next fold of wooded hills. Stone house and stone barn and stone corrals. You didn't see such masonry every day, yet not until Dude rode up to the house did he feel any great oddity about the place. That was when he saw the loopholes, narrowed to mere slits.

They sat their horses for some moments before dismounting and tying up at the long railing. There was no one about. Dude climbed the long flight of stone steps and knocked on the heavy door. No one answered. He knocked again.

At the fourth knock the door opened and Kate Taggart greeted him. She wore a long, dark green skirt and a sleeveless, light green blouse. Her dark hair, knotted on the back of her neck, gave her rouged face a slim look.

"The walls of this house are so thick you can't hear a thing," she apologized. "Come in. Let me take your hats."

For Uncle Billy she had a kiss on the cheek, for the others a horsewoman's firm handshake. As she led them down a hallway, past the staircase and into the parlor, Dude came face to face with a full-size portrait of a glowering man: high-peaked big hat, purple shirt, gray twill trousers tucked in black boots decorated with white steer heads. Big-knuckled hands on hips. Two big six-guns hung on a broad, silver-buckled belt.

"This," she said, "is a painting of my late husband, Big Jim. I had an artist come down from St. Louis to do it." She called up the stairway, "Boys! Boys! Company's here! Come a-runnin'!" Turning to Uncle Billy, "Now you sit right over there on the sofa."

Dude heard a clomping down the stairs, across the hall to the doorway, and his eyes fixed on the three surly riders of town. Each had the same glowering visage of the bellicose man in the painting, the same jutting brows, the same piercing gray eyes, the same heavy jaw, the same coarse, ill-humored mouth — distinguished only by age.

"I want you-all to meet my boys," she said, her mother's voice proud. "This is Monte — and this is Lucky — and this is Tooter."

Monte was the oldest and tallest. Middle twenties, Dude figured. Next in age and stature came Lucky, then Tooter.

"Just like stairsteps," she said fondly. "Tooter gets mad when I call him the baby."

Tooter glowered like the man in the painting.

Each shook hands, muttered "Howdy," and stepped back until they formed a front, Monte on the right, then Lucky, then Tooter. They had sat their horses in that same alignment, Dude remembered from town. Monte on the end, next Lucky, next Tooter.

"Now," she told them, beaming, "you boys go get Jackpot ready to show these gentlemen."

They left without word or change of expression, first Monte, then Lucky, then Tooter.

She seated herself beside Uncle Billy and squeezed his hand. "Can't tell you how plumb tickled I am to see you again, Billy boy. Now tell me about your friends." She favored them all her hospitable smile.

"Dude, there," the old man began, "is one of those Alamo Texans. Still calls the Great Rebellion the War Between the States. He's kind of on the circle now" — he dropped one eyelid in a knowing wink — "if you get what I mean. Seems his calves didn't foller the right cows. . . . Danny, there, is a song-and-dance man and can make a harmonica howl . . . has trod the boards of the Palace in Denver . . . Coyote, there, is the son of the chief of all Comanches. You saw how he rode today — got the best out of a tard horse. He's an educated Indian. Honor graduate of that Carlisle School."

"My," she said, sounding impressed. "So you're just traveling around?"

"Oh, we match a race now and then as we work toward Texas. Want to smuggle Dude across Red River if we can. He's homesick for wind and dust, hoot owls and rattle-snakes."

Amused, she leaned closer to pick lint off Uncle Billy's coat, her low-necked blouse showing smooth, white shoulders and an expanse of snowy bosom. "You're a sight for sore eyes, Billy boy," she murmured.

"And you're as pretty as ever — even pret-tier."

"Billy . . . you're such a tease," she laughed delightedly and squeezed him again. She had a provocative manner of laughing, brittle as it was. She straightened his tie, her hands lingering over him, and tweeked his cheek. "You'll never get old," she said.

"I can't believe you're the mother of three grown boys," he came back. "Why, you could be their younger sister."

She blushed prettily and looked down at her hands.

Dude listened, shocked. What was this? Was she part of the old man's shadowy past? Had there been a busted romance, with her marrying Big Jim Taggart?

When Kate said, "Although I cannot, in all modesty, believe one little word you've said, I can see that you're still a devil with the ladies," Dude cut in; "Indeed, he is, ma'am. He hasn't changed one little bit. That's the real reason why we've come to this remote part of the territory, and why we generally have to pass through towns at night."

"At night?"

"It's much safer."

"Safer?"

"Pinkertons," he whispered, his tone ominous, and let that stand for whatever it might mean.

"Why, Billy," she shrilled, "I didn't know you had a wife and family."

"It's not that," Dude supplied fast, ignoring the old man's killing look. "He's a free man. The rub is there's a widow woman back in Missouri with six kids that's draggin' her rope for him. Claims breach of promise."

"Billy," she shrilled again, giving him a nudge, "you *are* a devil!"

Dude was thinking still faster. "Why she's after him, I can't figure out. Did you ever know an old horseman that had any money put away?" There! He had managed to get that in.

Monte entered at that saving instant, behind him Lucky and Tooter. "Jackpot's ready for the showin'," he announced.

They trailed out to the main stone corral, Kate hanging on the old man's arm like a bride-to-be, the two of them chattering and giggling and as often whispering, their heads touching, carrying on enough to make a body sick. Dude could only wonder and vent his disgust in silence.

Monte opened an iron gate, and when everyone was inside, he carefully slid an iron bar across to hold the gate fast; and with Lucky and Tooter following, he opened another iron gate to a stall on the far side of the corral.

A rumble of hoofs, a volley of snorts, and

the gate opened and a buckskin stud shot out, the three "boys" jerking on the halter rope like puppets.

Kate Taggart yelled, "Hold 'im — you idiots! Want Jackpot to hurt himself! Tooter — you lend a better hand there!"

Buckskin stud and trio went tearing around the corral twice before order was restored. Dude was impressed. If Jackpot was an inch he was seventeen hands high, and if he weighed an ounce he weighed fourteen hundred pounds, all big bone and long muscle.

"Katy girl," Uncle Billy said, his tone syrupy sweet, "you've got yourself a powerful-looking horse."

"Glad you think so. You may not know sic 'em about widow women, but you do know horses. Jackpot holds records from here to Memphis and Springfield. Can't even match him, anymore."

"An old story with a good horse. What's his best distance?"

"Depends how far the other side wants to run," she evaded, "and how much they want to put up."

Cagey, Dude thought, cagey.

She played the old man a come-on smile. "Think you might like to match us, Billy boy?"

"It's up to Dude. Texas Jack is his horse."

"Well, Dude?" she smiled.

"Might — when Texas Jack is ready."

"When is when?"

"Week or so."

"How much might tickle your fancy?"

"Not much. A few hundred, maybe. Maybe less."

Arms akimbo, she wiggled her slim hips. "Where's that Texas brag and put-up? You talk like some Iowa farmer in a potato-sack race at the county fair. I won't lead this stud out on the track for less than a thousand, and I don't mean promises. I mean one thousand dollars in sight."

Dude fell to whistling "Dixie" and looking off at the hills. "I'd have to have odds . . . something like four to one."

"Four to one! You're out of your mind!" She was close to shrieking, instantly furious, her eyes narrowing to nailheads.

He said calmly, "Now wouldn't I be a fool to bet my tard ol' horse even money against your mighty Jackpot? Wouldn't I, ma'am?"

"We can talk about it later," she said, subsiding, "after we've put on the feed bag. Boys, take Jackpot back. See that he gets fresh hay and water from the springhouse. Now, Tooter, you help!"

At the house she showed them into the

parlor again, and when the brothers stomped in, she ordered them to the kitchen to "fetch the refreshments." Monte came in with a brown, earthenware jug, Lucky and Tooter bearing glasses.

"Thought you might like a bracer after seeing Jackpot," she said, fixing Uncle Billy a sidelong smile.

"I always have one little toddy before dinner," he said, as proper as could be.

"Pour your own medicine. Since you can't buy whiskey in town, we have to make our own. The boys call it Old Canyon Run."

Only Coyote Walking abstained.

Dude raised his glass. "Here's to a very lovely lady of the turf and the mighty Jackpot." She sparkled at the toast. He took one sip and felt fire scald his mouth, his throat, his chest, until it plunged a burning rope to the pit of his stomach, there to coil and smolder. A great flush overspread his face. Uncle Billy smothered a cough. Danny, after a taste, set his glass down.

The "boys" downed theirs at a single thrust, showing no more reaction than had they drunk spring water. Kate Taggart sipped. "I've always believed," she said, "that if a boy is gonna drink, let him start at home." She jerked. "Tooter, take your feet off that chair! Put 'em on the floor where they belong. Don't know why it is the baby boy is always the most spoilt."

Glowering, Tooter obeyed.

"And all of you boys," she barked, "take off your hats!" Noticing Coyote's abstinence, she remarked to Uncle Billy, "What's the matter with your Indian friend? He's not drinking."

"Never drinks when he's training."

"Other way around with most jockeys I've seen. Can he talk American?"

"Can he? I told you he's an honor graduate of Carlisle School."

"So you did. Well, I reckon my boys figured they knew it all, because every year when Big Jim started 'em in school again, they always quit after the first week and never went back."

A thin, meek-faced woman came to the doorway. "Supper is served, ma'am."

Kate Taggart looked at Uncle Billy and he at her, and he rose and bowed and offered his arm and she took it with a tilt of her head — enough carrying on, Dude grimaced, to make a body sick again. But as the couple stepped lightly toward the doorway, her sons crowded in ahead, Tooter the foremost.

"Boys!" she rasped, her voice like a whip. "Pull back there! Tooter, you're gonna get a talkin' to!"

They held up, glowering, silent, until the guests had passed.

Uncle Billy seated her, more mannerly than Dude could ever recall. Thus, at the head of the table, Uncle Billy and Coyote Walking on her right, and Dude and Danny on her left, and the "boys" at the other end, the hostess was about to commence dinner when Dude saw her freeze.

"Did you boys wash up and comb your hair?" she questioned.

With hangdog looks, they trekked to the kitchen. Dude could hear splashing and grumbling and tramping about. They clomped back shortly, their wet-combed hair slicked down, Tooter wiping his hands across his shirt front.

Family style! Dude hadn't sat down to such a spread since leaving the old homeplace on the Salt Fork — fried chicken, beans and ham hock, biscuits and cornbread, yellow squash sweetened just right, black-eyed peas, green beans and butter beans, potatoes swimming in lakes of gravy, grape jelly and plum jelly, coffee and milk. He dug in.

No one spoke for a long while. The brothers were literally shoveling away, chins almost touching their heaped plates. Of a sudden Tooter stopped in midmouth. His jaws continued to work. He swallowed and muttered, "These beans ain't salty enough, Ma," and pushed back his plate.

Something flicked across her face. Without a word, she turned and reached down behind her and brought up a buggy whip. Swiftly, she popped the lash at the ear of her complaining youngest. "Eat them beans, Tooter!"

He lowered his head and ate, wolfishly.

Afterward: apple pie, peach pie, cherry pie, blackberry pie, and more coffee.

"Tooter," Kate Taggart barked after the dessert, "pass the cigars — and wipe your mouth." As Tooter was rising to his feet, "And put in your shirttail — and buckle your belt!"

Lighting up and leaning back, Uncle Billy said, "I can say without doubt that Jackpot is the biggest and strongest-looking racehorse of my memory — bigger than Peter McCue. Mind telling me his breeding?"

"Been wondering when you would get around to that," she said, rolling her red lips. "Jackpot traces back to Sir Archy on his sire's side, and back to Gabriel through his dam. Can you tie that?"

"Thunderation, he's well-bred!"

"None better."

Dude, funning, made as if to leave. "We might as well go now, Uncle. Texas Jack is out of his class."

"Don't let me skedaddle you," she said. "I'll match you and let you choose the distance, anything up to a mile — but no four-to-one odds."

"Three to one?"

Her dark eyes seemed to ignite. "No three to one, either."

She had a temper, Dude knew by now. She was a mercurial person, shrewd and competitive, made so from rearing three surly sons and surviving in a horseman's slick world. He felt both admiration and wariness of her.

"How would you bet?" he fished.

"The day we match, this I'll tell you."

"To tell you the truth, dear lady, I'd rather have a head start than odds any day."

That triggered her unpredictable laughter, and still laughing, she stood and everyone filed into the parlor, she on Uncle Billy's arm. "Would it not be appropriate, Billy boy," she asked, "if Danny rendered us a number or two?"

"It would, my Katy girl."

Dude sickened at the valentine romantics. Now it was *my* Katy girl.

Smiling and obliging, Danny blew into the mouth organ and promptly swung into the tender notes of "Lorena," that song Grandpa McQuinn had said both sides sang during the War Between the States — yes, by damn it! — the War Between the States. As he finished, incongruous snores broke the quiet.

"Tooter!" Kate Taggart roared. Flashing up and across, she kicked the soles of Tooter's boots. "Now off to bed! Lucky and Monte can stay here!"

Tooter yawned and sat up. Glowering, he left the room.

As the evening waned and the outfit took its leave, and Kate Taggart saw them to the door, she pecked Uncle Billy on the cheek and said, "I'd like to match this race some Saturday, if for nothing else, to wake up the town. It's like a cemetery without head-stones."

"You'll have to work that out with Dude, Katy girl."

Riding through the darkness of the hills, Dude mused aloud, "Wonder what ever happened to Big Jim?"

"Your guess is as good as mine," the old man replied, his tone noncommittal.

"Didn't you know him?"

Dude waited for the ambiguous, the half-mocking, half-funning, yet always amusing, "Did I say?" But it didn't come.

They rode on in silence.

After a very long moment, Uncle Billy said, "That was a long time ago, Dude — a mighty long time ago," and said no more.

.

Chapter 18

Dude McQuinn could not define the feeling that bothered him, this uneasiness, this foreboding, this wrongness, while Blue Grass carried him along the country road. It was like a tiny voice cautioning him not to go through with the match race that was building.

Why would Kate Taggart, with the top horse of the region — if he could believe her brags — be so eager to match an itinerant outfit? And why would she make over an old gent years her senior, even admitting that Uncle Billy was an exceptional specimen for his age, as spry as a coon dog after his toddies and naps? Yet, could it be the revival of a faded romance from long ago, or was she after his place-by-the-f'ar money?

He had expressed his reservations about the match race to Uncle Billy.

"Well, it's your horse, Dude, pardner."

"Judge Blair's *our* horse, really. We've always worked together, been pardners. I just feel we're getting in over our heads."

"It's Kate Taggart?"

"It is. I don't trust her."

"First time I ever heard you say that about a woman. You're wising up to 'em. Sign of maturity, of horse sense." That evident but impenetrable saintliness began to slide into his face, that inscrutable look that always foretold the unexpected. "Well, I have been around the track a time or two. Just remember, this old hoss knows where the finish line is." He slapped Dude on the shoulder, and that was the end of the conversation, and Dude knew no more than he did before.

Dude turned in at the Brown's Mule sign painted black on the red barn and rode past the house and on to the well, dismounted and watered Blue Grass at the stone trough.

A red-faced woman waddled out on the back porch, wiping hands on her apron as she came, her friendly eyes inquiring. He took off his hat. "Is Light Ledbetter about, ma'am?"

"He's out on the track, gallopin' his race mare. He can't seem to turn his hand at anything else since he won that race in town."

"Well," Dude laughed, "I'm the fellow whose horse he beat."

"Go on past the barn. You'll find him goin' 'round and 'round."

Passing through a maze of corrals and sheds, Dude came to a bullring track. At this moment Ledbetter was working his mare around the far turn. When Dude waved, he galloped up and dismounted. Dude joined him as he walked the mare back and forth to cool her down.

"Have you matched another race?" Dude asked.

"May take her over to Fort Smith before long."

"She's fast. How's she bred?"

"Copper Bottom blood on both sides."

"That will do to bet on."

Ledbetter's eyes were curious. "What's on your mind this morning, my friend?"

"Need some questions answered, in confidence."

"Might — if you'll stay for dinner, then ride with me over to a neighbor's to look at his horse colt?"

"I think I can manage that," Dude smiled.

"All right, shoot."

"How good a horse is Kate Taggart's Jackpot?"

"He's cleaned out Fort Smith and Little Rock, the north half of Louisiana and the south half of Missouri. He's never lost at the quarter mile and he can go longer."

"Whew! A scorpion. Ever run Betsy Lou at him?"

"I've tried, but Kate's a plunger. Bets the moon. Heck fire, if I lost a thousand dollars I'd have to sell my farm." His jaws ground cudlike and stilled. "Aim to match her?"

"It's not final. Just talk so far."

"Pardon me for sayin' so, but Texas Jack can't stay with Jackpot. Not the way he ran the other day."

"He can run a lot faster when he's ready."

"We always think that, don't we?"

A windmill, its wheel groaning, its sucker rods slapping, pumped water into a stone trough by the barn. After Ledbetter let the mare drink her fill, he led her to a stall and rubbed her down from head to hindquarters, dumped oats into her feedbox, and climbed to the haymow. But a moment there, he stepped down waggling a hook-necked jug. He wore a devilish grin.

"My number one transgression. The second is tobacco. The third is two-fold: horse racin' and gamblin'." Taking the cob stopper from the jug, he passed it to Dude, who laid it over his shoulder, turned his head just so, and had a long swallow. The whiskey was smooth and cool, slightly sweet. He smacked his lips. "Light, you're as good a judge of whiskey as you are of horse-flesh."

"I see you know how to drink out of a jug."

"Learned on buttermilk."

They sat on bales of hay in the barn's cool runway, just talking horses, and directly Dude worked around to, "Light, can you tell me what happened to Big Jim Taggart?"

Ledbetter took a short pull at the jug and sat it down softly in the straw. "Big Jim was killed ten years ago when he robbed the Cherokee Gap bank."

"By a posse?"

"Never got that far. Moose Butler shot him as he ran out of the bank with the money bags."

A scene jumped before Dude's eyes: the three surly riders at the demonstration glaring at Butler, Butler glaring at them, virtually daring them. "So Big Jim was an outlaw?"

"Not officially till then. Never anything on him that could be proved. Everybody knew he was selling whiskey to the Cherokees back in the hills, rustling cattle and horses . . . driving 'em into Arkansas to sell to traders, who moved 'em on south. Some years before that when the bank was robbed, everybody figured Big Jim had a hand in that, too, but another man went to prison for it. That was a little before my time around here."

"How did Kate figure in all this?"

"I don't like to say this about a woman, but she was the brains. She was known as Queen of the Outlaws, though nothing could be proved."

"Huh — an outlaw queen. What happened after Big Jim was shot?"

The horseman's slow grin took hold again. "Kinda the retired queen then, you might say. Mostly horse racin'. Some whiskey peddlin'. Some weekends she runs poker games at the ranch for Cherokee Gap businessmen."

"What about her three boys?"

"Mean as hell — made meaner by ignorance. They've got the whole town buffaloed — Moose Butler excepted. Monte's the only one with much sense. But I figure the one they call Tooter is the most dangerous. He's another Big Jim on a smaller scale. If it wasn't for Kate, they'd all be in the pen by now."

"If we match this race," Dude said, "I'd appreciate it if you will be a judge?"

"Glad to."

"Who rides for Kate?"

"Tooter — and he's cob rough. He'll take

your horse to the outside if he can." Ledbetter passed the jug again.

Five o'clock had come when Dude reached camp to find Coyote and Danny working on supper.

"Where's Uncle?"

"Grandfather Billy," said Coyote, "taking bath he is at the creek."

"What's the unusual occasion?"

When Coyote was slow to answer, Danny said, "He didn't say."

"That means he's up to something."

Watching the creek while he unsaddled, Dude glimpsed movement. A figure departing the trees and brush — a ghostly figure, as one might imagine a Biblical patriarch coming out of the wilderness. A strolling Uncle Billy, clad in winter underwear, which he wore the year round, his uncut hair a snow-white mane, his legs like bowed pipe stems, a towel flung togalike over one shoulder. He was whistling that Yankee song, "The Battle Hymn of the Republic." He nodded to Dude and no more on his way to the wagon.

There he squinted into a small mirror hanging by the medicine chest and carefully trimmed his beard, still whistling, after which he splashed something from a bottle on his hands and patted his beard. Dude got a whiff of bay rum. In order, Uncle Billy donned white shirt and string tie and frock-coated suit, dusted his boots, crimped his hat, saddled Judge Blair and rode away.

"Wonder where he's going?" Danny speculated.

"Four to one it's the widow Taggart's," Dude said.

Past midnight Dude heard the old man ride up whistling that song and noisily unsaddle. Sitting up, Dude saw this figure lurch over to the water bucket and take a long, gulping drink, making as much noise as a horse, and start undressing, sounding like a man stomping snakes as he hopped first on one foot, then the other, struggling to remove his boots. After much grunting and cussing, he reeled past Dude to his bedroll, leaving a trail of sour-mash fumes.

Dude woke up to a voice and hungering smells — Uncle Billy's call to breakfast, and coffee boiling, bacon frying and biscuits baking in the Dutch oven.

"You hoot owl, you," Dude scolded him, "you slept in your boots and pants."

The saintly visage looked as fresh and guileless as a country girl at a pie supper. "Did you ever try to get your boots off when the air's damp at night?"

"And," Dude went on, merciless, "you threw your frock coat over the wagon wheel. Just look at that!"

"Now, Dude, pardner, don't you figure that's better than sleeping in it?"

"Besides, you came home roostered."

"Seems I recall something in the Good Book that applies to your assumption. It goes like this: Let him that is without sin among you, let him cast the first stone."

"*At her*, Grandfather," Coyote finished. " 'Let him cast the first stone at her.' "

"And there's another line from somewhere," the old man said, ignoring Coyote, "that goes: Come an' get it or I'll throw it out!" He turned to the breakfast makin's.

Afterward, he saddled the Judge and rode to the general store, gone a long time. Shortly before noon, a clerk delivered several packages at the camp for "Dr. Lockhart." That afternoon Uncle Billy again saddled up and rode to the barber shop. Upon his return Dude noted certain changes. The old man's long hair had been shortened to fashionable length and his beard tidied to a stylish point.

About an hour before suppertime, the old man took his packages behind the wagon. Muttered cusswords and grunts and tuggings marked this interval.

"How do you like it?" he crowed, parading out.

Dude pretended shock. "What is it?"

"For your information," came the affronted reply, "this is the latest round-cut suit made of brown, twilled Melton . . . and this," preening himself, "is a style A-linen collar. Note, if you will, the turned-down ends . . . unequaled for verve . . . and the four-in-hand green cravat of Japanese silk . . . and the handmade boots."

"You do look slick, Uncle."

"By the way, I won't be here for supper."

He rode off whistling that annoying Yankee song, heading for the gap.

"There," said Dude worriedly to the others, "goes a man with the most dangerous case of calico fever I've ever seen."

Each evening thereafter the old man slicked up and saddled out to the Taggart ranch, returning at a late hour, whistling and singing and stumbling around in the dark. In addition, he rode Judge Blair into town once every morning and afternoon, alternately tying the gelding in front of the bank and the general store.

When one morning, Dude gently broached the radical departure from Uncle Billy's usual habits, he was told, "You know, that fella never has got in the veterinary supplies I ordered. Right now I'm out of lobelia and fenugreek."

"Since when did the bank start selling horse medicine?"

A pained look. "You lost in Cherokee Gap? Don't you know the drugstore is right next to the bank, and sometimes the hitching rail is full?"

"And what's going on every day at the general store?"

"Friend Appleman has the saddle-horse fever. Wants me to advise him on how to buy when he goes to Springfield next month."

"I'd like to talk to you about something else," Dude said, awkward about it. Leading him beyond earshot of the others, Dude cleared his throat and commenced. "Now, Uncle, we've been pardners for a long time. You've schooled me in everything I know about runnin' horses. How to hang my head and hem and haw and look off and not act eager when talkin' match. How to size up the other man's horse and tell a horse's age by his teeth . . . to look for that long shoulder, that powerful forearm, that muscular stifle and deep girth. How to counter, up and down, and work around to your horse's best distance. Above all, how to make your horse look easy pickin's and get odds." He paused, swallowed, stumbled on,

"You showed me what can be at the end of the rainbow when a man's got two look-alike horses — one fast, one slow. How to match the slow horse a time or two, get him beat, then match again and switch to the fast horse — at the same time to keep from gettin' outslicked by the other side. . . . You showed me the sideways break — how to turn the Judge a little bit so he takes one short step first and swings into his start. . . . You've schooled me in all that." He swallowed again; his throat thickened. "I never told you this before, but my own father died when I was seven. Horse fell with him — we went to live with Grandpa McQuinn — mama and me. Grandpa raised me. Remember, he was in the War Between the States?"

"I'm not likely to forget that," Uncle Billy smiled.

Dude gulped, almost overcome. "You've been like a father to me. We've been through a lot together, the two of us and Coyote, and Jason back there, and now Danny. We've always stuck together. If one of us got in a tight, the others helped him out. We've been shot at, but never hit. We've been chased, but never caught. Along the way we've helped out some folks that needed helpin'."

"What are you trying to tell me, Dude?"

"It's that Taggart woman," Dude blurted. "I know she's a walkin' picture for her age and sets a good table. But . . ." He couldn't bring himself to say, not wanting to hurt the old man's feelings.

"But what?"

"She's after your money. I just know she is."

The old man burst into laughter. "What money?"

"The money you've saved back for your place by the f'ar. For that little hotel you used to talk about, you on the front porch with your feet propped up, watchin' folks go by. I want you to have that."

"That? Sure, I've put a little back. But Kate Taggart could buy and sell me forty times over."

"Richer they are, the more they want," Dude warned. "Besides, I don't want her makin' a fool out of you."

"Mean she has?"

Dude let that touchy one go by, deciding enough had been said. What more could he say?

It was not Uncle Billy's way to show affection. But now he placed a hand on Dude's shoulder and his voice carried an unusual earnestness. "I haven't forgotten what you told that Sweetwater Smith fella when he got the drop on us. You meant what you said. For a second there, the way you kept comin' at him, I was afraid he'd pull the trigger. Your Grandfather McQuinn brought you up right — be true to your friends and respect womanhood." He was studying the toes of his boots. "Just remember there are two sides to a coin and what —" He cut off at the rapid trotting of a horse.

Dude turned at the same time, seeing Kate Taggart pull up and step down from the phaeton.

" 'Morning," she called cheerfully, her greeting for the whole outfit. "Just wondered if we might talk us up a little horse race?"

She cut a striking figure, Dude was aware — flowered hat and veil, and a gray traveling suit that went in and out at the right places. Strolling toward them, she revealed a neat ankle. She drew the veil back to buss Uncle Billy fully on the mouth.

"It's up to Dude," he told her.

"Well, Dude," she said, playing her eyes upon him.

Somehow he felt he should back out now. In spite of that, he found himself responding to the old give and take, the jockeying for the advantage, partly, he sensed, because

Uncle Billy was for the race. And he heard himself saying, "How much you want to bet?"

"Make it easy on yourself."

"I won't run my horse unless I get odds."

"I might listen to something reasonable."

"I'll try to be. I won't start with four to one."

"You'd better not!" She had a tighter hold on her natural aggressiveness today, not that he failed to see its flash.

"But I will have to have three to one." He put it flatly, with finality, hoping she would throw it back at him and stalk away and the race would be off.

To the contrary, she looked to be running that through her mind. She paced off and back and said, "You take both hair and hide."

"Frankly, I figure I'm a fool to run you."

"Then why holler go at me?"

"Because I'm a gambler, and because I think my horse has a chance."

"Maybe you're betting the jockey?"

"Partly. But a jockey can't carry a horse over the line."

"Well, I'm a gambler, too. You've got your three-to-one odds. I'll bet three thousand to your one thousand. Tobias Appleman can hold the stakes."

"I'll have to go for that," he said, surprised.

Her dark eyes hurled amusement. "I figured you would."

"How far you want to run?"

"You can name it."

His mind reached back to Jackpot's impressive conformation: all bone and long muscle. Power. Distance. He thought of Judge Blair's quickness and the swinging break. He said, "Three hundred and fifty yards," and saw Uncle Billy jog his chin. At the same instant, Dude set himself for her to up the distance.

"You're on," she said, her eyes never leaving his face, his own unable to leave hers. "When?" she asked.

"Saturday?"

"I like Saturday. I want folks to see my horse run. What time?"

Strange, how he felt on the defensive, when she was giving him the choices. "Two o'clock," he said.

"Mind making it at three?"

"Three o'clock is as good as two."

"Guess Tobias suits you for the starter?"

"He does."

"The owners to pick a judge and Tobias the third one?"

Dude nodded, yet left uneasy by the rapidity with which the conditions were being agreed on.

She held out a gloved hand. They shook, her grip as strong as a man's. He didn't want to run her, but he was. Those deep brown eyes behind the veil seemed hypnotic, as hard as nailheads.

She went to the phaeton, stepped up and in and drove away, faster than she had come.

Chapter 19

The few days before a race were always periods of monotony and boredom. These seemed even more tedious to Dude, while Uncle Billy resumed his twice-daily rides to town and his evening calls on Kate Taggart. Except to leave the wager with Appleman at the store, and slipping out before dawn with the old man and Coyote Walking to work the Judge on a remote country lane west of town, Dude stuck to camp.

Friday evening came. In lieu of going calling, Uncle Billy occupied himself at his medicine chest, pouring and mixing. Behind the wagon he covered Judge Blair's blaze so that he became a look-alike Texas Jack, and painted a blaze on Texas Jack's face so that he was another Judge Blair.

"Kind of early, aren't you?" Dude said, looking on.

"What if somebody came snooping around here early in the morning?"

"Nobody ever has."

"There's always a first time."

The remainder of the evening passed without any departures from routine, the Judge tied behind the wagon where he could be guarded, the other horses picketed on pasture near the creek. The outfit retired for the night and slept soundly between watches, Uncle Billy by choice standing the last hours before daylight.

While the others busied with breakfast, Coyote went to the creek to bring up the horses for grain. He ran back, shouting, "Texas Jack — gone he is!"

"Gone?" Dude walked over to him. "Probably pulled his picket pin."

"Picket pin and rope are there — Texas Jack is not."

They all ran to the creek. Only the sorrel team and Blue Grass grazed on picket ropes.

"Let's fan out up and down the creek," Dude said. Scouting downcreek through the timber with Uncle Billy, he found no sign of the horse. When they hurried back, Coyote and Danny were waiting.

"Coyote picked up the tracks," Danny said. "Somebody led Texas Jack off."

Both anger and a sense of personal loss filled Dude. Poor Texas Jack! He couldn't outrun the proverbial fat man, but he looked like a racehorse. He was gentle and trustworthy. An easy keeper. All the outfit liked him. He was a friend. Moreover, he made the look-alike game work.

"All we can do now," he said, "is report it to the marshal."

Glum and silent, they plodded back to camp.

Even this early the town was taking on the appearance of a holiday when Dude and Uncle Billy started searching for Moose Butler. Vehicles of all makes and vintages parked helter-skelter. Families taking choice places under the trees for picnics. Kids on the loose. Hitching racks beginning to fill. Country folk come to enjoy the rarity of fun and entertainment in strait-laced Cherokee Gap. Tobias Appleman had strung a red-white-and-blue banner across the face of his store. And, with his keen eye for trade, a front-window display of cord lengths arranged in shapes of bridles and this placard:

SOLD ONLY HERE!
PROFESSOR GLEASON'S
WONDROUS EUREKA BRIDLE
IT WILL HOLD ANY HORSE
OR MULE
UNDER ANY CIRCUMSTANCES

Moose Butler was leaning against one corner of the drugstore, watching the milling crowd. He looked the part of a marshal: thick of shoulder, lean of waist, a long, straight nose, a firmly shut mouth, and shaggy dark eyebrows shading eyes of stern gray.

"It's my ol' Shorty horse," Dude explained the theft forthwith. "Dark bay, four white feet and a blazed face. I sure think a lot of that horse."

"That the horse Dr. Lockhart's been riding around town?"

"It is."

"Those markings make him easy to spot. But don't get your hopes up. By now your horse is likely over in Arkansas."

In camp, Dude saddled Blue Grass and took the road through the gap for some miles, questioning incoming farm families as he went. No, they'd seen no such horse. Other searches south and west of town also proved fruitless. By then the morning was wasted.

The day was going to be a scorcher, and the outfit led the Judge to the creek and tied him in the shade. Danny brought bread and meat and cold coffee from the wagon. There would be no preparations for a quick exodus, Dude said, because, win or lose, they were all going to look for Texas Jack after the race.

The tedium mounted with each minute.

Judge Blair dozed, standing hipshot.

Danny and Coyote played mumble-peg. Coyote lost and had to pull up the peg with his teeth.

Dude paced back and forth, his mind more on Texas Jack than the race.

Uncle Billy tinkered in the medicine chest.

At one-thirty Light Ledbetter rode up to say he was sorry about the stolen horse. He would keep his eyes open. He wished them luck and left.

At two-fifteen Appleman walked over to tell them that the third judge was a farmer living north of town. Name of Art Roff.

"Light Ledbetter's our judge," Dude told him. "Who's Kate Taggart got?"

"One of her hired hands. Well, good luck, boys."

By two-thirty the road was a river of race-goers. At two-forty the outfit saddled Judge Blair at the wagon. As they finished, Dude saw Kate Taggart ponying Jackpot by. Tooter was aboard the buckskin stud, Lucky trailing. Where was Monte?

Ready. Dude mounted and led his horse out on the road, Uncle Billy and Danny following on the sorrels. The crowd had thinned to a trickle. Behind them, Cherokee Gap looked like a ghost town.

The track was a short ride down the road from camp, just a stretch of prairie marked by two race paths. Today it could be the assembly point for a land run: swarms of wagons and buggies and horsemen and people afoot, a few on high-wheeled bicycles. Overall, the chattering excitement of a race-day crowd, the same whether here or San Antone, Dude thought.

Appleman arrived a step behind the outfit. He had found a silk hat to go with his Prince Albert suit for his role as the official starter. "Glad I thought of this!" he yelled at Dude, tapping his hat, hooking thumbs under his lapels as he flexed his knees. Stepping to the center of the track, he waved and shouted for the crowd to get off. At the same time, Marshal Butler began shooing people back.

Striking a pose, Appleman called to the pony riders,

"We'll now have the parade to post. Take your horses to the finish line and back, then we'll start this here horse race!"

Jackpot, excited by the crowd, made a lunge that cleared his side of the track at once. Boy, did he have size and muscle! Kate

Taggart tossed Dude a tight little vying look and calmly took the stud to the center of the track and on to the finish line, Dude content to follow.

Briefly, and the horses reached the starting end of the track. Kate and Lucky watched while Tooter kept the buckskin in check.

Dude looked around. Monte? Where was Monte? Not that it mattered.

With Uncle Billy at the start, Dude galloped downtrack to catch the finish. When he looked back, Monte still had not joined the Taggarts. The horses were evenly lapped as they walked up. Appleman was holding his silk hat high. Abruptly, he swung it down with a shouted "Go!"

A clean getaway. Judge Blair in the swinging break — first that short step to pull on, then the long stride. He outbroke the stud by a length.

Without delay, Tooter larruped away with the whip. Within the first hundred yards he had the buckskin's nose at the Judge's flank. Jackpot was truly charging now. He closed to the Judge's withers, to the Judge's head.

There Tooter began to bear right, to force Coyote to the outside. So Light Ledbetter had warned Dude. So Dude had warned Coyote. He saw Coyote give away a little.

Unless Coyote surrendered more ground, the horses would bump. If he surrendered too much, he would be off the track.

Dude punched the air. *Whoop at him, Coyote! Come on — you two! Get out of there!*

So late it seemed it would never come, Dude heard the screeching yell tear from Coyote's throat — savage, goading, calling on the Judge to run faster.

Nothing appeared to change, yet there was a change. Coyote wasn't giving ground. He didn't have to. He was tearing on. He had room. Tooter couldn't take him out because Tooter wasn't on the lead.

The horses were sprinting almost head to head along the rim of the track. Screams rose as the crowd curled back.

As the horses pounded by, Dude saw Tooter go to the whip again. He was laying on the leather every jump of the buckskin when they crossed the line. It was close, so very close.

Dude managed to weave Blue Grass through to the three judges. An argument was going on. Butler stood by like a referee. Ledbetter was shouting, "I tell you the bay won by a head!" A farmer was jogging his chin the same assent. A third man, obviously the Taggart representative, was hurling denials.

Butler stepped between them. "The bay horse won," he said.

Kate Taggart was suddenly there, yelling for everybody to get out of her way. "What the hell's wrong?" she shot at Butler.

"Nothing's wrong, Mrs. Taggart," he answered politely. "Your horse lost by a head. Two judges say he did and I say he did. I saw the finish." He turned to the crowd for confirmation. Heads nodded. Several voices said, "That's right!"

Kate Taggart was too stunned to speak for a moment. Then, "*That horse* beat Jackpot?" Incredibility and fury poured into her face, her reddening cheeks matching her rouge. Her eyes stabbed at her hired man.

He spread his hands.

A pale-faced young man pushed through the crowd to Butler. "Marshal!" he hacked. "The bank's just been robbed — Mr. Purcell an' his clerks are chasin' 'im right now! One masked man on a blaze-faced bay with four white feet!"

"Which way'd they go?"

"South — the south road."

Butler ran to his horse, the crowd flowing after him. Dude followed, drawn by an uneasy insight he wished to deny and could not. Catching sight of Uncle Billy, he waved him over. But, first, the old man had to know:

"The Judge win it? It looked close."

"He did — it was. Come on. The bank's been robbed, and something's fishy."

They kept up with Butler and the foremost crowd, Kate Taggart among them.

By the time they rushed to Main Street, Dude saw a knot of riders jogging up from the south road. Three men guarding a fourth. An uneasy sensation plunged through Dude . . . that horse?

Galloping close, Dude looked and looked again.

The prisoner was Monte and the blaze-faced horse he rode was Texas Jack. Squaring around, Dude searched Uncle Billy's face. Although the old man said not a word, his eyes seemed to shed an unusual light.

P. T. Purcell was puffed up with himself, two bulging saddlebags slung across the swell of his saddle, and he waited for the crowd to quiet a bit before he reported what had happened. Meanwhile, he kept brandishing a double-barreled shotgun at the glum prisoner. He said, "It was just a few minutes before three-o'clock closing time when Monte, here, came in. Naturally, I didn't know it was him yet — him bein' masked, but there was something about him that caught my eye." Jerking abruptly, he waved the shotgun menacingly. "Now, Monte, you just sit sight straight in that saddle and no monkeyshines — that's better. . . . Well, Monte he pointed this great big pistol at me, which as you can see I now have on my belt, here, and he growled, 'Gimme all your money. Stuff it into these here saddlebags.' I did just as he said, you bet I did . . . because that pistol was a-shakin'. . . . Then Monte he runs out and jumps on this blaze-faced horse, here. Well, I signals the boys, here, and grabs my shotgun . . . and all the time I am thinkin' —"

"Mind saving the details for later, P.T.?" Butler broke in. "First thing is to secure the prisoner."

"Well, if he's not secure now he never will be," Purcell huffed, evoking guffaws from the crowd.

"I'm not criticizing what you bank fellows did — great work! I mean the first thing is to take Monte Taggart into official custody. And put that shotgun down, P.T. It might go off!"

At that, Butler locked handcuffs on Monte.

Purcell lowered the shotgun, but went on talking. "It was that horse — that slow horse.

We caught Monte, here, before he'd gone a mile. My fifteen-year-old saddle horse outran that bay. We'd never caught him on a fast horse, with the head start he had."

Grim faced, Butler now rode over to Kate Taggart. He said, "I'm afraid history is repeating itself, Mrs. Taggart. Only this time I'm holding you as an accessory."

"Me? I didn't rob the bank."

"This robbery was well-planned. Timing was perfect, near three o'clock closing time, the town deserted. Just about everybody at the race, including me. You're the only one in the family with enough sense to have planned it. . . . I regret to inform you, Mrs. Taggart, but you are under arrest. Come along."

She turned stricken eyes on Uncle Billy, in that moment as appealing as Dude had ever seen her. "Billy boy . . . can't you do something?"

"Kate," the old man said, "life is just like a horse race. You win some, you lose some." He looked away at the last moment.

Her face contorted, her eyes raking over him like a file. "Go to hell!" she flung out and spurred to go with Butler.

Not long after, Dude and Uncle Billy were waiting outside the jail when the marshal came out.

"I've come to claim my ol' Shorty horse," Dude said.

"He fits the description, all right," Butler agreed, his attention shifting to the gelding. A quizzical expression clouded his eyes, puckered his mouth. "Lucky for you that horse is slow, McQuinn. Otherwise, if Monte had escaped, I'd be considering collusion charges against you right now, as well-known as your bay is around town — those white feet, that blazed face. . . . That's what I don't understand. Why would Monte, the slickest horse thief from here to Arkansas, steal a slow horse?"

"I'll tell you why," Dude said. "You'll have to admit my ol' Shorty horse looks fast."

Leading Texas Jack, they left Marshal Butler still scratching his head and made for Appleman's store to collect their money. Dude came to the crux almost wearily. "All right, Uncle. What's this new wrinkle all about?"

The old man rode on thoughtfully, and then he said, "You see, Dude, pardner, I used to know Kate back in the early days about the time she got hitched to Big Jim Taggart. That was before the marshal's time or friend Appleman's. . . . I and an old pardner drifted into Cherokee Gap with two look-alike horses. He was as slick a fella as ever switched the fast horse for the slow horse. Fine — except he had one failing. He liked to keep the double doors swingin' on all the saloons. Right off, we worked the switch on a loud-mouthed bird that was trying to outslick us."

"Of course," Dude mimicked. *"Of course."*

"Happened my pardner rode a real fast paint horse. Everybody in town knew that horse. So Big Jim steals the paint one night, next day robs the bank just before closing time. Gets clean away, outruns the posse like they're standing still — and my pardner goes to prison for the robbery."

"Whoa, now. Didn't he have an alibi?"

"Did — but nobody believed him. You see, he'd been on a two-day toot — even I didn't know where he was — and was sleeping it off in a shed behind a saloon. It didn't take as much evidence as it does now and justice was faster. Besides, there was some widows' money in the bank and public feeling ran high. My pardner went straight to prison from Judge Parker's court in Fort Smith."

"But how did Kate know about our look-alikes?"

"She remembered it from the old days, when my pardner spilled the beans to her how we worked the switch. Boy, was she pretty! So when our outfit hit town she sees right off a way to set up the robbery by matching the race at the same time."

"So that's why she gave us three-to-one odds," Dude said, let down. "I didn't talk her into it at all."

"Kate figures we'll switch the fast horse for the slow horse the morning of the race, like in the early days. To get around that, she has Monte steal the fast horse at night. . . . Don't forget, she also wanted to win the race . . . Only I had painted Texas Jack the evening before to look like the Judge, remember? All the time they thought they had the fast horse. Remember how she liked the Judge's conformation?"

"Why didn't you let me in on this, you hoot owl?"

"Because I wanted you to act natural and carry on when you reported the theft, which you did. You're a natural-born actor, Dude."

"More like a dumbbell. But whoa, again. How did you know the Taggarts would rob the bank?"

"I didn't for sure. I just figured they might and use our horse, which I'd made certain was seen often around town. Kate knew that. Furthermore, the horse was a way to link us to the robbery — that collusion thing. Butler was smart to pick that up."

"So you were setting her up, too?"

"Same as she was us. Why not, after what she and Big Jim did to my old pardner?"

"That was still a long shot, figuring they would rob the bank."

"Better odds than you think. You see, Dude, pardner, crooks are great hands to repeat a pattern once it ever worked. And if Monte didn't rob the bank, they still had the race won with our slow horse against the speedy Jackpot — so they thought."

They rode on and tied up in front of the store. Dude hesitated. "Uncle, there's just one more little question before we break camp for Texas."

"What in the world could it be? You've already asked more questions than a country boy at his first county fair."

"Were you sweet on Kate before she married Big Jim?"

A guardedness played at the corners of the old man's mouth. But a partial grin lurked there as well. "Now did I say?"

The employees of Thorndike Press hope you have enjoyed this Large Print book. All our Thorndike and Wheeler Large Print titles are designed for easy reading, and all our books are made to last. Other Thorndike Press Large Print books are available at your library, through selected bookstores, or directly from us.

For information about titles, please call:

(800) 223-1244

or visit our Web site at:

www.gale.com/thorndike
www.gale.com/wheeler

To share your comments, please write:

Publisher
Thorndike Press
295 Kennedy Memorial Drive
Waterville, ME 04901